THE SWEETMEAT SAGA

THE SWEETMEAT SAGA

THE EPIC STORY OF THE SIXTIES

g. f. gravenson

TOUGH POETS PRESS
ARLINGTON, MASSACHUSETTS

Cover photo by Marc Miller
Cover design by Victoria Dudley

ISBN 978-0-578-38325-5

This edition published in 2022 by
Tough Poets Press, Arlington, MA USA

FOR TESSIE

Between angels and a million brothers in the dust,

Who would not choose orange soda?

—Jack Pitts

PROLOGUE

On April 24, 1966, Pookie and Paul Sweetmeat, rock idols of America's youth, mysteriously disappeared from their hotel room in New York City. What follows is the documented account of subsequent events.

where were you

                                                        when the news broke
            america
                                            when the news
                broke america
                            when
    were you
                                            down downing a shot
                                            in murphy's on east 83rd?
        rattling home
    on the long island
                            watching your dinner defrosting?
america?
                            taking in the wash
                                                    were you
        hoedown downing a shot
        from your coverall pocket
                                            america
            were you when
                            filing snap-apart forms
    you heard the news
                    (it was four on the coast)
                                                    come in california
        california here
                                                    come in texas
        texas here
                            when the news broke
                                                    alabama
            can't you get that sharper clara
colorado
                    supervising the table setting
                    the boston matron sticks her finger
    america
            turning the crud
            encrusted dial
                        watching the tube suddenly ignite
                        in a pale-blue flame
                                                        florida
    frames tumbling like a curtain of pickup sticks
                                        can't you get that
            clearer vera
    iowa
                            illinois
                                plug-in
        (sssssssshhhhhhhhhh)
                                        staring vaguely into
                                        the void of a two-hundred-
                                        and-twentyfive-squareinch
                                        cathode tube
        in america
                        sitting down
        plugging in
                (the toaster-size tv replacing
                the plastic floral arrangement)
                                            america
        shut up!
                                            (sssssssshhhhhhhhhhhhh)
boiling a bag of broccoli
                        when the news broke
                                                new hampshire
        (it was six in the corn belt)
                                (time beep)

NOW NEWS WITH SEYMORE SAVAGE
can't you get that clearer vera
sssssshhhhhhh
hhhhhhhuuuuuuuussssshh   "we were just sitting down to"
"fertilizing
the back forty when the bulletin comes in on my transistor"
idaho
taking out the burnt potatoes
when the news broke america
"good evening
i'm seymore savage..."
sunshine came softly through my window
when at that very moment
a woman is dancing around
her washing machine
you know what i mean
dig dig this
hy frisbee
yeah hear this now
hy frisbee pricks up his pavlovian ears
to five bells rung repeatedly on the teletype
"split for action city
but first let's take five"
hy frisbee
news director of WAGH new york watches the letters
B U L L E T I N
spit out with two
five-bell signals
"...seymore savage
the date is six
the month is may
the year is 1966
the news in a minute..."
(the sound of
nibbled nubleys)
(can't you get that finer dina?)
SAVAGE
just as the story hit the wires
stopped in for a beer at maxie's
B U L L E T I N
making it with
sealing wax
i nearly flipped total-like
when i heard it
"good evening
i'm seymore savege
the date is six
the month is may..."
"but right now a
word from our"
just about six as i remember
B U L L E T I N
e-lec-tri-cal
ba-nan-na
messing your
mind
her washing machine smiles back
making it friends with
"...in a minute..."
on my car radio

my world is empty without you babe

good vibrations
excitations

1901
MONTEREY CALIFORNIA (UPI MAY 6)

UNCONFIRMED REPORT THAT SWEETMEATS HAVE BEEN LOCATED XXX

(MORE)

hy frisbee feels his
heart beat like a strobe

but right now a
word from our sponsor

(ssssssssshhhhhhhhhh)

VIDEO   AUDIO

OPEN TO A SURGEON COMING OUT
OF AN OPERATING ROOM.   DOCTOR

Whew...I'm glad that mess is over...

MOVE IN ON DOCTOR WALKING
DOWN HOSPITAL CORRIDOR.
CUT TO INSIDE OF WASH-UP   Blood all over the place...
ROOM AS DOCTOR BARGES THROUGH
SWINGING DOORS.   But I'll get clean in a jiffy

ding-ding-ding-ding-ding

across the width and breadth
of

blast your mind
blow you blind

i dig i dig!

sitting down to eat
when we heard the news

on my way home

plowed when i heard
1901
MONTEREY CALIFORNIA (UPI MAY 6)

(MORE SWEETMEATS)

hy frisbee watches the teletype
sputter forth in a news orgasm
while on the coast
like a samba that sways so gentle

oooooooooo
(i thought it was a gag)

john wayne stands in an army barracks
doorway and asks: what do you mean
my orders were cancelled?

ok let's blow it

across the dearth and bitch of america
1901
MONTEREY CALIFORNIA (UPI MAY 6)

(MORE SWEETMEATS)

REPORT REACHING UPI CONFIRMS FACT THAT SWEETMEATS CAR

HAS BEEN

FOUND ABANDONED ON U-S HIGHWAY 1 FIVE MILES SOUTH OF

BIG SUR

CALIFORNIA.

growing stoned

hey
you've got to hide your love away

we was just sitting down to eat
when we

hey
you've got to hide

when we heard the news

my eyes were suddenly
opened as if the sky

rhode island here

THE SWEETMEATS, DARLINGS OF THE TEENY-BOPPER SET

HAVE BEEN THE OBJECTS OF A TWO-WEEK NATION-WIDE SEARCH AFTER

THEIR REPORTED KIDNAPPING IN NEW YORK. MAX VOGEL (RHYMES WITH

MOGUL) SWEETMEATS MANAGER SAYS HE QUOTE HAS NO COMMENT UNQUOTE.

publicity
stunt

sure sure

PAN AND ZOOM TO A CAN OF
DIGITDOUCHET

hy frisbee
tears off a ragged patch of teletype

lookin' for a special treat?

(it takes two baby)

NOM	WIE	WU	THI	ABC		DR
121½	14¼	54½	15	2s63-2000s63		5¼

chance
make general repairs
on all your property

for each house pay $25
for each hotel $100

baby what i said

right now a word from our

cool town

"while in saigon today
ground action was limited to"

"i love you all"
--shirley temple

(dissolve into a grease pit)

can't you get that better yedda?

brought to you by
YUM kipper herrings

kirk douglas throws a spear at an
onrushing christian

but right now a word
from

<u>VIDEO</u>   <u>AUDIO</u>

PAN AND ZOOM TO A CAN OF
DIGITDOUCHET.   ...With Digitdouchet.

DOCTOR TAKES CAN OF DIGIT-
DOUCHET AND SPRINKLES SOME
OF IT ON HIS HANDS.   Gets your hands spotless.
CUT TO DOCTOR'S FOOT OPERATING
WASHBASIN PEDAL. CUT BACK TO
WASHBASIN AS WATER SPLASHES IN.

                                                while at
                                                that very moment
3,000 some-odd miles to the west
                                        clyde rawlins
                                        station manager of KCUF monterey
also hears five bells on the teletype
                                        and chances to glance down at
1901
MONTEREY CALIFORNIA (UPI MAY 6)

(MORE SWEETMEATS)

REPORT REACHING UPI CONFIRMS FACT THAT SWEETMEATS CAR HAS BEEN

FOUND ABANDONED ON U-S HIGHWAY 1 FIVE MILES SOUTH OF BIG SUR

CALIFORNIA.
                                        wild as mountain dew
                                        geetah pickin wid yew
            shut that goddam thing off and
            come to the table!
                                                the city lights
                                                the pretty lights
                        when the night has come
            time goes by so slowly
            and time can do so much
            are you still mine?
                                    okay you beggars out there in radioland
                                    this will be sonny swingle sayin' it's
                                    been a groove to be with you today
                                    yes time goes by so slowly
                                    and time goes by
                                    then until the four o'clock news is over
                                    with jim skinner (wwwwhhhhhooooooooeeeeee)
                                    hold your marbles until i get back
clyde rawlins
exudes a cry that is heard
                                    clear in the studio
                                                        news beep
            "i was sittin in the office
             y'know like not doin' much
             when my girlfriend brendah
             called me and says hey has
             you heard the news and i says no and she says..."
MOGUL)
                                    hy frisbee does a bit of last minute
                                    editing and rushes in the copy to
                                    seymore savage who casually
                                    is watching the monitor

VIDEO   AUDIO

                        A fifteen-second scrubup and I'm all
                        set to
                                                    get a load of
                                                    this!
            "we were just sitting down to dinner
             when my son melvin heard it on the"
                                            can't you get more green
                                            arlene?

make the scene
shop around
                              "just keep those beers coming"
        blasted me skyhigh

                                        and i was saying
                                        yeah yeah yeah

                    VIDEO   AUDIO

MEDIUM CLOSE UP OF DOCTOR WASHING
HANDS.   A fifteen-second scrubup and I'm all
                                    set to...

FAST PAN TO A PAPER TOWEL DISPEN-
SER. ZOOM IN TO DOCTOR PULLING
TOWEL OUT.
                                        liddle red ridin' hood
                                        what big eyes you have

        (*that's all folks* scribbled across
         the end of a terrytoon)
                                            "while in saigon today
                                             ground action was limited"
            (wwwhhhhoooooooeeeeee)
                                    seymore savage scans the bulletin
                                    and nods his head in comprehension
while out on the coast
clyde rewlins
rushing in to the news studio of KCUF
stumbles over a capacitor
and watches his shoes shoot up above him
like clay pigeons
                                    oooooooooooooommmmmmmmmmmmmmmmmmmm

pppppppppppphhhhhhhhhhhhhhhh
                                                    AUDIO

                                        Get dressed and outa here.
            we was listening
            to the news on tv
                                    "i was leaving work a little early--
                                    you know
                                    friday and all--
                                    thought i'd get an early start on the
                                    rush hour"
        when i
        say that something
        i want to hold your hand
                                                            groovy
ok ok
hold sweetmeat
                                                ok hold sweetmeat
                hold the sweetmeat interview
                somethings just come over the
                wire
                                            pauline farnsworth
                                            WAGH-TV weather girl
                                            overhears the order over
                                            the control board
        "did they say the sweetmeats have been
            found
did they!"

<u>VIDEO</u>

CUT TO MEDIUM CLOSE UP OF
DOCTOR DRYING HANDS.

"viet cong and south vietnamese
regulars clashed in a bloody
battle forty miles outside of..."

lamb chops for dinner when i put on
the radio and it was just coming over

shut that goddam thing off

hi darling
what's defrosting?

and come to the table

run the bulletin in for a lead
then pick up the interview

got that?

clyde rawlins
picks himself up

just as jim skimmer is going on with the news:

'evening friends
jim skinner here with
five minutes of the latest
news from the KCUF newsroom

(it was four on the coast)

when the news broke in california
the kids getting back from school
angels in miniskirts
devils in military jackets

strolling in limbo
passing a joint

you mean they were
walking by a tavern?

i mean they were
sharing a marijuana cigarette

oooooooh really!!

hey there georgie girl

<u>AUDIO</u>

Then it's a night out with
my girl...

<u>VIDEO</u>

CUT TO MEDIUM CLOSE UP OF DOCTOR
AND NURSE EMBRACING IN A PARK.
ZOOM INTO NURSE'S FACE AS DOCTOR
RUNS HIS HAND OVER HER CHEEK.   NURSE

(Excited) No rubber glove smell!
i was workin da swing shift
and some guy was plain the radio

pauline farnsworh snaps her
gelatin-pampered fingers
and darts for the dog-eared
almanac on the editor's desk

well
what kind of a day was it in vietnam?

(a day like all days
filled with those events
that alter and illuminate
our lives)

viet cong and south vietnamese
regulars clashed in a bloody

"baked meatloaf!
nothing's
defrosting you
creep!"

i think i was listening to seymore savage
it was a friday night
friday may 6th to be exact

hy hy
get a load of this!

hy frisbee reads the line
beneath pauline farnsworth's
immaculately cared-for nails

SWEETMEAT, Pookie, & Paul
Entertainers Born: May 8, 1945

it seems like only yesterday

DOCTOR

so we put on the tube
right away so as not
to miss

like i thought they were dead
i really did
two weeks like just dropped out of sight
i mean
like i thought someone bumped them into groundsville

two weeks and them
dumb cops couldn't
find 'em

but the kids knew all the time

hey
has that report been confirmed

it's so confirmed
it's had its bar mitzvah

aw
the kids knew all along
and you can put that in your pipe

(sssssssshhhhhhhhhhh)

DOCTOR

Not on your life...

VIDEO

CUT TO MEDIUM CLOSE UP OF DOCTOR
AS HE HOLDS CAN OF DIGITDOUCHET
UP IN FRONT OF HIM. ZOOM IN ON
CAN.

Not when I use...
Digitdouchet. It's the one
hand cleanser I can depend
on to get my hands really
clean.

CUT TO CLOSE UP OF NURSE'S FACE.

NURSE

You mean to tell me you walk
around with that can of
Digitdouchet on you all day!

thirty seconds
ok ok
tell savage
he's got a
minute and five

                   65 seconds check
                                        hy frisbee shakes his head
                                        "what the hell is that supposed to mean
                                        pauline?"
"hy
 don't you get it
 May 8 1945
 May 6 1966..."
                              a publicity stunt that's all it is

    scanned the points
    for a cartoon
                                                               points?

    points you know
    like channels
                                        her teenybod boobs
                                        bobbing bra-less
                                        beneath a blue blouse
(visions of pookie)
                                              for a mind excursion
                                              not an incursion
                                              take FEEL UP

      clyde rawlins
      shows jim skinner the bulletin
                              regulars clashed in a bloody
                              battle forty miles
push grandma closer to the set
                                        two balls of rice are
                                        compared for firmness
                                                   (visions of paul)

    some great men have worn long hair
    and beards
                                   ho chi for instance

    is god dead?
                                   burnt his draft card

    and if you doubt the principles
    on which our government was based on
                                              it's doubtful you
                                              belong here
fight for the right to be an armenian in armenia
                                        set fire to the draft boards
              washington jefferson
              and who else
                                   "for chrissake pauline what is it!"
    "they'll be twenty-one on sunday"
                                   "who will!"

    "the Sweetmeats
     May 8 1945
     May 8 1966
     doncha get it?"
                         a rumor had it that pookie was (ssshhh) pregnant
i had heard that paul
received his notice to report for his physical
                                        that's all it was really
                                        purely physical

i remember the day
a friday it was
                              i was out in the back yard
                              when it started to rain
              twenty seconds
    clyde rawlins
    runs back to the teletype room as jim skinner tries reading the
    bulletin while also reading the news

                                        "south of monterey...oh...
                                        make that
                                        south of the demilitarized zone"
        here it is kids
        cartoon hour for all you kids out there
        age 6 to 60

                                                    cue in
                                                    i love a cartoon
                                                    theme

                when the first impulse flashed across
                america
                each town became an axon
                each city a ganglion

                                                B U L L E T I N

        five bells rung
        repeatedly

                                    it was curtains for them
                                    both of them
                                    pookie was knocked up
                                    paul was drafted

            it was the end of the road

                                        for chrissake pauline
                                        what does that have to do with it

                                                    i wanna see the wwwaaaaaa
            (the sound of nibbled nubleys)

                would you get the kid away!
    it was just
    six o'clock

                        i was having a shot in maxie's tavern
                        waiting for the game in new york to come on

        oh yeah
        the mets were playing the dodgers
        and koufax was pitching
    1902
    MONTEREY CALIFORNIA (UPI MAY 6)

    (SWEETMEATS)

                                                    fifteen seconds

                    VIDEO

        CUT TO CLOSE UP OF SHEEPISH
        LOOK ON DOCTOR'S FACE AND HOLD
        UNTIL WORD DIGITDOUCHET.   NURSE

        IN SYNC WITH DIGITDOUCHET   Haven't you heard about the
        POP ON PICTURE OF TOWELETTE.   new Digitdouchet Handy Towelette?

        ON WORD PERSONALIZED PACKET   Same wonderful Digitdouchet hand
        TOP ANIMATES TEAR AND FLYS   cleanser in a personalized aluminum
        OFF. TOWELETTE POPS OUT FROM   packet...
        TOP OF PACKET.
                                           ...So handy for purse or pocket.

                                                (SWEETMEATS)

                                                THE SWEETMEATS CAR, PAINTED
    IN HELIOTROPE AND CHARTREUSE XXX
                                           ten seconds
                come in alaska

                                                        alaska here
                come in virginia

                                                    virginia reads you

"can't you get that more green
arlene?"

all the people say
like the sweetmeats
were kidnapped but ah
never believes 'em

nine

VIDEO

CUT TO CLOSE UP OF NURSE HOLDING
PACKET UP BEFORE HER.

(SWEETMEATS)

THE SWEETMEATS CAR, A 1952 CADILLAC

DELUXE, PAINTED IN

HELIOTROPE AND CHARTREUSE WAS FOUND

BY CAMPERS

eight

hy
they'll be 21 on sunday

so what

legal-aged adults

it seems just like yesterday

the
sweetmeat
twins

kid stars of yesteryear

the shirley temples
of the fifties

remember

seven

how cute they were
on the horn and hardart
children's hour

remember remember the sweetmeats

clean cut american kids
both of them

ok give me an audio level

seymore savage glances over the lead-in
and nods he sees control room's signal

"for chrissake pauline"

jim skinner

six

come to my door baby
your tears and your shame
stick to your own kind

"south of the demilitarized zone
action was light with only sporadic"

have a soul party
turn yourself loose

you're driving me crazy

(health may be a hazard
to your cigarette smoking)

five seconds

"but hy
it only makes sense"

PAINTED IN HELIOTROPE AND CHARTREUSE WAS FOUND BY

"for chrissake"

                                    plug in iowa
                                                    iowa ready
                              illinois
                                                    illinois here
            all ready here
                                              four
systems check
range azimuth and elevation
                                                          tracking
                  NURSE

       Get with it...Get with New Digit-
       douchet Handy
                                        sporadic fighting in the ying
                                        yang valley
   and they'll all come home eventually
                                        oh sure
                                        just like that
            sitting down
            tearing back the aluminum cover on your tv dinner
                                                          three!
                  VIDEO   AUDIO

                        DOCTOR AND NURSE TOGETHER

stand by for blastoff
                                              so i say to you one and all
                  (seymore savage clears his throat)
                                              stand by in studio A
            ok baby
            bring it up
                                                    two!
                  sharp focus
                  captain
                                              VIDEO

                                    CUT TO DOCTOR RUNNING HIS HAND
"pauline shut up already!"
                                              insane baby how my mind
                                              grooves
            jim skinner finishes the vietnam story
            and

                  hang on...
                                                          one!

                        DOOTOR AND NURSE TOGETHER

                        ...H-E-T. Digit...douchet!
                  VIDEO

       MATCH DISSOLVE TO PACKET
       WIPE ON WORD *DIGITDOUCHET*
       TO CLOSE
                                        oooooo   oooooooooooo
                  hang on...
oooooooo   oooooo
                                        now...
                                              blast off!

we had just sat down to dinner

                                        friday fish dinner
            when it came over the tv
                                oh you know
                                that network news commentator
                                whatshisname
        "a bulletin has just been handed me"
                                        when we heard the
and margie
my next door neighbor calls across the fence
                                some guy had his transistor on
        driving home from work when this bulletin
                                    out of sight
        way uptight
                    (a press agent's dream)
                                        ladies and gentlemen
                                        a bulletin
    a report reaching our studio
                            remember?
teletype
prattle
punctuating
twilight winding smoke-gray tendrils
                            above plumcolored west virginia hills
        ding-ding-ding-ding-ding
                                the whole nation knew
        max
        MAX!
            for chrissake max
            give me the story
                            i only heard it myself on savage
            come on max
            you owe me a favor
                            shel
                            i don't know any more about it than you
        max-eeeee babyyyyy!
                            i'm catching the first flight out of
                            new york to join them
(max vogel
sweetmeats manager gives sheldon klingerman a fine-tooth brush-off)
                                        max-eeeee!
(shel klingerman artificial disseminator of the news
was for years for those of you who don't remember
the sweetmeats' press agent)
                            has just been handed me
        "on a silver platter
        a once in a lifetime publicity stunt and the guy clams up"
                                                SAVAGE
            jim skinner said they found the car abandoned
                                                SAVAGE!
            near big sur
bug sur?
                                    sure in california
                                    where all them creeps is
        boss
        i'm not going to california
                            you're going savage
                            and you're taking farnsworth
                            with you

                    aw for chrissake hy
                    i promised my my mother i'd
                                        quit stalling and get out to
                                        the airport

bbbbbrrrrrrrrrrrooooooooooommmmmmmmmmmm
bbbbrrrrrrooommmmmmbbbbrrrrrroooommmmm
                                marvin tempest
                                leader of the muffler roughers:
    those weren't no campers what
    found the car
                    bbbbbbrrrrrrrrrrrrrrrooooooooooooooommmmmmmmmmmm
    that was i
    (and the gang)
                                                    did you hear
                                                    the news
                    well you heard it first on KCUF radioooooooo
                    you little dewy-crotched flower people you
(sunny swingle
KCUF's inimitable
and sometimes inimical afternoon d.j. does his diurnal bit)
                                                WOW!
                    but don't you all get uptight about it
                    just because their jim jar was dug up it's
                    too early to tell william or william tell
                                                WOW!
                    only we'll be bringing you all the latest
                    right from the scene of action and reaction
                    like KCUF is sending our own jim skinner
                    down there right now
SKINNER
GET THE HELL IN HERE!
                                like a poem poorly written
                                couplets out of rhyme

        there i was just a sittin
        gettin me a shine

                                        when it came over the tv
    "well
     you can imagine my surprise"
                                max vogel hails down a cab
                                and tells the cabbie he'll slip him five
                                if he can get to kennedy before eight

        pay the ticket too?
                                yeah that too
                                just step on it and put on your radio

    he's so fine
    gotta be mine

                    VIDEO   AUDIO

        OPEN TO DECK SHOT OF DEEP SEA   ANNOUNCER (VOICE OVER)
        FISHING BOAT FISHERMEN HAULING   WAVES IN BG
        NETS IN.

                                        When the herrings are running

                    i want you to run down to big sur
                    and do a remote from there
                                            i won't do it
                                            clyde
                    take the station wagon
                                            get williams
                    there's no time to get williams
                    this story is breaking now

15

ding-ding-ding-ding-ding

　　　　　　　　　　　　　　　　manny makemore in chicago
　　　　　　　　　　　　　　　　creator of the pookie and paul dolls
　　　　　　　　　　　　　　　　gets a call from his wife

　　　"oh i'm so glad i got you in"

　　　　　　　　　　　　　　　　"what is it honey
　　　　　　　　　　　　　　　　　i was just on my way to the barber"

　　　"they found the sweetmeats"

　　　　　　　　　　　　　　　　"what!"

　　　"not actually the sweetmeats
　　　　just their car"

　　　　　　　　　　　　　　　　"ok honey
　　　　　　　　　　　　　　　　　tell me very slowly what you heard"

i couldn't get the kid off the phone
he mustuf called every friend he knew

　　　　　　　　　　　　　　　　　　(at&t reported the heaviest
　　　　　　　　　　　　　　　　　　　load of calls in its history)

　　　　"i couldn't get through"

　　　　　　　　　　　　　　　barbed wire fence and rescued ten
　　　　　　　　　　　　　　　americans trapped inside

　　shel klingerman puts a call
　　through to timothy queen
　　at ths fire island
　　hideaway

　　　　　　　　　　　　　　how'd you get my number shel baby
　　　　　　　　　　　　　　it's unlisted you know
　　　　　　　　　　　　　　and besides
　　　　　　　　　　　　　　i don't think we have anymore to
　　　　　　　　　　　　　　say to one another after that frightful
　　　　　　　　　　　　　　bit of cheese you put into last monday's
　　　　　　　　　　　　　　quote column unquote

look i'm sorry about that timothy
really i am
i didn't mean to put you down like that

　　　　　　　　　　　　　　well what seems to be the matter

what do you know about the sweetmeats'
disappearance

　　　　　　　　　　　　　　why ask me shel baby
　　　　　　　　　　　　　　i don't know a thing
　　　　　　　　　　　　　　i told the police everything i
　　　　　　　　　　　　　　knew

you were with them the night before they--

　　　　　　　　　　　　　　oh for criminy sake shel
　　　　　　　　　　　　　　read your own column
　　　　　　　　　　　　　　you have that story already

about a movie wasn't that it timothy
you were going to make a movie about them

　　　　　　　　　　　　　　oh i don't know
　　　　　　　　　　　　　　a movie or a portrait
　　　　　　　　　　　　　　we hadn't decided...
　　　　　　　　　　　　　　something delicious though
　　　　　　　　　　　　　　say what is this
　　　　　　　　　　　　　　the second degree?

it just might interest you to know that
they've been found

　　　　　　　　　　　　　　no kidding!

　　　"well
　　　　my first reaction was it's a hoax"

　　　　　　　　　　　　　　i never believed they were
　　　　　　　　　　　　　　kidnapped in the first place

of course not

but as soon as my kid heard it
(we had the tv on during dinner)
he jumped up and ran out the door

silence is replaced
with the steady hum
of cathode tubes

kitchens and living rooms phosphoresce
flicker
with the grayblue shroud

(can't you make that ghost disappear
dear)

(hamlet sees his father appear on
an aspirin ad)

hot dog!
groovy
i dig it dig it dig it dig it dig arthurjohn needs baldhead sally
ok ok
whhhhhooooo
honey
put on the radio won't you

when i saw it coming out
i flipped like it was a
double fakeout

ding-ding-ding-ding-ding

clyde rawlins
remembers how it was

"another bulletin comes
out about ten minutes later"

B U L L E T I N

(MORE SWEETMEATS)

SWEETMEATS CAR ABANDONED

NEAR BIG SUR CALIFIRNIA CLAIMED TO BE

FOUND BY MARVIN TEMPEST

WHO HEADS THE MUFFLER ROUGHERS.   TEMPEST

CAME ACROSS THE SWEETMEAT

CAR

<u>AUDIO</u>

when the herrings are running
you can be sure Yum is there
where all the action is

max vogel is tied up on the
59th street bridge

"look buddy
it's like this every friday night"

"why aren't they taking their pills?"

warm springs west virginia
(population 10,061)
is 83% tuned in

i was
flabbered...   "and what is your name?"
rosie
wallace...   "and where do you go to school?"
right here
at central...   "and what grade are you in?"
i'm a
sophomore...   "and what do you think of..."

use the tuner oona

                        remember
                                they were interviewing the kids
        waddya mean

                                                        commies
                        that's what i said
                        a goddam commie plot
                                        "and what do you think of"
        a plot
                                they're everywhere
        did you see that shot of
        pookie wearing a miniskirt
                                        they were focusing on her knees
i mean i wouldn't let my daughter
                                winning the hearts and minds of
                                sixty million american youngsters
        general ochre
        chief of the 69th national guard battalion
        stationed at monterey's camp ord
        gets a beep on his walkie-talkie
        between the 14th and 15th hole on the
        pebble beach golf course and says to his caddie
                                        "hold it sambo
                                         i just got a call"
                (crackle) "general ochre sur"
                                        "ochre here"
                        "colonel caper sur"
                                        "no
                                         ochre here"
                        "i mean i'm caper
                         colonel caper here"
                                        "for chrissake man
                                         why don't you say so"
remember
pookie posed bareass in foreplay magazine
                                        forest jagoff
                                        publisher of foreplay
                                        gets a buzz on his console

        forest honey
                                sure...
                                connie?

        wendy...
        connie went home with
        diarrhea
                                oh hey yeah wendy what's up

        sweetmeats have been
        found
        thought you'd like to know
                                oh say hey yeah
                                i'll put on the telebishion hey wendy hun
(mocking) what forest hun
                                whassatime
        sixish
                                b.c. or a.d.?
                                        america's telstar
                                        satellite is
                                        jammed with calls
        couldn't get through
                "i kept thinking of pookie being forced to do
                 all sort of unnatural acts for those hoods"
hy frisbee is trying to get
a fifteen minute spot for a
news special

<u>AUDIO</u>   <u>VIDEO</u>

STYLES TRIO PLAYS GRASSLANDS THEME
INTRO   OPEN TO SUNRISE SCENE OF DESERT
                                            AS SUN SPEEDS UP OVER HORIZON.
              VOCAL GROUP (SINGS)   FAST PAN TO HOGAN AS COUPLE
                                            EMERGES.
my first reaction was
the mafia was holding them for ransom
                                                      (paul must've put up a
                                                        terrific fight)

          surfin shack
          afternoon
                                            "woody wilson there?"
          naw
          he's lining up
                                            "can you call him in?"
          he won't like it
          surf's up
          who's this
                                            "marvin tempest"
          oh yeah sure marv
          i can call woody
          to the phone
                                            "make it quick"   (duals roaring in the
                                                                    background)
      ba-by together
                        geetah picker
                        quicker 'n spit
captain francona
state police officer
near big sur township gets a call on the radio car's receiver
                                                        "captain"

                                                        "i just got a
                    "francona"   call from the
                                                         (gulp) fbi"

          calling all cars
                        (or as ralph nader would have it)
          recalling all cars
                                            timothy queen's cabin cruiser
                                            "will of the lisp"
                                            steams him towards his private jet
                                            sea plane anchored somewhere in
                                            long island sound
shel klingerman is pulling all stops
he telephones a swami sahalami
the great near eastern yoga mogul
and more recently the sweetmeats
astrological advisor
                                            i'm sorry
                                            swami sahalami is in meditation

          don't give me this meditation
          jazz
          i know he's around
                                            who should i say is

          tell him mr. klingerman
          and if he doesn't come around
          mention paris summer of fifty-two

on your toes
anything grows
but not when you're
protected with
DIGITDOUCHET

ok you sweetsmellin little cop-out artists out in
radioland
this is sonny swingle back again for another lucy juicy
hour of the very best sounds and rounds discwise
and while we're on the subject of being wise
are you going to be matched tomorrow night
at monterey's central high school computer bust out?

nitty-gritty

sugar xxx
leader of the ethnic dukes
gets the word at his los angeles headquarters

sugar baby

uh

how you

uh whossiz

william 83X

83X?

uh

hollit

whasmadder

gotta find yer name
in ma book here man
see who you really are

uh

"look buddy waddya want me to do
fly over the traffic?"

pollution builds stronger bodies 8 ways

well you can imagine my surprise

i wasn't going to go out on a
limb

jim skinner
packs up the KCUF station wagon
mouthing an occasional curse

a curse for all occasions
my friends is the phrase
i don't need god

and how many of us use that curse daily
yes daily
how many of us think that by backsliding it we can make a go of things
well my friends you are sadly mistaken if you think backsliding is synonymous
with upgrading...

(the speaker is none other than reverend cecil
buttermilk practicing his sunday sermon to his
wife who he believes is listening to him in the
kitchen but who is presently chatting to her
neighbor across the buttermilk's back fence)

conjugate the verb said

gladly
i said that you said that he said
so she said that they said that
we said

exactly who said it
give me all the facts

it was on the seymore savage show

    do you mean to tell me
    the fbi gets their infor-
    mation on the seymore sav-
    age show!

                           i don't know captain
                           that's what they told me

seymore savage and pauline
farnsworth catch the pan am
helicopter out to kennedy

                        (please
                          the word is *hecticopter*
                          the children may be listening)

       oh sure the children
       the children
               the children were gluesniffing their little brains
               out while their older brothers and sisters were
hold it
HOLD IT!
        "that's editorializing
         strike it"

                  hy frisbee runs his hand through his
                  graying crew-cut and then pounds his
                  desk
         "i got less than four
          goddam hours to do this
         thing and i get gluesniffing"
                     let's keep to the facts
                     just the facts
  the sweetmeats never were accused of gluesniffing
  smoking pot dropping acid yes--but never gluesniffing!
                   hey who won the
                   detroit game
  it could have been any night in any month in any year
                    only the times were
                    changed to protect
                    the innocent
  it could have been in any home on any block in any town
                    only the thymes were
                    changed to provide
                    the incense
  it could have been a smell of tobacco even
                who ya kidding
                paul was a head
       did he say paul was ahead?
naw
a head
like dope
          "this KCUF"
                    "yeah"
         "finally got through
         this is chief broken wind"
charles victor
vietnam hero steps off the plane at kennedy
just as max vogel reaches the airport
                  hold it
                  one more of these
      hey
 hey   hey victor
          give us another with the
          stewardess
                  get another with
                  the stewardess

```
    hey how about waving
                                        c'mon wave
        wave        ok ok
got it                              hey charlie give us a big grin
            one more before the
                                        get him over by the mikes
    hey stop your pushing
    hey
                            ok fellows give him air give him some room
    ok over here
                    private victor
                                i'm glad to be back in the states
                    private victor
                    i understand
LOUDER
                i understand you're going
                to be awarded the distinguished
                medal of honor by the preeident              (move back)
                on sunday
                how do you feel about that
                                            i'm very glad
                what was your first reaction
                when you got off this plane
                                        i was glad to be back
    and what about that stewardess (laughter)
                                        i'm glad to be home
        (do you have a reservation sir?)
                                    "this is chief broken wind"
        (a reservation sir?)
                                    "broken wind"
        (sir?)
                                    "me got story to tell about
                                        sweetmeats"
would you hold on for a moment"
                            like the whole country was holding its
                            breath
                            you could feel everyone inhale at once
        a stillness filled the air
                            save the incessant bells that jangled
                            incessantly
    rinnnnnnnnggggggggggggggggrrrrriiiiinnnnnnnnnnggggggggggggggggrrriiiiinnnnnnnnnnnnnnnnn
nnnnnnnnnnnnnnnggggggggggggggggggggg
                                                        hello
miss pitt's residence
                                    is miss pitt in
who shall i say are calling
                                    whom
just a minute please
    (there's a miss whom
     on the phone ma'am)
                                    hello?
...miss whom?
                                    olive
                                    this is carmella
carmella karma!
how nice to call
my maid said a miss whom
was on the line (the idiot!)
                                    have you heard the news
...it's so hard to get good help these days
```

*these days friends it's who you
know
and how many of us friends know
god*

*that's right god GOD GOD!
how many of us really know the good lord!*

<u>VIDEO</u>

<u>AUDIO</u>

(FOOTSTEPS SFX)

OPEN ON HAZY SHOT OF DOCK.
PAN AND ZOOM TO FISHERMEN
WALKING DOWN DOCK. CUT TO
MEDIUM TELEPHOTO OF FISHERMEN
WALKING AWAY FROM CAMERA.

rrrriiiiinnnnnnggggggggg

seymore savage
and pauline farnsworth run down the ramp into the waiting plane

just as
timothy queen's
jet takes off

while in dallas texas
doctor mountmother
world-famous psychiatrist
gets a call from one of his
"psychotic children"

doc?

ohhhhhheeeellllloooo
this is doctor mountmother

gona kill myself
doc

ooooooooooooo
who is this

stuart

oooooooooooohhheeelllllooooo
stuart

gona kill myself
doc

ooooooooooooo
don't do that

doc
they found the
sweetmeats doc

oooooooooooooooooooo

i need to kill

did chicago play today?

they lost 6-3

i had five bucks on them

a bunch of bums

well that night i had tickets
to the philharmonic concert
but my two kids began acting
strangely so we cancelled

my son lawrence (larry)
ran out the back door

i mean
we had given them up for dead

what was it?
two weeks?

i didn't believe the news

*who cares i said to
myself*

woody wilson here

                  woody
                  it's marvin tempest   (duals revving)

yeah marv
what can i do for you

                  me and the gang gotta have a place
                  to crash tonight

what's up

                  we're in big sur
                  me and the gang found the sweetmeats' car
                  off a road

no kidding

                  and this place is crawlin' with fuzz

        rrrrriiiiiinnnnnnnnnnngggggggggggggggg
        rrrrrrriiiiiiiiiiiiiinnnnnnnnnnnnggggggg

                                  did you hear

   the news

              jim skinner is driving the twenty or so miles
              from monterey to big sur with a station wagon
              full of radio remote equipment

(cut and trim
 the lamp)

                          the sun was going down
                          at kennedy airport
                          a golden balloon being
                          pierced by needle skyscrapers

   while in chi-town's loop
   manny makemore calls for his limousine

                          never knowd
                          how'n it was all right
                          seein' as two weeks passed

   QUIET
   QUIET ON THE SET
               sssssssssssshhhhhhhh
we have a daughter who's fifteen
and very impressionable

                i mean we all were at that age

once it was francis x bushman
and rudolph valentino

                    very impressionable

    you don't want to give up those
    memories

        the dreams you grew up with

                  booth and bernhardt

                              we all

23-skidood
        a part of the past that was your very own
     reach out
     reach out for me
             serving up his lips on a silver platter
      the girl with the
      zoom bazoms
            (i remember hanging up a picture of
            lana turner on my foot locker)
grable and gable
         harry james and jeanne crane
                    william boyd
                    and harold lloyd
     gabby and helen hayes
            "the generation gap
            is a lot of crap"

cut that word

what word hy?

the word crap you fool!

hold it for a moment fellows

QUIET

QUIET

scene 36

take 4

ACTION!

i love you i love you i love you

forest jagoff
steps into his sauna
and finds a guest from the last
night's party sprawled on the floor

okay let's send it down south and see if it votes

"and how are you juicy ones
from the loose goose of radioland
sonny swingle here with..."

david cohen
leader of S.H.A.M.E.
(students hindering american military efforts)
hears the news over his car radio
while driving home from berkeley
and realizes that his old arch enemy
general ochre will probably be there with the national guard

(who
incidentally
was that
moment

FORE!!!

teeing off the 16th)

"general
sur..."

"uhhhhh
dis is da general's caddy
kin ah help"

sugar xxx
leader of the ethnic dukes
gets the word

you sure man

as sure as heaven above

and the plane carrying seymore
savage and pauline farnsworth
is finally air-borne

carrying among others
max vogel (rhymes with mogul)
sweetmeats' manager

you couldn't tell the forest from the freeways
it was so crowded

"driving up from l.a.
took us until midnight"

and even then we couldn't
get through the roadblock

a roadblock men
set up a roadblock

(captain francona is instructing his men
to roadblock every intersection around big sur)

captain francona

francona here

washington is calling

put 'em on

              "captain francona"

                    "yessir"

              "have you instructed
               roadblocks be put up"

                    "yessir"

              "general ochre from
               fort ord is being
               instructed to take a
               detachment of men..."

    FUCK THAT GODDAM TRAP!

            while in another part of the forest

ric gland
and
girda loins
together for the first time in melvin eliot's LUST WEEKEND
break for coffee after an afternoon of shooting

                this is swami sahalami
                what blessings can i
                bestow on you

      you can stow those blessings
      salami
      i know what the score is

hit the road jack
and doncha come back no more

                (whatya say)

and doncha come back no more

          the kid jumped out of his seat and
          beat it out the back door

    damn kids

      remember
      when hemlines and knees had something in common

  what have they done
  to american morals?

          and then paul began rolling his
          own brand of cigarette

why i watched them every wednesday
night when they were kids
on the sweetmeats' family hour

        it was good clean family entertainment

    and we spent many a
    wednesday night
    listening to them
    on radio

        and then TV

  tv

              woweee

   don't give a damn

      i must kill
      doc

           oooooooooooooooooooo
           not yourself stuart

      i shouldn't kill
      myself doc?

           nnnooooooooooooooooo

mayor meyer
mayor of big sur
(and presidential hopeful in '68)
gets a call from carmella karma

      in short (or in shorts)
      in those first full futile momemnts
      everyone who was anyone had heard the news

```
          and were getting briefed on
          (or getting their briefs on)
                                                   the news
no tern was left unstoned
                              "i want complete coverage
                               we got a 15-minute spot after the
                               11:00 news"
      ding-ding-ding-ding-ding
                                            B U L L E T I N

                                            (MORE SWEETMEATS)

                                            BIG SUR CALIFORNIA (UPI MAY 6)

                                            FBI REPORTS ROADBLOCKS SET UP ON
ALL HIGHWAYS LEADING TO
                                            AND FROM BIG SUR.
          over here
          over here another stanchion
                                                        get another horse
                                                        over here
                 let's go men
                 we don't have all day
                                            colonel dipper
                                            presently circling the earth
          brentin strong
          vietnam correspondent
                                      major macho
                                      cuban exile leader
all get the news
                                                  and even
                                  mah felluh amuricuns
                 gets the news
                                            "all god's chilen
                                             getteh have news"

          EXTRA!  EXTRA!
                                            (as the sunset swept across the
                                             midwest in a sickle of clouds)
           "russell
            it just came
            over the radio"
                                                        may 6 1966
a date to remember
                                  russell smith
                                  and meg
                                                        even the smiths
          the john does of monterey california
                                                        even the smiths
          insurance salesman smith and his wife
                                            hell
                                                        even the smiths
          parents of linda and louis
                                                        get the news
not to mention mom and pop smith
                         (parents of russell)
paidup members of senior citizens
anonymous
                                       you little painted-flower-power
                                       people
                                       try this on for thighs
```

red and blue means me and you

                                          "fantastic
                                          fantastic
                                          i see hawaii"

synchronized pulse type pattern and random jammers

                                                get the news

      i'm gona get me down there

                                at the hop hop hop
                                let's go to the hop

  rock rock
      let's go

                  <u>AUDIO</u>   <u>VIDEO</u>

      Crass beer is good beer...
                                PAN AND ZOOM
let's goooooo

            if i shouldn't kill
            myself doc should i
            kill you?

                                    ooooooooooooooooooo
                                    nnnnnnnnoooooooooo

       linda smith is upstairs doing her homework
       louis smith is tossing a baseball in front of their home at
1432 pleasant
street
                            when they get the news
         and by the time dusk fell
         on monterey
              "i'm going to kill
                the sweetmeats"
                                  "ooooooooooooooooo"
     everybody who was anybody
                         when
         coma liddle bit closer
push grandma closer
to the
                      ZOOM AND PAN
                                pookie's bared knees
      (a necklace of carlights winds about the
       highway leading to big sur)
                                paul's open shirt
    running girlfree in the meadows of our dreams
                                     soaked
with the sweat of our hopes
                      remembering
                      remembering
   when we first heard the news
                        they had been
       o god!
                        found!!

PART ONE

AUDIO	VIDEO
(SFX OF ROOSTER CROWING)	OPEN ON ZOOM TO BEDROOM WINDOW OF SUBURBAN HOUSE.
(SFX OF ALARMCLOCK)	CUT TO ALARMCLOCK JANGLING ON THE SIDE OF BED AND A HAND FUMBLING TO TURN IT OFF.
WIFE (V.O.)	CUT TO WIFE STANDING IN THE BED- ROOM DOORWAY.
(Brightly) Wake up...wake up...	
(D.V.)	
Wake up darling...time to do your bit at the office.	
HUSBAND (V.O.)	
Ooooohhhhh!	
WIDE (D.V.)	TRUCK WITH WIFE AS SHE WALKS TO THE BATHROOM.
I know just the thing for my sleepyhead...something brand new!	

                                        charles victor
                                        hero of hill 457
                                        arrives at the
                                        new york hilton

private victor
private victor sir
                                can we have a shot of you saluting
                                back at the concierge

          the who?   the concierge ehhh
                                       that man over there

          oh
          the guy at the door
          sure!   is this your first visit
                                             in new york private

          yeah
          everything looks big
(laughter from the
 press corps)
                                       and your mom and pop are
                                       meeting you?

          yeah
          mom and pop are meeting
          me
          the government flew them
          all the way from iowa
                                       (keokuk born and raised)

after a hearing that lasted 10 hours
the board of education of fenster township
suspended a 17-year-old honor student from
the fenster high school today for having
sideburns that they considered too long

ric gland is standing on his head
as gerda loins aging alky starlet
slips quietly into his trailer

(swami sahalami sees all
 swami sahalami sees all)

sheldon klingerman goes over his handwritten notes
for sunday's Klingerman's Kolumn while waiting for
swami sahalami to begin his midnight séance:
              they did that little toe dance together
              and danced their way into our hearts

our hearts tapped
                together with scotch

                              (remember the cute little
                               kilts they wore)

    they couldn't have been

                        more than four or five when they
                        first appeared on the horn and
                        hardart children's hour

sam and fay taught them one of
their vaudeville numbers remember

                              (less work for mother
                               so she'll understand...)

      and then arthur godfrey's
      talent scouts

                  (tap-tap-tippity-tippity)

                              "and danced their way into

   our hearts"
                  the silent fifties
                  years spent in prayer
                  for eisenhower's latest recovery

                                          hopalong cassidy
                                          bridey murphy
                                          ernie kovacs
                                          howdy doody
                                          the big bopper
                                          dick nixon

(where are they now?)
                  there was peace at last...
                  a piece in our times
WOW!
get a load of the cover story

                        POOKIE'S SEX SECRETS
                            REVEALED!

                                          (she menstruated)

                        CAN PAUL EVER FORGET
                        HIS FIRST REAL LOVE?

                                          (fifth grade teacher)

                        THE SWEETMEATS CAN NEVER
                        FORGET HIS KINDNESS

    (frank olson
     the motorist who administered
     first aid to the kids at crashsite)

                              it was a big time for the kids after
                              sam and fay's curtain rang down

watching them on ed sullivan
from between your toes america

                        "we knew more about pookie's training bra
                         than she did herself"

      for two or three years
      they were mr. and myth america

                        (still darlings to camping fags)

took them into our hearts
and sucked the breath out of them

                                        (*their world was alive*
                                         with the sound of muzak)
"i mean they were so *square*"
                        "so goddam howard-johnson-good all the time
                         i just couldn't accept it after a while"
    (i didn't need a six-
     button blazer anyhow)
                                        it wasn't natural the whole thing
        something phony about them
                                by then other groups were lip-syncing
                                their teeth into protest songs
but not the sweetmeats
                    no sir not them
                    they were still on top of ole smokey
                    in their ivory tower of innocence
    "who needs them
     i said"
                            couldn't care less that they dropped out of sight
            slipped into the back recesses
            of our collective minds as the decade turned the corner
                                        "*swami sahalami sees*
                                        (*he peers into his ball*)
                                        a couple...yeessss...a man
                                        and a woman
            (gasps from those assembled)
"*the sweetmeats?*"
 asks klingerman
                                        "*too dark to tell...*
                                        i see an outline...
                                        the man is doing yoga"

            paul!
                                                            paul!

    remember when he came to the recording session
    wearing a bananapeel on his head
                                        (something had happened
                                         in those three years
                                         in seclusion)

and pookie had fulllllllllllly developed
                                she made tammy look like
                                francis the talking mule
grooving bra-less with her new
roach holder
                                        (something had happened
                                         all right)
    "put me through to sheldon klingerman in new york
     at the world-herald-tribune-sun-pm-mirror-dispatch
     this is chief broken wind of the cannabis tribe"
                                        (something that was making
                                         the grass look greener in
                                         the other fellow's yard)
i mean they literally *looked different*
                                paul was thinner and taller and
                                gaunter with his black hair falling
                                to his shoulders
"pookie was stacked!"
                        (is that all you can ever think about)
"and didn't care who knew"
                                        she was after love and lysergic
        "some of my best lovers are
         high public officials" she once said
                                        and paul wrote all new songs
        "the word 'fuck' has never
         killed anyone in vietnam" he said
                                        mah felluh amuricuns
carmella karma wants to be sure the president
has gotten the news

"operator
 please place a call to lady bird johnson
 i'm not sure of the number but the address
 is 1600 pennsylvania avenue in washington"

                                        "would you spell that
                                         last name please"

"surely
 J-O-H-N-S-O-N"

                                        "1600 pennsylvania
                                         avenue?"

"that's correct"

                                        "one moment please"
while at precisely that very moment
                                olivia pitt also
                                puts through a call
                                to 1600 pennsylvania avenue
  and both of them get a busy signal

                                        "the line is busy
                                         will you wait?"

    common noise sweep and pulse generators for each
    jamming type can be utilized with separate amplitude
    controls and switches
ah
i
see!
                        things are goin' so fast these days
                        it's hard to keep up from day to day
    things were
    slower years
    ago
                            (mom and pop smith
                             father and mother to russell smith
                             visiting him on their annual trip to monterey
                             from cowpie idaho
                             talk things over after dinner)
                        yesh mom (pop smith has trouble
                        with his new dentures) t'aint at all
                        like it wach when we wach kids

    things were
    slower years
                        an altogether different mom
                        don't ferget that
                        different as day is from night
    what say?
                        i said DIFFERENT AS DAY IS FROM NIGHT
    oh yes...
    yes...
                                        it was the best of times
                                        it was the worst of times
        and the moon is the only
        light we see
        stand by me
                                pot and pan
                                        oooh
                                        look
                                        at the sunset

manny makemore flying at 30,000 feet
in his private piper
glances out the window of his cabin
and watches the sun set over the pacific
                                        "GREAT"
        "but will it last ric?"
                                "gerda
                                 gerda"
        "our happiness
         will it last ric?"
                                "roll over
                                 let's do position 17"
    e-ter-nal-ly
                turning this whole crazy land upside down looking for love
spending a won-
der-
ful evening at the top-of-the-six's
                                    as the gray-green light flickers
                                    out of the eastern coast
        and matresses prepare for a massive
        onslaught of tired bodies
                                        the end of a busy busy week
            my love
    my love
                        goodnight my love
        my love
                    (do you think they'll find the sweetmeats?)
    put out the television
    and come to bed
come
                                                    to bed my love
                windows open slightly
    a dog barks
                    and fifty million eastern-seaboarders
                    yawn in unison
    it's been quite a week
                                                    quite a weak
                                                    (cough)

        chchchhhhhchhhrrrrhhh
                            and begin to wonder
                            when they will finally drop off
    somewhere a radio blares:
                            AUDIO
                    YES FRIENDS,
                    CRASS IN A GLASS HAS CLASS --
                    CRASS BEER THE ONE BEER YOU HAVE
                    WHEN YOU FEEL LIKE IT
                                        ball 2 strike 2
                                        on mosikdyzki
                                        here's the pitch

            AUDIO   VIDEO

                                        OPEN TO PITCHER ON BASEBALL
                                        MOUND THROWING IN TO HOME PLATE.
        (SFX OF BALL HITTING   MEDIUM CLOSE UP OF
        CATCHERS MITT AND ROAR   BATTER STRIKING OUT.
        OF CROWD)
                                        ZOOM IN TO PITCHER WALKING OFF THE
                                        MOUND AS TEAMMATES SURROUND HIM.

36

AUDIO   VIDEO

            AANNOUNCER V.O.
         (GRADUALLY DIM TO OFF SFX)

Another win for big Bill Grospekski
...and another headache for...
                                    CUT TO INTERIOR OF GROSPEKSKI'S
                                    KITCHEN.
Mrs. Grospekski   MRS. GROSPEKSKI STANDING OVER WASH.
              the game was over
              and on that dry maywine
              night
                                             couples walked home
                                             silently each and all

the men dreaming of young cheerleaders with
bared knees running girlfree in the meadows
                                                      and the women
                                                      ah the women...

the women dreaming of their daughters
don white
whispering down aisles of babybreath
                                    to marry some dark man on a dark horse
           (while both had given up
            on their sons and lovers)
                                             louis smith
                                             18-year old son of meg and russell
                                             gets high with some of his friends
                                             in the parking lot of the hires
                                             root beer stand
     "hey lou
      y'hear about the sweetmeats?"
                                                  "yeah"
                "hey put the radio on"
                                                      "we win the baseball
                                                       game tonight?"
     "how the fuck do i know"
                          "any more grass?"
     "this is the last joint"
                                                  "we lost 6-2"
                "figures"
                                                      "coach shaffer"
                "shithead"
                                             (laughter all around)
                          "match?"
oooooooooooooooo
stuart be careful
dr. mountmother thinks as he races to stuart's apartment
on dallas's south side
                                                  dallas
                                                  where it had all started
                                                  this insaneness of ours
                     dallas
                     that three years after
                     still smelled to high heaven
                                                  dallas
big D dallas
           where it all started going wrong
                                                  dallas

my oh yes
      callous dallas
      who saw all and said nothing
                  who could only distribute his
                  picture on a wanted-for-murder poster
  and who even
  when they got their man
             weren't satisfied
                  ("should've plugged jackie too")
dallas
and the death of a dream

              my oh yes big D dallas

VIDEO	AUDIO
MEDIUM CLOSE UP OF A COWBOY TAKING OFF HIS HAT AND WIPING HIS FOREHEAD WITH HIS SLEEVE. WITH HIS OTHER HAND HE PULLS OUT A PACK OF GRASSLANDS. MOVE IN ON PACK AS HE POPS UP A CIGARETTE AND PLACES IT IN HIS MOUTH.	(SFX OF CATTLE MOOING) COWBOY (OVER) When I reach for a Grasslands my problems seem insignificant. Not even them cattle bother me.

(mah felluh amuricuns)
          jim
          jim can you read me
                      "sure clyde"
          where are you now
                      "'bout five miles
                       north of big sur"
          what's happened
                      "best as i can tell
                       a roadblock
                       traffic's backed up
                       for miles"
          can you get in?
                      "not unless i drive
                       on the beach"
          do it for chrissake!
forest jagoff
downs a martini
                  BINGO
                  i win!
                  whadda i get?
and pushes the button that rotates
his circular bed
              "francona here"
  "captain
    the CIA just called
    to ask if the FBI called"
             manny makemore is thinking:
             if the sweetmeats are dead
             i'll come out with an embalming set

        AUDIO

CRASS BEER HAS LESS BUBBLES--
LESS BUBBLES MEAN MORE BEER
DELICIOUS BEER
THE BEER THAT MADE CALUMET CITY FAMOUS

(MRS. GROSPEKSKI)

It certainly is a chore to get Bill's
uniform clean...

<u>VIDEO</u>

SHE HOLDS UP UNIFORM. CUT TO
CLOSE UP OF UNIFORM ON WORD
CLEAN.

See those stains. That's dirt. Pitch-
ers' mound dirt.

CUT TO MEDIUM CLOSE UP OF MRS.
GROSPEKSKI ON WORD *BUT*. MOVE
IN AS SHE TAKES BOX OF *NEW*
OFF WASHING MACHINE TOP.

But I've got just the thing for those
stains.

       linda smith is in bud halley's car
       parked in front of the smiths'
       house

  "why not lin?"

      "i just don't want to bud"

  "aw shit
   don't give me this innocent
   crap"

      "i just don't want to"

  "give me a kiss then"

      "not here
       my folks are still up"

  "we'll drive..."

      "uh-uh i gotta go in now"

  "what about the computer bust"

      "i'll let you know tomorrow
       call me"

david cohen
leader of SHAME
(students hindering american military efforts)
driving down u.s. highway #1 meets the convoy
(the general's car and two jeep escorts)
taking general ochre back from
the pebble beach golf club
and decides to lead the convoy
but at a conservative 10 mph

        "what the hell's the matter"

   "sorry general
    there's a slow car in front
    of the forward jeep"

        "well get him outa the way"

   "jeep number one
    jeep number one
    can you read me?"

"jeep one"

   "can you honk
    repeat
    can you honk"

"roger"   (beep beep)

        "that ain't much of a honk"

   "is that the loudest
    it will go?"

"affirmative"

        "you honk too
         and get jeep number two also"

while back at the ranchhouse
   we were turning in for the night

```
turning
on for the night
                                                turning out

        the light
        for the night
                                                turning on the burglar alarm
    putting out the cat
                                we were
                                                turning in

    a note in the milkbottle
a kiss
on the doorstep
                                                    a hand
                                                    in the icebox

            a finger
            in the hotbox
                                we were flushing toilets and gargling
    douching and praying
                                        unplugging the network
                                        of our minds
if the number of undefined overflow symbols
                                    is few
the assembled object deck can the be relocated
elsewhere by the relocatable-program loader
                                            jamming random
                                            dream
                                                pattern

    the noises of the night
                                                            crickets
floorboards
                                an unknown tapping in the walls
        dog bark
                        and the constant prattle of the mind
    now thinking
    about the bills
                            the kids
                            and the wife
                                        the girl he loves and the
boy she loves
                    and all the things that had that day happened
        drifting from
        east to west
                                            a sirocco wind of dreams
                        and sleep
time to go in now pop
                                    (russell smith tells his dad)
                                                        yeah
time to go in now
                        what's that?
                                    "by placing the clutter pattern
                                    on the photo-multiplier tube
                                    pickup..."
        hey
    get another shot from here
                                                    private victor
                                                    private victor

            another shot
put your arm around
the chambermaid
                            "eveything's so big"
```

"any more booze"

"hey fellows
he's got to sack out"

"hey charlie
let's have a smile"

"c'mon fellows"

"any youse guys got
a 'J' on him?"

"one more for the press corps"

hahahahahahaha

hey one more
just one more

c'mon one more

it's two in the morning

saturday may 7 1966

hey c'mon

brentin strong
vietnam correspondent (or stringer if you wish)
squints into the sweatstreamed sun
then hurriedly pencils a wire to hy frisbee
in new york

WAGH NEW YORK

NEW BATTLE LOOMING YING YANG VALLEY TOWN OF FUC HUE STOP

CAN GIVE YOU FULL HALF HOUR COLOR FOR SATURDAY SAVAGE STOP

IMPERATIVE WIRE BACK STOP BATTLE HOURS AWAY BRENTIN STRONG

and gives the
wire to his
honcho

"take this note to francona and wait for an answer"

"but marvin..."

"don't give me any shit
if francona gives you trouble or tries to bust you
tell my shithead friend that we'll have 10,000 muffler
roughers from oregon here before sundown
tomorrow so he better play ball with us"

hello?

how

how?

this is chief broken wind
of the cannabis tribe
you sheldon klingerman?

that's right

me been trying to get you
all night

i've been at a séance

c'mon klingerman
sahalami gets his dope from me
which is the reason i'm calling

wooden beads beards boots buttons

bells wire-rimmed

spectacles

shoulder satchels sandals fringed

capes berets and
australian hats

you're putting me on

putting you down

taking me up

                                        faking you out
asking me in
                        jerking you off
                                                        sending us over
        every dollar taken out of an american bank
        results in a loss of $3 to the american banking system
                                                keeping them high
        pill time america
        pulls open the mdeicinecabinet
        (suffering as it does from insomnia)
        and upsadaisies a downie
                                        china's "cultural revolution" and
                                        leadership struggle have evolved
                                        their own baffling vocabulary
                sssssshhhhhhhhhh
                can't you sleep?
                                        fluffing the pillow
                                        the boston matron
operation code not a valid
mnemomic
                                and who's to know
                                america
        goddam motherfucker
                                                the dreams of generations
                                                embrace in the national concern
                                                for the sweetmeats
            hold me hold me
                            do you remember?
            hold me hold me
            she said to paul
                                she was lost in the woods
                                remember
their first movie
made when they were only 8
                            remember?
hansel and gretel
starring the sweetmeats
                                                        remember?
                                                        how could i forget!
                i mean
                they were more than just kid actors
                                                        thrown clear of the
                                                        crash
remember?
                        mr. and mrs. sweetmeat die
                        and the twins survived
they were driving
back to connecticut
after doing a show
                        the kids couldn't have been more than 10 at the time
        the sweetmeats
        orphaned!
                                        a terrible tragedy
                (i always thought the crash
                 screwed them up a bit)
                                        horrible simply horrible
        "we watched them every tuesday night"
                                                THE SWEETMEATS
                                                BROUGHT TO YOU BY DIGITDOUCHET
                                                THE SOAP BURSTING WITH
                                                DIRT-DESTROYING BUBBLES...
                                                DOUBLY-BUBBLY GOOD

"right opposite milton berle"
                                    but even before that
                                    remember
                                    the sweetmeats on radio
          do i?
                                              "right opposite fanny brice"
              every tuesday night
              at eight (or was it wednesday?)
                                              a very devout family
      the kids went to church religiously
                                    a terrible accident
                                    took their parents away
          and how they cried at the grave?
          remember
                                              perchance to dream
          so tell me
          why should i hurt you
                                    hello?
you have just told me a
                                              breakdown my tuner
                                    hello montana?
              cq
              cq
                                              anyone out there?
      on a tour of one-night stands
                              (brentin strong decides that even without
                               confirmation on his telegram
                               he'll join baker battery
                               as they make their way to fuc hue)
while back in the steaks
                  america sleeps
                                    restlessly
                                    fitfully
                                    the conscience of the king to catch
          hello? hello?
                                    sorry sir
                                    new york is still sleeping
hello?
                  saturday may 7
                  dawns its early light on bermuda
hawaii is putting
out the lights
                        and on that divided continent between
                        on that ill-defined
                        ragged coastline east and west
                        that incredible silver sweep of the 49th
                        that snake of a river where our latin-american friends
                        curse our every breath
    "time to call it a
     night"
                                    ("not again honey
                                     how much sex do you think
                                     i can take
                                     anyhow?")
          a last long look in the mirror
          at another wasted day
                                    do you think they'll be found?
                  maybe
maybe baby
go to sleep
                        harold
                        i was just thinking
                                              go to sleep
                                              already

```
          ho hummmmmmmmm
                              GOT TO GET SOME SLEEP GODDAMIT
    boom boom of thr sonic
    stabilizer
                                  the range-coordinate (time-shared vector)
                                  indicator flashes green
          colonel dipper
          struggles with his fly zipper
                                        (bars are closing in oregon)
the nation
for those few brief minutes out of every day
when it is completely at rest
from shore to shore
                                                  can't sleep"
          can't keep awake?
                              take COMPOZE-NODOZ
                                                      for your
                                                      schizophrenia
          "well folks
           that's it for the late late late show
           helen twelvetrees in..."
                                          i was just thinking selma
                                          just a theory though
               for chrissake go to sleep
                                              (yawn)
       honey
       just one for good measure
                                              GOT TO GET SOME
GO TO SLEEP
                          stop that snoring henry
     (the bitch farts in
      her sleep)
                                            the forest animals
                                            are all tucked inside
                                            of disneyland
                  the bedbugs and barflies
                  and thoughts of sugarplums
                                        dance into
        minds endless in their thoughts empty
                                            fold the final newspage
               push the last button for the night
                                        that time
  that minutia within minutes
                          the national image crumples up into a
                          fetal position
       put out that light!
                                          turn down that raga!
          sssssshhhhhhhhhhh
                                  and shuffles
                                  and sniffles
                                  and sputters
                                          off to sleep...
```

                                        "still can't get the damn thing
                                         closed"
"ground control here colonel
 did you turn the zipper control
 lock-on sensor?"

                                        "i didn't touch a goddam thing"
"please control yourself colonel
 amateur radio operators may be
 tuned in"
                                                    morning
            the morning of may 7 1966
                                                    a light spring haze
                                                    as lazy as a nigger's ghost
                                                    strays along the breakwater
                                                    then sniggers up the coast
                    the sun
                    a yolk rising from fiery butter
                                                    lays an egg in the sky
            a platter of platitudes
            served with the grinds of yesterday's coffee
                                                        people come to understand
                                                        it's a new day
water splashes in basins and commodes from here to
dayton
                                                                    an eye
                pops open
                                    a cigarette is groped for
        a dream come true
                                                                        america
            wet from the dew drops spun from the subconscious
                                                            an eye
                                                            for an eye
                                                            pops
                out of the toaster commercial
                                                radiating bursts of brilliance
(the milkman cometh)
                        as the quartz-lamp flickers off
                        much as it had flickered on
                        the evening before
    but on the coast
    it was only 4:10
                            "c'mon ric
                             enough is enough"
                                                            "gerda gerda
                                                             gerda"
                            "i don't dig this kind of
                             kama sutra crap"
                                                            "gerda (gurgle)
                                                             gerda"
        clyde rawlins
        dreaming that he hears a telephone bell
        is jarred awake by a telephone bell
                                    (the station has been off the
                                     air for better than three hours
                                     and clyde has sacked out on the
                                     couch in studio a)
    "clyde..."
                                    "yes...jim?..."
    "yeah clyde listen..."
                                    "where the hell have you been?"
    "the station wagon got
     stuck in the sand..."

45

"for chrissake jim how'd you do a stupid thing
     like that?"

"anyhow the national
 guard got me out and a
 general by the name of
 ochre spelt o-c-h-r-e
 was personally in charge...
 in command get that?"

                              "huh?"

"...gimme that phone
 son..."

                              "what's going on?"

"whosis now?"

                              "clyde rawlins
                               station manager of KCUF"

"this is general
 ochre"

                              "yes general?"

"we got your man out of
 this quicksand here
 and there was this
 favor here that i
 thought of in return..."

                                        (reverend buttermilk has been up
                                         all night writing his sunday
                                         sermon)

          ~~reality the kids of today~~
          ~~openly seek god but god in~~

                              when in reality the kids of today
                              want god more than ever before
                              they are hungry for god
                              they need god as -- one bearded hippie
                              told me recently -- "soul food"
                              that's what he said friends
                              he needed god as "soul food"
                              now what did he mean by "soul food"?

               a 35¢ egg and a cup of java
blini and
bacon

                                                    elephant meat

          hamhock
          'n beans

                              what's yours?

     i'll have some orange juice and

                              (the most mouth-watering taste-tempting
                               flapjacks this side of howard johnsons)

               cup of black
     one of them there buns
               i'll have

                                        two up on two

          maggie
          the eggs are hardboiled
how's the
eggs dear

                                             mmmuuummmmmmmpphhhhh
                         some maple syrup?
     pass the sugar bud
                    and brush your teeth at every meal
   but sometimes that's impossible
                                             sometimes
          you don't wake up in your own bed
                                   sometimes

```
            the breakfast parodies itself
            like a bad commercial
            and the day begins as a comment on itself
                                            bleak
                                            unresolved
            the same motions and the same stale cornflakes
            the rain of raisins its own raison d'etre
            hailing into a hollow bowl
                              as the toast pops on the hour
sometimes
            the day that's impossible at every meal
                                                    breakfast
```

AUDIO	VIDEO
...wash your hands after every meal...	BUSINESS MAN CHECKS HIS WATCH. TRUCK WITH HIM AS HE WALKS AWAY FROM RESTAURANT.
Sometimes there just isn't time.	ON WORD *ISN'T* MAN STOPS DEAD IN HIS TRACKS. CUT TO MEDIUM CLOSE UP OF HIS SNAPPING FINGERS ON WORD *TIME*.
That is, before there was Digitdouchet...	ON WORD *BEFORE* HIS RIGHT HAND

```
  over his left heart
  a pledge of allegiance
                  to our national anathema
                                    just as
francis scott offkey
and the rest of them boston tea smokers
for which they stand on the fifth
                        drinking a fourth
convened the first joint session of congress
        jefferson with his hair tied behind in a ribbon
        washington as well
(in the style of current change)
                                        salutes you at daybreak
        manny makemore
        paces the night away
        from his suite on the 38th floor of the mark hopkins
        wondering whether his put order on united fruit went through at 28½
        wondering whether his helicopter pilot will show
                              "and the home of the brave"
good
MORNING
good
morning
good morning and here's the news at 5
                              a new fight looks imminent for u.s.
                              troops of the 242nd infantry brigade
                              situated in the ying yang valley 30
                              miles north of saigon
                                          informed sources
                              said today
        pauline farnsworth
        staying at the hilton
        gets her wake-up call at 5
        and has room service ring 1320
        to get seymore savage "off his fat ass"
```

ugh?

                    savage get off your ass

                                                            whossis?

                    it's pauline stupid!
                    let's get going!
                    those guys from tv control
                    are gonna meet us at 5:30
                    remember?

                                                            ugh

while at the new york hilton
a sunrise away vietnam hero
charles victor has his head split open with the parting of the window curtains

                                                            AW!

and tried to put that fragmented shrapnel night together
which like the stench of the room
seems to have put a decidedly pall-like atmosphere
over everything

                                                "get up private"

            "huh awwwwwwwww"

                                                "you meet your mother
                                                 in an hour"

            "oooohhhhhhhhhhhhhhhhh"

                                                "let's go!"

    (the sheets are stripped off victor's bed --
    the most common tactic of getting soldiers
    out of the sack on a cold winter's morning)

                                                "...and he's still
                                                 sleeping!"

            "zzzzzzzzz"
    (this being the new york hilton in the month
    of may the most common tactic of getting
    soldiers out of the sack just didn't work)

                                                "victor get up!"

            "za party's in za next zzzz"

                                                "oh my god!"

    everyday oatmeal for breakfast
    and on sunday oatmeal for brunch

                                            a regular habit with
                                            those kids

        oatmeal that stuck to your ribs
        because the sweetmeats ate it

                                            good and good for you

but not just any ole kind of oatmeal

                                oh no

these were *special* oats

                                oatmeal personally endorsed by
                                the entire sweetmeat family

        YOU'LL SAY "OATERRIFICS" WHEN YOU TRY
        MAREZIE OATS -- THE OATMEAL THE
        WHOLE SWEETMEAT FAMILY ENJOYS EVERY
        MORNING.
                (they said a box of Marezie Oats was found strewn all over the
sweetmeat death car)

                                swami sahalami sees all

            and you mean swami
            that the sweetmeats are
            still alive?

                                i predicted their parent's death
                                do you remember that?

            yes of course

                                in exactly the way it happened

            yes

                    it was no coincidence gentlemen
      about the sweetmeats swami

                   they are alive
                   that is all my ball shows now
                   but more messages are forthcoming

(until 10 days ago the village of les
 choux was a dull place
                 as dreary
                    a housewife said
 as its name
         which means cabbages
then it awoke to find itself an international
center for gypsies)

                             ooooooooooooooo
                             i can't find stuart

            dr. mountmother
            has spent the entire night
            searching for stuart on dallas's
            south side

                         ooooooooooooooo
                         i bet he's gone to big sur
                         to kill the sweetmeats
                         i remember what he said
                         once about hating them from
                         childhood
                             something about the
                         oatmeal he had to have at
                         breakfast every morning

       those cold winter mornings
       of our childhoods
               the howl of seasons whoring its broken frame
               against the clapboards
                       the shutters
                             the windowpanes
the cold security of
family breakfasts of oatmeal hot as pigiron
                  lumpy and molten
                  and sour tasting
                  unless deserted in sugar
     you took them into your heart america
     and loved them every morning with every bite
                             they were the way
                  you dreamed your family
               to be
      the way it always came out happily
                     (because of a good breakfast)
      the way it always signed off
                          on radio

MUSIC: #1 THEME UP: FADE FOR

92 ANN: Now here are all the sweetmeats to say

           their goodnight prayers.
                       chief broken wind
                       up at the proverbial
                       crack of dawn
                       instinctively reaches for his
                       peacepipe lying on the table
"ugh
where the hell is that fucking peacepipe?"

                                        when at that very moment
                                        stuart
                                        psychotic (but basically
                                        very nice) mass murderer
                                        gets off a dallas-to-san
                                        francisco flight and walks
                                        straight to the rent-a-cars

            SAVAGE
            SAVAGE GET UP
                              seymore savage raises an eyelid that looks
                              like yogi berra's catchers mitt
                              and sees two pauline farnsworths
                              one out of each corner of his eye

sonny swingle has the
saturday afternon
"golden fifty" show
so he's still sacked out

                        visions of forty-five's
                        spinning on the turntable of his
                        mind

      and sugar xxx
      leader of the ethnic dukes
      and "prime minister" of watts
      is up and about
      (fermenting trouble no doubt)
                                      so are mom and pop smith
                                      parents of russell smith

   "what a beautiful morning
    come shee the beautiful morning mother"

                                              "what's that?"

   "iiiii saaaaaiiiidddd
    cooooommmmmmmeee sssseeeeeeeeee aw never mind"

                                        hy frisbee back in new york
                                        is at WAGH-TV studios looking
                                        over teletype for overnight
                                        news breaks

0230
MONTEREY CALIFORNIA (UPI MAY 7)

BIG SUR IS ALREADY FILLING UP WITH THOUSANDS OF TOURISTS AND

PUBLICITY SEEKERS AS WORD OF THE SWEETMEATS CAR FOUND ABANDONED

ON A SIDEROAD SOUTH OF THIS RESORT AREA HAS BEEN CONFIRMED BY

THE FBI. THE ROAD LEADS UP TO WHAT LOCAL RESIDENTS CALL "THE

STONEHOUSE," A MANSION ON THE MOUNTAIN SUMMIT OVERLOOKING THE

PACIFIC OCEAN. SHERRIFS DEPUTIES ARE WAITING FOR MORNING BE-

FORE ATTEMPTING TO CLIMB THE 2280-FOOT MOUNTAIN (NAME NOT YET

KNOWN).

                                        but later it was determined
            parnassus
                          this hill they made a mountain
            this hope this dream
                          they say...
                          they say the hope was half the hill
            that if you could carry the dream half way up
            the reality of it would carry you the rest of the way

they say
(not having ever climbed it for sure)
                                        but that's getting ahead of our commercial
                        AUDIO

    No foolin'...when you want
                                                            VIDEO

    good beer...beer with class...   HOLD ON BEER BEING POURED INTO
                                                STEIN. DISS ON WORD *CLASS*
    ask for CRASS! Crass Beer!   INTO TRADEMARK TO END.
                                                                hey honey
                    get me another beer
                    will ya
                                                (the power of suggestion)
            pertaining to a storage device in which
            the *access time* is effectively independent
            of the location of the data
                                        "gerda...
                                        gerda it's almost daybreak..."
                "ric for chrissake
                 let me get some sleep!"
                                        "i love you love you love you love..."
    carmella karma
    is still trying to get through
    to the president (of what you ask?)
                                        she still believes
                                        in that innocent untouched spinster mind
                                        and body (wrinkles around the eyes belie
                                        the fact that she's 50 if she's a day)
                                        that soul pristine-pure...
    she still believes in (gasp!)
    god, country, the presidency, the warren commission report, and apple pie
    in that order
                she is the eleanor roosevelt of boredom
                                                            AUDIO

                                        ...and Yum Kipper Herrings are
                                        so good for you... Have some
                                        with every meal.
        "eef i do hear dot herring ad again
         i myself will go loco
                        turn it off dot radio"
                                            (the speaker is major macho
                                             head of the secret cuban
                                             exile organization based
                                             in the basement of the
                                             fountainebleau hotel)
        "good
         now what is ze report?"
                                        "san juan 6 san josé 4
                                         inning number 8 *el mucho*"
        "i mean about ze sweetmeats *stupido!*
         have they found them"
                                        "no señor"
        "then we carry out plan *numbro 3*"
                                        "si señor"
    what time you got
                    'bout 5:30 marv
    time for the muffler
    roughers to get going
    wake the gang

                                      huuummmmmm
                    lord have mercy
                    honey you're my joy
                                                huuummmmm huuummmmm

          i'm gonna make you mine
                                    sherry baby
start each morning
                                                  oooo baby

              yesterday
              all my troubles seemed so far away
                                        "how each song seemed to be
                                         written just for you"
          they really knew how to push a song
          those two
                    they knew 'where it was at'
                                      (the above was going through the trite
                                       mind of sheldon klingerman at
                                       that very moment
                                                he's busy writing
                                       sunday's Klingerman's Kolumn for
                                       the New York World Herald Tribune
                                       et cetera)

      "so that's the story son
       and my men can put that
       sound truck right back
       in the sand"
                                  "i can't do it general
                                   i'd be violating fcc regulations
                                   if i let you say that over the air"
      "not even the part about
       commie-dominated kids"
                              "general ochre sir in all respects
                               surely kids wearing long hair today..."
      "covering up small miniature
       radio receivers that implant
       orders
            yessir i believe that"
                                    general ochre had possibly in mind
                                    david cohen
                                    leader of s.h.a.m.e. (page 24 for stand-fors)
                                    and the general's arch enemy
                                    presently in the general's protective
                                    custard
              (military brutality
               MILITARY BRUTALITY)
                                            if that commie fuck
                                            doesn't shut his mouth
                                            i'll put my M-1 in it!
mah felluh amuricuns
                          forest jagoff
                          wakes up
                          believes that he's dreaming
                          and falls out of his own arms
with the help of a bellboy
pauline farnsworth finally
gets seymore savage out of bed
                                          "look at this 'thing'
                                           it's not even a human being
                                           look at the filth on him
                                           covered with lice"
                      "military harassment!"

          paul said that

                                        paul said that?

          not paul from the bible stupid
          paul of pookie and paul
                                   paul had shoulder length hair
                                   just like a girl   (giggle)
(from the back you couldn't tell
 one from the other)
                         he used hair net on it
                                             he was a goddam fag
                                             that's what he was!

             good riddance to both of them!
                                   goddam commies
when paul got his physical for the army
20,000 girls signed a petition asking the findings be made known
                                      "only mom and dad sweetmeat
                                       and pookie ever saw him nude"
              but everyone saw pookie naked
when she was
painted on
                         then they dragged her across a canvas
and gave the painting to
the marezie oats company

                                         she was a whore!
              a saint!
                    i hope to god they're both alive
     may god have mercy
                    or at least pookie
     may non-god have mercy
                                     (i'd settle for just paul)
     may non-non-good have mercy
                                 and so it went through the
                                 morning of the seventh
                                 may seventh ninneteen hundred
          and sixty-six
a good year
          good for death
          (though sixty-seven even bettered it)
                                     the coopers went on strike
                                     when they heard of the
                                     plastic casket
          yeah
               umph through the ricepaddy
                              (knock on wood)
               listening for the cat pad
               stalk death beyond the jungles mouth
a little kipling
in all of us
(or a little conrad)
                         the big buck sergeant got the first blast
          was this at danang or
          detroit buddy?
                    in those concrete canyons crying
                    the days wash
                    the little green islands within whose wells of tears...
where'dya say
that was?

                                        hey shaddup an let da
                                        poet say somethin'

(let each man tell it his own way)

                                    brentin strong:
                                    from vietman:
"this is brentin strong with baker battery
 of the 549th infantry battalion on the outskirts
 of fuc hue dead in the heart of the ying yang
 valley
        arrival of fresh viet cong regulars here last
 week marked a new and potentially crucial phase
 in the war..."

                                    N E W S   O F   T H E   D A Y

        BIG BATTLE LOOMING NEAR SAIGON

            By Melven Ford
        Special to The New York Herald Post etc.

    SAIGON, VIETNAM, MAY 6--
    Informed sources said today

                                        carmella karma
                                        from california:

    i remember waking up just as the
    sun rose that saturday morning
    i had been up all night trying
    to get the president (of what you ask?)

                                    N E W S   O N   T H E   H O U R

    BIGGEST BATTLE OF THE YEAR NEAR SAIGON

                                            informed sourcerers
said today
                        if you don't love me
                        love me like you usta do
        tell me don't love me babe

                                        sent out among the stars

                        for news he returned
                        emptyhanded
                                    a period of waterfalls and cymbals

        crashing against eardrums
                        drums of our ears

                                                    drumming up
                                                    business

                (flints
                 the noise silencers
                 reported a 37% rise in business
                 the day pookie's and paul's latest flip
                 CONTEMPLATION ON A BUDDHA'S NAVEL hit the racks)
                                                    drumming
the strange music of flutes and sitars against unwilling ears
                                                "pure noise!"

                        sounded like a river
                        if you floated with the water
        down the DNA canal
                        to the beginning
                        it sounded more like singing
        down the NRA canard
                        hard if you had to work
                        in the thirties like a jerk
                                        soda watertowning it
            (how ya gonna keep them down on the farm
             after they've seen t-v
                        -----hay--------)
                                        "goddam creeps listen to that
                                        there commie gook music"

a time when things were clear-cut

                                    when good and evil
                                    was as clear as the nose on your race

a time when we knew our enemies
as well as we knew ourselves

                                    "fought the krauts and the japs
                                     to preserve the right of my kid
                                     to call his old man a fascist!"

REMEMBER PEARL HARBOR YOU NO-GOOD BUM!

                                         when roosevelt was running
                                         with a guy named fala

zane grey
and faye wray
                sammy kay
                        martha raye
                                turhan bey
                                       dennis day
                                           janet leigh
                                                   sam and fay

WHO?
                      sam and fay sweetmeat
                      that vaudeville team
                      don'tcha remember?

                                       got married
got married don'tcha remember
in an absolutely *super* wedding

                                       on one of his furloughs
for better and then for wurst

                                       returned to fight in the
                                       battle of berlin
and nine months to the day (so they say)

                                       with sam still away
out popped the twins

                                       the very day
                                       the war ended
the very day

                                          sugar xxx
                                        of the ethnic dukes:

"ah was born on the very same day man
 but like a few years before man
 but nobody remembers my birthday man"

                                         (interjection
                                       sorry)
                                          "line check"
we have our axioms and our method of deduction modus ponens
these are the ingredients of a mathematical system et cetera

                                           "checks out sir"

                              "i want t' be sure
                               the 69th is fightin' ready"
(general ochre is moving
 his troops out)

AUDIO	VIDEO
ANNOUNCER	ANIMATION
Sometimes it isn't enough for a beer to claim to be the best...	OPEN TO TROPHY ROOM PANNING QUICKLY OVER ROWS OF TROPHIES.
Sometimes you have to prove it!	

woody wilson
surfer:
> "i was up at the crack or dawn
> stoked with the view of these
> be-u-ti-ful sets coming in..."

(timothy queen
a-c-d-c:)

we arrived in my jetliner just
as the sun was rising

stuart
with a short circuit:

i knew then that i had to kill
a feeling came over me like i
had before
> *deep in my stomach*
like i was suddenly very hungry

"gerda loins
setting star:
> as far as i'm concerned
> gland spelled backwards
> spells 'drip'"

david
cohen
setting
pretty:
> hey
> will one of you guys call the a.c.l.u.
> for me
> i gotta get outa here

hy frisbee
in new york:

"about nine in the morning or so of the
7th a bulletin came over the wires..."

0857
MONTEREY CALIFORNIA

(UPI MAY 7)

A DETACHMENT OF NATIONAL

GUARD SOLDIERS UNDER THE COMMAND OF

GENERAL OCHRE (PRONOUNCED

OAK'-ER) HAVE ARRIVED AT THE SITE

WHERE THE SWEETMEATS ARE

BELIEVED TO BE HELD HOSTAGE. A NEW

REPORT CONFIRMS THAT THE

SWEETMEATS ARE ALIVE AND UNHARMED.

ORDERS HAVE BEEN ISSUED

TO ALL LAW ENFORCEMENT AUTHORITIES...

and so it went
into the morning of the 7th

"hello mabel?"

"i know i heard
they're alive"

glorybe

did they say alive and unharmed?

i was listening to news
over breakfast when it

came over the air

i was out in the garden

(pruning her prunes
the boston matron)   *and den i heard on da radio*

penny lane is
in my ears and
in my eyes

```
        i flapped out when
                                    hold it hold it!
you mean to tell me
you first heard them alive and well
the next morning?
                                           not their voices actually
                                           but the radio said so
then they could have been
                                              it was never established
                        sunshine came softly
                        through my window today
                                                 that morning of
                                                 may 7th 1966
           it could have gone either way
```

```
"jim
 jim come in"
                                           "i read you fine clyde"

"what's happening"
                                           "don't really know
                                            i'm caught in a
                                            traffic jam about
                                            two miles from the
                                            stonehouse"

"can you get in there
 with the portable
 transmitter"
                                           "are you kidding
                                            it's bumper to
                                            bumper all the way"
```

AUDIO	VIDEO
...imagine my hands are no strangers to grease and grime...	MECHANIC HOLDS UP PALMS TO CAMERA. DOLLY BACK UNTIL IN SYNC WITH WIFE SLIDING IN ON RIGHT. MCU OF WIFE AND MECHANIC.
My wife here came up with the answer to a mechanic's prayer...	ON WORD *PRAYER* CUT TO ECU OF PRODUCT.
Digitdouchet...cuts grime like crazy!	

                    prayer alone can't clean up our cities
                    or stop the dope and vice
                    or stop the murdering and raping
                                              no friends
                    it takes more than prayer for god to hear us
                                                        it takes
(rev. buttermilk underlines this passage)
                                        the positive action of the will
                                        or what i call
                                        spiritual dynamicism

                now what do i mean by
                spiritual dynamicism?

                                                    (gerda
                                                     i got that feeling
                                                     again)

ladies and gentlemen (would you watch the cable mac)
in just a few minutes mom and pop victor
mother and father of charles victor
will step off that airplane now taxiing
at the far end of the runway

                                                    "mom
                                                     dad!"

and private victor will see his parents
for the first time in two years

                                                    "MOOOOOOOOMMMMMM!"

(just a minute charlie
 they can't hear you from in the place)

                                                    "DAAAAAAAADDDDDDY!"
                "hey
                 what's that kid on?"
                                        ground control
                                        ground control

    "ground control here colonel"
                                        i can't sleep
    "just close your eyes and..."
                        N E W S   O N   T H E
H O U R
                CAUSES OF THE RIOTS FIND REMEDIES IN VIET
                ENDED IN DEATH TODAY IN SOUTH AFRICA SWEETMEATS
                CHIEF OF STATE STRENGTHENING OF HOT PUR-
                SUIT PROPOSED SURCHARGE ON INCOME TAX SPACE
                NATION DIE HE SAID COST OF STEEL INCOME KILLER
                                        (but first a word
                                         from our sponsor)

          AUDIO   VIDEO

    ...mah felluh amuricuns. So the   PAN DOWN FROM EXECUTIVE SEAL ON
                                        APRON TO BARBECUE PIT WITH ROAST
next time you-all are throwin' a   PIG SLOWLY TURNING. PULL BACK TO
                                        SHOW JAR OF *INFORMED* IN FOREGROUND.
bar-be-cue, be sure to slime yo'
                                        CUT TO ANIMATED JACKASS LOGO WITH
porker with *Informed Sauces*...the   *INFORMED SAUCES* POPPED ON TO END.

sauce that gets it straight from the

horseradish's mouth. Y'all git some.

                                                    the civil rights
movement has saved us temporarily
                                what we do now is drag out one of the old
plots and add a new sociological
dimension by casting a negro in the role
                                                    louis smith
                                                    turns on
                        (the television
                         of course)
                                                    the television
                                                    (natch!)
                just in time to catch
                major macho before the microphones
                                                "dots right si si si si
                                                 i myself know where ze
                                                 sweetmeats are located"
major
                                major macho
                "major..."
                        ("hey one at a time")
        major
                        "major macho sir
                         did you say they were
                         kidnapped?"
                major
                                                "si kidnapped"
by who
                        "by who sir?"
                                                "coo-ban agents"
that's what i said mac
the stonehouse is on
roughers turf
                better get
truckin' before
there's trouble
                                listen tempest or whatever your name is
                                we don't want to have any trouble with
                                your group on this thing
                                                just play ball
                                with us this time
                                                (please?)
okay men
don your gas masks!
                        (please!)
rubber hoses -- out!
                                marv
                                marv old man...
                                        mayor meyer
                                        mayor of big sur
                                        feels the dam break
                                        in his armpits
NAPALM!
                                MARV!
                                marvin listen
                                i'll talk to francona i'll talk to francona!
at rest men
                forest jagoff
                is brushing his teeth
                with a scotch-flavored toothpaste
                humming along to songs of the perfumed garden

"francona here"

"eh
 sorry to bother you frank..."

"who's this"

"eh meyer
 major...i mean mayor meyer mother..."

"dammit
 drop dead"

"it went...went dead...dead...fellows?"

(why does violence always
 precede the commercials)

VIDEO   AUDIO

CUT TO ASTRONAUT TRYING TO
SPEAR HERRING FLOATING IN SPACE.   Herring spearing makes the long
                                     hours pass for our men in space.
copulation in free space is considered
unlikely and fertilization even more so
says a new report titled *the scotch tape revolution*

                                                (whatever goes up
                                                 must come down)

        ok keep movin'
        keep movim'

                                        you there
                                        g'won beat it

  keep the roads clear
                              HHHHEEEEEEEEEYYYYYYYYY!
        "who yah shovin!"

                                            move it
                                            mac
                                                        ok ok
                                                        break it

        up yours
        you motherfucking hunkie
cocksucker
                                    (there they were as big as life
                                     lined right across the highway)
                        break it up!
                                        it was a public highway you know
    at first i thought there had been
    an accident so we waited for a
                        break it up!
                                            the road was just
                                            jammed
WWWWWWWWWWWWWWWWWHHHHHHHHHHHHHHHHHHHHHHHHHHHEEEEEEEEEEEEEEEEE
                                            and sirens blastin'
        ok folks
        let's break it up now
                                        common sense in the matter
    then someone up front passed back the news
                                            *didn't i tell you to
                                            get behind that barrier!*
    that the highway was blocked
                            move it
                            move it!
ok folks
you'll have to clear this area

                                                hey wait a minute
                                                this is government
                                                land

                    was that true?
                                that's what they said
                                over the radio

                                                        "clyde
                                                         now listen very closely..."

                    "go ahead jim"
                                                        "there's an argument brewing
                                                         whether the stonehouse is
                                                         on government property"

                    "what about it?"
                                                        "the stonehouse may be in
                                                         big sur national park
                                                         if it isn't
                                                         then the national guard
                                                         has less authority than
                                                         the state troopers
                                                         unless of course the guard
                                                         is mobilized in which case
                                                         the sherrif's office has no
                                                         jurisdiction over the FBI
                                                         except by executive decree"

(anyhow
 it looked like someone or other was going to be busted)

                                                            but let the sweetmeats'
                                                            manager max vogel
                                                            tell it like it
                                                            really was:

        "i was trapped in my car just like all the others
         even though i got an early start that morning
         the events of the last half day were almost more than i could bear"
(woops)

                        AUDIO   VIDEO

                                                    CUT TO BLACK. OPEN INSIDE CABINET.
                                                    DOOR SWINGS OPEN. FOCUS ON WIFE'S
                                                    FACE, THEN HAND AS IT REACHES
                                                    FORWARD TO PICK UP BOTTLE. FOCUS
                                                    BACK TO FACE FOR WINK. BLACK. CUT TO
                        WIFE   TORSO SHOT AS WIFE TURNS IN SYNC
                                                    HOLDING PRODUCT TO CAMERA. FOCUS
    ...A FEEL UP in the morning   ON PRODUCT.

    contains just as much caffeine   POP ON WORDS *AS MUCH CAFFEINE*. POP OFF
                                                    ON WORD *BUT*.
    as the usual breakfast stimulant
                                                    ON WORD *BUT* POP ON WORDS *NON-HABIT*
    but isn't habit-forming. Best of   *FORMING*.

    all...
                        "if the CIA doesn't put in
                         a request typed in triplicate
                         one copy going to the justice
                         depsrtment..."

                                                        "ooooooooooooooooo
                                                         stu-artttttt
                                                         stu-artttttttttttt"

    we hear a lot from that texas butcher
    appearing on television with barbecue
    sauce all over his face
    but we know by the congressional record

that he spoke of the *yellah threat*
many years ago
well brothers
that fat hunkie is going to find out
something about the *black threat* this summer

"what's your name soldier?"

"lewis washington eh sergeant
 william lewis washington suh"

"can you tell me something
 about what's up ahead?"

"uh
 looks like a batallion of
 gooks to me"

yes friends
you'll see hate literally dissolve
before your eyes
and an end to all of those
petty jealousies and distrust
yes friends
god has provided me with the
answer
god has personally told me to share my
good fortune with you and so help me
i will

AUDIO	VIDEO
Yes...you'll feel clean...	CUT TO COUPLE HOLDING HANDS ACROSS CANDLELIT TABLE. PULL
really clean...with the one	BACK, DISSOLVE INTO DIGITDOUCHET CAN THAT IMMEDIATELY SLIDES TO LEFT.
handcleanser cleaner than soap...	POP IN TOWELETTE ON RIGHT TO END.
Digitdouchet--can or towelette.	

now
back to the news

MEDICAID COSTS CHAIRMAN OF THE JOINT REPUBLICAN
FORECAST RAIN CONTINUING SAY A PASSENGER TRAIN
CLASHED WITH RIOT POLICE HURLED ROCKS ARRESTED
REPORTEDLY READY TO IS STILL FIGHTING IN SAVE
THE CRITICALLY ILL BOMBING IN NORTH VIETNAM POPE
THINK A TAX HIKE IS NEEDED NOW 100 MEN ARRESTED
CIRCLING THE GLOBE

"ground control here
 colonel
 we have the hypnotist
 you wanted on the phone

"swami sahalami sees all
 your wish is my command"

"swami listen
 i saw your act about seven years ago
 when you were known as
 melvin the mental wizard"

"on some of my karmic
 voyages i'm known by that
 name yes"

"it was up at the concord
 on my honeymoon
 you were
 performing as a hypnotist"

"that is entirely possible"

                                        "well you hypnotized me that
                                         afternoon and i went right
                                         to sleep"

"it is a gift of the third plane"

                                        "i have to get some sleep swami
                                         do you think you can do it
                                         again?"

"i have hypnotized royalty
 my services do not come cheaply"

                                        "money is no object swami
                                         the space agency will take
                                         care of it"

"i'm sure of it...
 but what i can use more than that
 is what they now call 'exposure'"

                                                    downtown
                                         things will be great
                                         waiting for you

            movie shows
            downtown
                                      downtown
                  just listen to the
 bossa nova
                                        "hey let's go downtown"
            the saturday voices of the stockpiling
            public:
                                                a sale at gypp's
                "$2.49
                 marked down from $2.99
                 marked up from $100 for the gross"
                                        out and go out and
honey
i'm going downtown to buy
                              to see
            to hear
                                        to feel the pulse of
                                         pursestrings
               vibrating with the jingle of jangle
                                        (in towns of only 5,000 or so
                                         minor traffic jams develop
                                         on friday nights and satur-
                                         day mornings)
      right off the farm
                          names like: mr. and mrs. albert corley
                                       randy lewis
                                       mollie die
                                       lenzy moore
                                       ella mae mitchell
            swarming like caterpillar tractors
into
social butterflys
                    "clem
                      clem there's a sale of bathing suits down at dixon's"
to see and be seen
                  to be believed
                              cancer: this is your period
                              to buy your dreams

olivia pitt doesn't put much weight
on her horoscope (not as much as she
does on herself) yet she instinctively
turns to it every morning in her newspaper

                                        virgo: a day to make decisions
                                        stay clear of geminis

   decisions she muses *what kind of decision
   should i make?*
           i haven't decided anything
   for years

                          just as well
a decision for miss olivia pitt
is a decision for the nation

                   (or at least what we should hope
                    our nation to be)

    indivisible with liberty and
    justice for the haves

                                       the haves?

       you know man
       like the haves and the have nots?
you mean
your huddled masses yearning to breathe freeway air?

                        i mean sir
don't fire until you see whitey in their eyes

                (or black men in their wives)

    i mean sir
    justice is blind
    what she doesn't see won't hurt her

                  (miss olivia pitt
                   recalls she played
                   justice last year
                   at a d.a.r. fund
                   raising supper)

i mean all those hunkie faggots
who think they own this goddam country

               well sir or madam r.s.v.p.
               my grandfather was a slave
    and his father was in this country
    long before your mick mother came over on the boat

                          (they all came
                    over on boats)
    buried their cattle and turned under their potatoes
    and added them all to the melting pot

               which simmered for generations
               in a hatred stew
    until a war provided a necessary stopcock
             to end all wars
    and another
    and then another
    and then once more
preserving (or at least trying to)
the ideals won so hard by the first war for freedom

                  *linda smith just turned
                  16 and junior at monterey
                  central high school gets
                  a call*

hi lin
what'cha doin'

                                        reading history
                                        got a test on monday

goin' to the dance tonight?

                                        sorry i can't go with you danny
                                        i got a date with bud

is he going to the dance?
thought maybe you wanted to
go down to the sur tonight

                                        you'll never get in
                                        the highway's all blocked

that's just what the radio says
so you don't go down there

                                        well thanks anyway danny i'd like to
                                        but i really made a date with bud...
                                        kind of...

ALL RIGHT MEN
FALL IN!
                    "eh general ochre sir"
                                                        "what is it captain"

                    "the men have already fallen in
                      sir"

                                                        "well they're sloppy
                                                         have them fall in
                                                         again"

     "again eh?"
                                    "i said mother
                                     russell wants to know if you want
                                     t' go downtown wich us"
     "how's that?"

                                    ma smith's voice tinkles like a little bell
                                    cold in the empty belfrey of her mind
senility becomes her

                                    pa smith's mouth is filled with a thousand
                                    clicks from a hundred metronomes
his dentures keep time
to the monotony of his
senior citizenship

                                    together down the garden path of life
                                    shouting and lisping
                                              fortunately blissfully
                                              ignorant of the 20th century
                                              from the great war on

          only you
          can make the world seem bright
          only you
          can make the darkness light

                                        (a bit of solid gold
                                          for your golden years)

     ok ok
     i get the bit
                    health education and welfare (but mostly you-know-what)
                    for septuagenarians who still like to go dancing
remember
          the sweetmeats donated over five million of their records
          to old age homes throughout the country in just three years!

                                                        a record
                                                        number
                                                        of records

sheldon klingerman writes:
                        they were an enigma...
                        in a world of conformity
                        they were unconventional
                        in a world of tired hackney phrases
                        they were candles that lit the darkness
     (didn't adlai stevenson
say that about eleanor?)
                                        when managed news became
                                            the credibility gap
                   but pookie and paul
                   always told it like it was
always hit the nail on the
thumb
                                        "rules say that the local
                                         sherrif's office has pre-
                                         cedent"
               "well why don't the sheriff
                go up there with his depu-
                ties"
                                        "he can't get through the
                                         traffic"

     yes friends
     life's road is paved with opportunities
     opportunities to find who we are
     and who god is
                   just the other day a stranger
     came up to me and said *reverend buttermilk*
     you talk a lot about god as if you know him
     better than you do yourself
                        and i said
     i *do* know him better than i know myself
                                    because
     i have divine intuition of him
                        heavenly   intuition
                        everlasting intuition of him
     and i have only earthly knowledge
                            only *earthly* knowledge
     of myself
                                    (you are going to sleep
                                     you are going to sleep)

              (i just yawned swami
               keep it up)

                                    (the wheel of the dharma
                                     turns slowly for you)
novus ordo seclorum?
or how about annuit corptis?
                                        both are running downhill
         "keep eyeglasses from sliding down your nose!
          inconspicuous flesh-colored foam pads adhere
          instantly to nosepiece of any frame
                            peel off
          only when desired
                        use on eyeglass temples too
          relieve pressure spots
                        ease weight of hearing
          aid and other heavier frames
                        6 pads in a set"
                                        did he say
                                        six pads to the set?

                    how many to be gross about it?
                                              who ya pushin!
    get your fucking hands off me you goddam creep!
                                                          hey
                                                          more beer
            you goddam fucked-out whore
                                      don't give me any of your lip
            ma-ma   (ma-ma)
                                  the bastard wanted to borrow my lawnmower again
    ding-dong-dell
    pussy in the well
                      pussy all over the place
                                          "if i don't get that raise next"
                ok ok stop shovin'
                              move to the back of the bus
        hey over here
                      "so i said that she said that he said"
    saturday morning
    me an' my kid usually
    go fishin' down the creek
                                  just sits by the television all day
                                  and watches baseball
        justsitsby the   television
                                          all
                                                                  day
            the count on raukcjcnvky
            is two balls and two strikes
                                      came in with a pound of dirt on him
      "aw i gotta work on saturdays
       painting with my pa"
                                  who ya shovin!
    ok ok no offense
                                                      (you headshrink
                                                        holiday)
            but he won't see a doctor!
                                      oooooooooooooo
                                      stttuuu-aaarrrrrrrrrttt
                                      where did that lunatic
                                      go
                                        (dr. mountmother en route to california)
    "jim what's happening now?"
                              "they're tossing a coin to see who goes in
                              and get them
                                          but they can't agree on the coin"
        meg
        i just heard on the radio
        that federal marshals
        are going in to get the sweetmeats
                                          russell
                                          are you going to help me with
                                          linda's trunk or not
        can't you wait till after lunch
                                          that's what you said last
                                          saturday
    (last saturday in fact
     russell smith was in
     frisco on a business trip)

where at that very moment
manny makemore
is eating a couple of 3-minute eggs
in the mark hopkins diningroom

having coffee with him is his secretary
pearl gottlieb who flew into frisco late
friday night at her boss's urgent request

"i want you to buy an expensive
portable recorder somewhere around
here and be back at the hotel at
exactly noon"

"boss what's up?"

"honey
i don't even know
but if i can get into the place where
they got the kids i can make a tape
and take some pictures maybe
that's
all i want
the damn things will sell like hot
tamales"

OK OK once more with feeling
QUIET ON THE SET

(ric gland star-director
of The Lust Weekend has gerda loins
read her lines again)

"...but don't you see *amor*
that my people are not like you
they are proud yes...
but they are also humble
you are asking the impossible of me..."

OK THIS IS A TAKE

(clap-board strikes)

"hello is walter there?"

"hey have you heard?"

ringgggggggggggggggg ringgggggggggggggggg

hello?

information
i'd like the number for...

"this is a recording"

well...
this is a recording of a recording you stupid fuck!

i remember...

i was fifteen when the sweetmeats were born

knew them from the time they
appeared in their first movie

THE SWEETMEATS AT
TUMBLEWEED RANCH

(remember how they rescued the colt
from the quicksand?)

or how about THE SWEETMEATS MEET
ABBOTT AND COSTELLO

HAHAHAhahha

i remember the scene

making the scene
in the sixties
they were a pair those two!

a good thing going
like they knew everyone
who was everyone

(why are we continually putting them in the

                                                --but honey--
                                                        past)
they're not dead
they couldn't be
                                if anyone touched a hair on pookies head i'd
    "until i read in the papers
     they were caught smoking those terrible things"
                                                i'll kill the guy
                                                who sold them
                                                    that stuff
        a pope meddler
                    a mute diddler
                            a dilly dally
                                    and a flub-a-dub
                                                rolled into one!
that's what it does to you
it makes you freak out like paul
                                        remember that son-of-a-bitch
                                        refused to serve in the army

        (goddam fucking commie)
                            just sat down before the induction center
                            and burnt his draft card just like that!!
        this generation!
                        and then burnt a dollar bill
        lawdy!
                    and then burnt a poem by carl sandburg
                                            "why i recall a time
                                            them sweetmeats
                                            used to write
                                            poems about
                                            the flag"

                        OUR FLAG
                            by them sweetmeats
the flag is red
the flag is blue
the flag is white
for me and you
                    it has stars
                    of forty-eight
                    one star for every
                    single state
                                        it has bars
                                        and it has stripes
                                        and it has strikes
                                        and it has strips
                                            dragging the last butt
        into another world
        screwing the left behinds in their left behinds
        tossed out on the street
        evicted from life
                    all those unwilling to share the phantasy
                    for lack of the admission price
all those
who heard the news at noon

N E W S   A T   N O O N

modulated by video output
power-setting crank knobs

                          HANOI TO INVESTIGATE DEFENSE DEPARTMENT TWELVE
                          WHITE MEN IN POWER FAILURE POSTPONEMENT COUNT
                          DOWN MUSICAL WORLD

  radar antenna beam pattern

                                          aircraft scintillation noise

            TWO INVESTIGATIONS UNION TOLD THEIR
  COST BORNE BY EMPLOYERS BEAT NEGRO PRESIDENT
  CHOSE FOREIGN POLICY

                  signal decay with range and blip-scan
                  effects

                              EFFORTS OF FEDERAL MARSHALS CALLED
                  IDENTIFIED AS ROBERT WILLIAMS TO RESCUE THE
                  SWEETMEATS

VIDEO	AUDIO
OPEN ON CITY CONSTRUCTION SITE.	
ZOOM IN TO TWO CONSTRUCTION	BKG OF CONSTRUCTION NOISES
WORKERS OPERATING PNEUMATIC	AND JACKHAMMERS
HAMMERS. CROSS DISSOLVE TO MCU	
OF FRONT VIEW OR WORKERS.	
	"well sweetie
	you can just imagine my chagrin
	when i found i couldn't get in"
"because the roads were	
blocked mr. queen?"	
	"roads?
	as yes the roads
	completely blocked you know?"
about as blocked as stuart's	
childhood	
but perhaps we should	
let him tell it	

i was a few years older than them
they were born when i was five or so
so when i was ten or so my mother began
harping on me to be as good as them
she said they were half my age and so polite
if the sweetmeats can be so polite and eat
their marezie oats then i can be too
and if i did anything wrong
she'd tell me the sweetmeats were watching

naw
i don't hold no grudge
against 'em

                              (marvin tempest talking into a KCUF microphone)

i and the boys
or is it me and the boys
anyhow
me and the boys decided to
lay our claims to the south
side of the sur as rougher turf
in 1964 my predecessor murry mowglis signed a treaty with several of the
home owners in the area promising not to mess up their gardens or nothing
or break in and wreck their places in return for the stonehouse which we
were to take possession of in 1967
                              "that's whut whitey think
                               in the meantime we hit the stores
                               of them motherfuckers and run...
                               hit 'an run just like them vc's do"
        you can't walk anywhere
        these days even in broad daylight

                                        the streets are so unsafe
        it's a crime
                        millions of crazy people out there
                        and you call *me* paranoic!
raping and mugging
where will it all end
                              "right in broad daylight too!"
            everything from marijuana
            to yellow jackets

                                my little girl who---eee
                                come and give me love
                                i can't stop whooo-ooooo

        i read just tte other day that a 14-
        year-old girl was fatally stabbed to
        death by a burglar

                                                terrible!
        or was it the other way 'round?

                                                just as bad
            i don't know what's gotten into them
"when i was
 their age"
                    these niggers you know
                    think they own the world

                                        goddam international conspiracy
                                        by those goddam commies
                                        to subvert america's fifty
                                        largest cities

                    mind you
                    i'm not blaming this recent lawlessness
                    as part of an organized movement
hey
hey you!

                                                    goddam kid swiped an apple
                                                    just like that

        putting up the wash when a perfect
        stranger comes up to me and says
                                        in broad daylight
                                        just like that
where will it all end
                        it was a time for visions
                        of sugarplums dancing in beds
                        of coast-to-coast televisions
                        dancing in heads
                                a time for sugarplums
                                dancing in bowls of cereals
                                sugar radiating bursts of
                                brilliance
                        a balanced breakfast
                        a balanced lunch
                        a balanced dinner
                                dancing down the enzyme highway
                        dancing their way into your hearts
        coast to coast
        they danced
        white scrubbed clean americans
                                (the kind norman rockwell would have
                                 if he could have)
        their tummies filled with 100%
        dancing sugarplums
                        their middle class bellies
                        radiating bursts of brilliance
a time for visions:
of a balanced breakfast:
                                    toe-tapping tangerine juice
                                    cooled to the peak of perfection
        chicken's eggs *au continental*
        anyway you like 'em
                                sausage and bacon and corn fritters
        toast rolls bagels
        individual butter patties
                            "a stack of jacks"
a number 3
                                the breakfast special
        "draw one"
                                the breakfast special
                                coast-to-coast
        "all aboard"
                                chugging the sweetmeats
                                through outmeal mountains
in a time of visions

AUDIO	VIDEO
VO SWEETMEAT THEME (FEMALE)	CUT TO GROUP SHOT OF POOKIE DOLLS VARIOUS POSITIONS. CUT TO
...just like Pookie does in	MCU OF POOKIE DOLL. OTHERS DIS-SOLVE.
real life. Watch how she	DOLL ANIMATES. DOLLY BACK ON THEM.
combs her own hair with real	SLIDE IN LITTLE GIRL BEHIND WHO

       water...then lets *you* set it   APPLIES ROLLERS. ZOOM IN ON
                                        ROLLER.

       for her...just that way you   DISSOLVE INTO ECU PROFILE OF DOLL.
       want it. There! Isn't she   POP ON SPARKLES LINES IN SYNC.

       lovely!
                        "well if you ask me
                        i think she was a no-good little turnip
                        and it serves her right
                                      i heard from somewhere
                      she had had two abortions and a miscarriage!"
carmella karma is
childless (and had had a mismarriage)
                      "...and you know of course she had her
                        nose fixed..."

likewise carmella
though it didn't improve her face any

                    "nope
                     don't recognize you
                     can't let you through"
      "look officer..."
                    "francona"
      "francona
       you're letting other
       members of the press in"

                    "they're personal friends
                     i don't know you folks"
      "i'm seymore savage and this
       is pauline farnsworth of
       WAGH-TV national network news"
                    "i can read that on your card all right
                     but i'm not sure..."
bbbbzzzzzzzzzzzzzz bbbbzzzzzzzzz
                    "hol'it" (he reaches in his car)
bbbbzzzzzzz
                    "francona here"
(captain i got another call from
 mayor meyer
        he wants to speak to you)
                    "yeah put him on"
(eh captain this is mayor meyer eh ah
 i have marvin tempest here alongside
 of me who wants to say a word or two)
                    "WHO!"
      marvin tempest
      in a pot of tea
            in a sea of pot
                 smoking duals
                 across state lines from here to
                 boston
          (where after lecturing at harvard
           he joined adams house proctors in
           an old fashioned tea party)
                  "WHO?"
makes me feel so good
everytime i see that girl
yyyeeeaaaahhhh what can i do   marvin tempest with his
                      12-point beercan top medallion
                      his flip-top necklace
                      his studs and his daisy roots

    rrrrrhhhhhhhhhooooooooommmmmmm

                                              dragging the dawn
                                              down deserted roadways
            (beercans staring like one-eyed cats
             in the blackness)
                        rrrrhhhhhhhhhhhooooooommmmmmmmmm
                                              he is marlon brando
                                              and james dean
                the lone eagle and paul revere
                                    rrrrrrhhhhhhhhhhhhooooooooooommmmmmmmmm
        splitting the night
        with the cries of our dead longings
                                    (...as much caffeine as the
                                     usual breakfast stimulant...)
"well friends
 god has an answer
 and he gave us that answer through his son jesus christ
 jesus said
 come unto me all ye that labor and are heavy laden
 and i will give you rest
                        i will give you rest
                        i will give you rest...
 now god wanted you to
 come to jesus so that jesus could give you rest"

                                                      AUDIO

                                    Beer as bright that last sip

                                    as it is the first.
(major macho guzzles down a CRASS
 and wipes the foam off his beard with his sleeve)
                                              "dots what i say
                                               coo-ban agents of ze CIA"
                        "major
                         do you mean counter-revolutionaries or..."
"major
 did you say working *for* the CIA?"
                                              "part-time"
                        "part-time?"
                                              "si
                                               free-lance basis"

            (did he say bases or basis?)
                                              "ze sweetmeats were
                                               working for us ourselves"

                        "as revolutionaries major?"
                                              "anti-counter
                                               revolutionaries"
"what kind of revolution major"
                        "what kind..."
                                              "i no can discuss dot at
                                               zis time"

the steady bombardment of this base camp in the
paddy fields south of saigon where about 2,000
marines are braced for an expected north vietnamese
attack turned out to be the prelude to a heavy
shelling a few hours later
                        large artillery shells pounded down on
                        the sand-bagged bunkers and the airstrip
in the distance you can
hear communist mortars rout out the last defenders of fuc hue
the town that must be won back if the ying yang valley
is to be opened once again

                                            so slowly
                                            and time can do so much
                                            are you still mine...

sonny swingle arrives at
KCUF studios to do his
"golden fifty" afternoon show
                                            lonely rivers sigh
                                            wait for me wait for me...

humming *unchained melody*
one of the all-time goodness
goldies and a best 300-pick selection
                                                            whhhoooooooooeeeeee
                                                            i need your love

                    quite oblivious to the fact
                    that no one
                                not even the engineer
                    is there

                                                    "i'll engineer myself
                                                    just like the old days"

in the old days *(francona is saying)*
te-ve creeps like you wouldn't have
a icecubes chance in hell to get in there
but i'm lettin' you in cause i like you

                                            (seymore savage slips the captain
                                            a jackson and drives on)

                    <u>AUDIO</u>   <u>VIDEO</u>

            (ANNOUNCER MALE)   OPEN ON MLS FRONTIER WOMAN
                                        IN BACKYARD SCRUBBING CLOTHES.
In the old days washing the
family's clothes was an all-
day affair...

                                        CUT TO OVERHEAD SHOT OF WOMAN
Rough on the clothes...but   RUBBING CLOTHES ON SCRUBBOARD.
rougher on the lady of the
house...   CUT TO TORSO SHOT OF WOMAN AS SHE
                                        STRAIGHTENS HER BACK.
                                                    "like the whole thing
                                                    is to keep your back
                                                    loose"

            (woody wilson is explaining
             the fina art of surfin')
                                                    "the largest wipe-out
                                                    factor is not a bad
                                                    curl as is popularly
                                                    thought
                                                            it's a stiff
                                                    back"

            (his class listens attentively
             to this man who's become a legend
             in his time)
                                    ten years ago woody wilson
                                    hadn't the bread for his own board
he was like any other gremmi
stoked with the sight of those big sets spilling in from the sea...
surfin' was just a baby then
(though mark twain was said to be jazzed on the idea)
known only to those sullen slit-eyes to the west
but fate was to annex them to the coast of california
and where the waters met surfin' overnight grew up
                                                            well sir

woody wilson stowdaway
goin' to hawaii
woody wilson got no lay
arriving in hawaii
                              but he made a deal with the hawaiian police
let me stay woody wilson said
i'll work to pay the fare back
in six weeks time i'll be out of the red
(and down to the shore with my rucksack)
                                          with a hey and a hi and a hodad ho
                                          with a hey and a hi and a ho
                              0100
                              MONTEREY CALIFORNIA

                              (SWEETMEAT BACKGROUND)

                              BIG SUR CALIFORNIA, LONG A FAVORITE CAMPING
AND ARTIST RETREAT
                              BECAME CALIFORNIA'S BIGGEST TOURIST ATTRACTION
TODAY AS THOUSANDS
                              JAMMED THE HIGHWAYS LEADING TO THIS SMALL (POP-
ULATION 534) TOWN
                              ISOLATED IN THE BEAUTIFUL LUCIA MOUNTAINS 20 MI
SOUTH OF MONTEREY.

VIDEO	AUDIO
MOVE IN ON GROCER AS HE STOKES POT-BELLIED STOVE.	...population only 500 some-odd you wouldn't think I get requests for...
CUT TO SHOULDER SHOT OF GROCER.	kipper herring. But I do.
MLS OF GROCER AS HE STANDS. TRUCK WITH GROCER AS HE WALKS BEHIND COUNTER.	Folks here are pret-ty persnick-ety...

fuck 'em
if them homeowners won't honor their agreement
were goin' to make their front lawns look like
disneyland

                                              AUDIO

                              ...only one cigarette that stands
                         out as superior...

                                        (olivia pitt is on the
                                          telephone again)
        "now you ask
        what harm can come of that?"

        "cigarette smoking leads to
        marijuana smoking"
"nonsense"
        "roberta
        i read somewhere that cigarette smokers are 23% more inclined
        to smoke marijuana than non-cigarette smokers in the 10-14-year-
        old age range"
"terrible"
        "and in the 14-18-year-old age range the figure trebles!"

                                                  and
                                                  trembles

at the thought of those mod-bods
beating time to the message of love
eminating from KCUF studion in the mellow-yellow voice of sonny swingle

hi!

> *sonny swingle sending it your way this cra-zy saturday*
> *vibrant morning crazy with the sounds that abound*
> *the groove of the louvres in music masterpieces*
> *the solid gold from our treasure library (whhoooooo-eeeeeeee)*
> *here they are for linda and mel judy and bob chris and the gang*
> *the sweetmeats and*
> *rockaround the bo tree*

(record plays)

(clyde rawlins bursts in)

"where the hell you've been clyde
i had to open this morning"

"sorry sonny
i was sacked out in
studio b" (yawn)

"what happened last night?"

"jim is down at big sur
i was up all night"

"what did he say"

"as far as he can tell
the sweetmeats are safe
but no one's seen them"

"kidnapped?"

"that's just it
no one knows for sure"

"when did you hear from him"

"about two hours ago
he was moving up towards
the stonehouse"

two hours before that
chief broken wind
had put through a frantic
call to KCUF

(yawn)

(this KCUF monterey)

(yeah)

(this is chief broken wind
of the cannabis tribe)

(yeah
what can i do for you chief)

(me got a story about the sweetmeats
that'll blast you through your hogan)

(okay
shoot)

(too dangerous to talk about over phone
i'll drive down in my pontiac and tell
you face to face)

bumper to bumper
america was moving
that saturday noon

traveling rainbow roadways
to get to the pot on the other side

chickens and gold

spilling onto velvety asphalt ribbons
leafing through the clover

chrome-plated
america

                   was on the move
                   spider bugs
                   zipping down the freeways
                   animated suspension
                   kept up by tension
                                               "turn right after second left"
"keep to the right"
                            no parking 8am to 8pm except on sunday
     tow-away zone
                      hey buddy!
                                                          bbbbbbbbbeeeeeeeeeeeeeee
    hey hey buddy!
                      eeeeeppppp   bbbbbbbbbbeeeeeeeeeeeppppppppppp
wanna drag
                               speed limit 45
bbbbllllllllaaaaaazzzzzzz!
                                          metered one hour parking
          hey bub
          can't park here
                               sssssssswwwwwwwwwwwiiiiiiiiiisssssssshhhhhhhh
     flashing fishtail
     into water-rippled mirages
                                        "good riddance you goddam fool"
             thinks he's king of the road
             i'll show him a thing or two
rrrrhhhhhoooooooooo   oooooooommmmmmmm
                               "COCKSUCKER!"
        out of sight america
        was bumper to bumper that midday
                                              hosing down their hopes
                                              polishing their promises
   "listen to that kitten purr..."
                            america was there
                            examining engines
                            tying-up tailpipes
                            cleaning the carpets
        on the move america was there
        bumper to bumper in a desert of dreams
                                              "sy sy
                                               over here"
             "pauline
              where the hell have you been"
                                              "with the production
                                               crew"
             "i just talked to frisbee
              we have a half-hour special
              set for 10:00 tonight"
                                              "great
                                               we just taped
                                               marvin tempest"
             "is the road clear yet"
                                              "are you kidding!"
(as clear as adams)
                   "what this country needs is a good five-cent nickel"
      and now
              N E W S   O N   T H E   H O U R
                                              the sound of
                                              nibbled nubleys

DISPUTE UNCONCERNED REPORTS NOT IN FAVOR AND THE U.S. SAYS
WHITE HOUSE DEAN RUSK SAYING THAT DIPLOMACY SOUTH VIETNAM
SEX FOLLOWING BLOODY FIGHTING SOME 50 MILES THE SWEETMEATS
ACTIVELY SEEKING PEACE TESTIFY BEFORE A CLOSED RULING OUT
PRESIDENT JOHNSON WAR TAX INCREASE PLAN TO BENEFIT SPACE
PROGRAM PARTLY MILD TODAY HIGH 60-65 AND AGAIN ON SUNDAY

CUT CUT CUT!

honey
walk through that line again

and remember p-l-e-a-s-e please
you're brokenhearted from losing
the only man you ever loved
eduardo eduardo eduardo
keep thinking that okay honey

okay
take three

(clack)

"oooooooo
if i don't get through this
car jam i'll never find stuart
i hate this traffic
hate it hate it *HATE IT!*
it makes me feel so *confined*"

AUDIO

WOMAN

But since I discovered NEW,

washdays are fun days again...

in fact, *I'm* going out right now!

manny makemore checks chicago
after catching the 9:30 news

"did that shipment of sweetmeat
sweatshirts come in?"

i'll check boss

"and stevens
i want tou to get hold of a guy named quinn
he's in my phone book
makes pocket flashlights
tell him i want to see him monday
and stevens..."

yes boss

"what did xerox open at?"

but boss
it's saturday!

"saturday you little fleshapods you
sonny swingle bringing it all to ya with grooves of love
wwwwwhhhhooooooo-eeeeeeeeeeeee!
saturday
the day you'd rather mow than smoke wwhhhooo-eeeeee and
shed your academic robes you little diploma-happy fools
saturday wwwhhhoooo-eeeeeee
and you know about the computer bust tonight don'cha
central high school a date at eight um-ummmm bring your
bird or your cage only three washington's for the both
of you um-mmmmm (you crazy little hobbits you) be there
and here's number 42 for sherrie and louis..."

79

go on men
cut the line
                (captain francona has just given the
                 order to cut the electricity lines
                 leading up the mountain)
do they have
a telephone
up there?

                                        ...Hello, Mrs. Grospekski?

        "naw
         dis is sugar xxx
         whossis"
                                        "muhammad 73x"

        "oh
         hiya larry"
                                        "do you like eggs and
                                         lox?"

        "i like locks and yeggs"
                                        "dig
                                         see ya baby"
stu-art i brought you an oatmeal cookie
stuarttttttt stuarttttttttt it's doctor mountmother
                                        HOLD IT HOLD IT CUT CUT! ! !
                                        who the hell are you bud

ooooooo
i'm doctor mountmother
i'm looking for a patient of mine
                                        well look somewhere else
                                        we're filming here

ooooooo
certainly
                                        (fucking idiot!)

actually stuart is a moron
not an idiot
                                he had the mentality of ages
                                a product of scrambled genes

        (or scumbled jeans)
                                a walking brussel sprout

    and sprout he did
    a lincoln and two
                                dumb as they come
                                but a great basketball center

  in fact
        he shot as many points in one game
        as the total on his algebra final
                                                and was elected to
                                                the student senate

    "his name burns brightly in the hearts of all
    who knew him at tulsa's davis high school"
                                        this basketcase
                                        with a basketball

well sir

         he racked out so many brownie points

(his nose dribbling
 down the court)

         that two colleges (two mind you!)
         bid for him and were it not because the korean war was
         over and that the vietnam one not started

were it not for
the grace of god

         there go he to the college of his choice
         on a basketball scholarship no less
         when destiny would have been a good deal better off
         having him go to war (the war of his choice no less)
         and finding some way to have him conveniently step on a

punjab spike
but there was no war
by the grace of eisenhower

         and stuart was on his way for a b.a.

                  ba sheepskin

AUDIO	VIDEO
...here on the open range. But there is. There's a real hankering here for YUM Kipper Herring.	SHEEPHERDER PUTS DOWN HIS SHEARS. CUT TO BENCH AND PAN FROM SHEARS TO HERRING JAR.

      "i majored in art history you know at (can i mention
       my school)..."

                          "that's not
                          what we want
                          to know
                          mister queen"

                          "what about the
                          sweetmeats?"

  "um oh no?"

      "um well (did anyone ever tell you you have lovely
       eyes) pookie and paul were going to star in this
       mad little movie of mine called 'the sweetmeats take
       a trip'
           a spoof on their old travelog one-reelers"

                          "did they sign?"

      "oh they were hot to sign
       but then these new developments intervened"

"why are
 you here?"

      "well frankly (can i be frank with you) i was in
       the neighborhood so i thought i'd drop in"

                    hey
                    there's max vogel
                    their manager!

   mr. vogel
   mr. vogel

                "mr. vogel would you mind
                  answering a question..."

      mr. vogel
      i'm from upi

        we have some mikes set up over here
        mr. vogel

max

                         "over here sir"

        "just a couple of things i want to say gentlemen"
mr. vogel

          (have you been in touch with)

                                   "first of all i want to say
                                   that timothy queen has never
                                   signed up the sweetmeats for
                                   anything and if he does without
                                   my consent i'll bring him to
                                   court"

      "have you been in contact with
       them sir"

                                    "i've eh
                                   been kept informed"

                 (by who)
     "by whom sir"

                                    "a mutual friend"
         "are they all right"

                                    "i can't say anything
                                   more about that now"

mr. vogel
        mr. vogel
                                    "that's all boys"

      "are you going to try to see them sir"
                                    "i'm going to do more than
                                   try
                                     i'm *going* to see them
                                   as their manager i have
                                   a *right* to see them..."

                                   "before *anyone else does*"

          "sir..."

        ("does that mean sir
         you're going")
   LOUDER!
             "does that mean you're going
             up the mountain yourself?"
                                   "i'm leaving right now"

   mid america
   its muddled middle class
        stranded in midtown
            (or middle of the roading it to town)
mewed its way
against the pantsleg of casper milquetoast
its cat-grin of smug complacency
looking over backyard barricades
or down the mainstreet of ghosttown

                                while machines of the mind
                                      gave way to machines of the muscle
              "machine and muscle drove the cars
               and lawnmowers the floor polishers and the cattle prods
               the go-karts and the motorboats
               the pruners and the weeders..."
                                            americans were relaxing
                                            stretching out

        taking five

                                                  saturday american
                                                  beercan in hand
                                            stretching out
                                            on chaise longues

        catching forty
                          dying the midday death
                          of gout of the house
                          laxing and relaxing over the width and girth of the
                                            land
(meanwhile
 back in outer space)
                          "the zipper is still stuck
                          i think a tooth is missing"

                                                  say again?
                          "i think a tooth is missing"

                                                  please clarify
                                                  do you have a
                                                  toothache colonel?

                          "negative
                          i believe a tooth on my
                          zippered fly
                                      eh
                          say over
                          i believe a tooth on my
                          fly zipper..."
(zap your virile
 while we hear a commercial)

                    1. SOUND: TRAFFIC SOUNDS UP; FADE AND HOLD

                    2. ANN: (DRAMATICALLY; OVER BKG.) We're at the

                                   crossroads of the world -- Times

                                   Square -- to ask Mrs. Lloyd Simpson

                                   of Salt Lake City...

                    3. WOMAN: (INTERRUPTING) It's not like that at

                                   all. We're in a recording studio!

                    4. ANN: (RED-FACED BUT DETERMINED TO GO ON)

                                   Eh...that is to say...to ask Mrs.

                                   Lloyd Simpson of Salt Lake City, Utah

                                   what she thinks of...

                    5. WOMAN: (INTERRUPTING) You got the name right.

                                   But I come from Denver. I told you

                                   that when I signed the release.

"i want you to know that the new
 truth-in-advertising bill came about
 as a direct result of my talk before
 the WC's (*ed. note. Wmnen Concerned*)
 back in 1958"

                                        the speaker is carmella karma
                                        chatterbox to thousands

"we made sure they popped on the
 word *dramatization* on all those phony
 interview commercials"

                                            hi there

        hi (houseowner opens door a crack)

                                            *i represent central homeowners
                                            insurance company*

        *i see
        you're a representation*

                                            i'm a representative

        *i see and
        this is a dramatization?*

                                            *no
                                            this is the real thing
                                            i'm really selling insurance
                                            didn't you call earlier?*

        *there have been so many phony
        salesmen around here lately
        i'm sure you can understand
        my concern*

                                            no really (he laughs)
                                            here's my card

        *hhhhmmmmm
        could be forged*

                                            here's the company's i.d.

        that too could be...

                                            *my driver's license
                                            passport
                                            birth certificate
                                            laundry ticket...*

        hhhhmmmmm

                                            *say...
                                            what kind of insurance did
                                            you want anyhow?*

            life

                            assure your personal safety when you're
                            alone at home or traveling dark
                                                    lonely streets

"step right up folks
 15¢ apience
 50¢ for the 3 of 'em"

                            "large giant economy size"

        (get yours whule they last)

                                                90-day warranty
                                                on everything
                                                but parts & service

                i'll take three

                                        keeping up with the joneses

        a find!
        a real find!

                            buddy
                            this is a real cream puff

not a scratch on 'er
                    look
                    have you ever seen a basement *without* a crack
                    in its walls?

                                                       posters to cover
                                                       cracks with
            incense indian bells water pipes stick-on tattoos
                                                       forehead jewels
                                                       lights and bead
                                                       necklaces
cracks to cover posters with
                                        the kitchen sink
                                        and the sickening catch
            the madness of an outmoded
            motorboat
                                                installment books filled with
                                                green stamps
        (america was turning out its pockets
         of resistance)
                                                guerrilla warfare in
                                                supermarket aisles
                    a sneak attack on stockpiles
picking the spent
shells off the empty shelves
                                        shooting the works
america
                            into the life-line blood-flow of the economy
            "use our layaway
             plan"
                                        "buy now pay through your nose"
    everyone a winner
                        so easy to play
                                            all you need is what
                                            the joneses got
                        no money to start
"and in only two weeks time
 they noticed a difference
 right before their eyes"
                            (their investment paid off
                             again and again)
                                                as we hurried
                                                past them america
        from market to market
                        stocking our stockings with stockings
                        our pockets with pockets
rubbing asses with the
masses
                        mobbing counters for the cashiers
                                                hurrying
                                                before it rained
        dollars and cents america
how can you think
of money at a time like this!
                    "it's now thirty minutes since max vogel
                     manager of the sweetmeats headed off alone up the
                     narrow winding road leading to the stonehouse
                     reported to be the place where the sweetmeats have
                     been held for two weeks now
                     vogel has the assurances of law enforcement officials
                     gathered here in big sur that they will not use force
                     to bring out the sweetmeats if their abductors release
                     them unharmed
                     so far no word from the stonehouse
                     when asked what kind of force would be used if vogel
                     is successful state police chief francona said
                     it all depends on what they got
                     this is pauline farnsworth big sur california"

remember
remember
                                        it was back in 1960
                                        when the sweetmeats
                                        made their last cross-country
        thirty cities in thirty days
                                (they drew bigger crowds than
                                 kennedy or nixon that year)
        thirty of our largest cities
        from new york to spokane
                                        traveling in three
                                        huge vans called the
                                        sweetmeat caravan

        one for pookie
        one for paul
        one for the equipment
                                        (while maxie followed
                                         in his rolls)
"i remember the sweetmeat caravan
 like it was only yesterday"
                                boy could those kids sing anything

   "revival gospel c&w jazz blues
    folk opera rock bop you name it"
                                        pookie could belt out german
                                        lieder on request
            (and she did in milwaukee once)
                                        and paul could yodel
jesus could those kids play
                        "guitars banjos pianos flutes violins
                         washtubs french horns jew harps you name it"
    those kids could do anything
                                                and frequently did
"but it was always good clean fun
 the sweetmeats never got in trouble"
                                        "until just lately anyhow"
        they were such good kids
        the kind of kids i wished i had
good kids
                                not a bad bone in their bodies
                                they were all the time doin' good
        like the time they flew to huntington
        west virginia 'cause they heard the
        town couldn't raise the money for a hospital
                                        (well sir
                                         they raised enough for
                                         two hospitals)

        or the time they gave the proceeds of one of
        their hit records to the red cross when that
        earthquake buried that greek town
                                remember?
                                        or entertaining our boys
                                        in korea
                                                how 'bout that?
well
i remember that they *didn't* go to vietnam
                                                "yeah what about
                                                 that!"
            "yeah
             and what about all this shit about
             paul trying to beat the draft"
                                        "goddam tools
                                         that's what they was"

well i recall the time when they sung *america*
at the headquarters of the *daily worker*

        and what about the time
        pookie unwrapped bandages
        at the red cross center

    if you think i believe the story that
    she's pregnant you have another thing coming

pookie
couldn't
be pregnant

        "a girl like that wouldn't get
        in a position like that"

    they were good kids
    until a couple of years ago

        don't know what got into 'em

  (smartass kids
   robbed us blind)
        never lived up to potentiality
"and had everything
 going for them too"

        let's cut out this sentimental
        crap and get the news

N E W S O N T H E H O U R

CONTRACT NEGOTIATIONS ACTION AT FUC HUE SAYING
FORCED TO ASK ONE MILLION CIVIC LEADERS OF RACIAL
UNREST AND TO PROHIBIT MAX VOGEL UNEXPECTED THE
THIRTY FIVE AS ALLIED ATTACK ON U.S. TROOPS AS
PRESIDENT CEREMONY CLEAR WITH A HIGH OF SIXTY

        "i don't know why they're
        not sending troops in"

   "olive
    didn't you hear the news
    their manager is going up
    to talk with them"

        "did you know that max
        vogel was a card-carrying
        communist in the '30s"

   "i don't understand..."

        "it's as clear to me as
        bottled water
                he's in
        with them"

   "with who olivia?"

        "the communists of course"
woody wilson is on the
phone with clyde rawlins:

      i'm telling you rawlins
      i saw it with my own eyes

        okay let's have it
        again

      i was out at the break
      say a hundred yards from
      shore

        yeah

      when i look behind me to
      scan the heavies and there
      clear as day i saw it

  (knock)
        go on
      not the whole submarine
      just the conning tower

first it was the
periscope
    now it's...

okay okay
just the periscope
but i'm sure it was there

(knock knock)

look wilson
there's someone at
the door

i think we're being
invaded!

yeah okay

i think the reds are...

look wilson
i gotta go now

(knock knock knock)

pearl hrbor!

(click)

"who is it?"

"chief broken wind"

"come in chief"

"how"

"aw not bad
how's it with you"

"could be better
this friday me found out
my medicineman really
an m.d. in disguise"

"ha ha ha
not bad chief"

"but seriously me have
story about sweetmeats"

"shoot"

"story so big costs much
wampumpeag"

"fifty"

"ten bucks"

"forty"

"twenty"

"cash"

"twenty-five tops"

"okay listen
about three weeks ago..."

"if it's really a scoop"

115 SOUND: CROSSFADE TO

AUDIO

SALLY (ON EDGE)

I don't know what to do, Joan. I'm

always so tense, so nervous. This

morning I really blew up at the kids...

and for no good reason.

JOAN

Maybe what you need is a vacation.

                    SALLY

          But we took our vacation just last

          week.

                    JOAN

          Then have you tried this vacation *in*

          a pill? LET DOWN. It's better than

          aspirin...Better than codeine.

the lighter the
burden of sanskaras
the higher the experience of consciousness

                                        beyond the body into
                                        cellular timelessness

          protein memory sequences
          setting off biochemical raster scans

                                             VIDEO

              AUDIO   CUT TO CU OF THE SWEETMEATS
                                     DOCTOR'S KIT. KIT TOP PEELS
     ...playing doctor and nurse just   BACK; ANIMATES OPEN.

     like Pookie and Paul do. You'll

     have so much fun giving pills out   CUT TO GIRL DISPENSING PILLS
                                         TO HER PLAYMATES.
     to all your friends. And when

     there's an emergency...)

     "just barely jim   "clyde come in
      where are you?   can you read me?"

     "any word?"   "i'm at the bottom of the hill
                                      waiting for vogel to get back"
     "have you heard anything about
      hemp mats?"   "they've spotted him coming down"

     "hemp mats"   "what?
                                      say that again"

     "h-e-m-p-m-a-t-s"   "can't read you clyde
                                      spell it"
     "floor mats woven out of hemp
      an indian guy says he delivered   "what the hell are they"
      50 of 'em up to the stonehouse
      about three weeks ago"

     "keep your ears open jim
      it could break this story wide
      open"   "haven't heard a word about them"

     "swingle says it's dynamite"
                                     "hemp mats?"
     "make love in them?!
      you smoke them you fool"   "do you make love in them?"

                                        marvin tempest:
          (the fuzz has closed off the main
           road to the stonehouse but i know
           another way)

                                        gerda loins:
          (ggggooooooooodddddddddddddddddddd
           is this guy gland a lousy lay
           i wish i could get out of my contract)
swami
sahalami:
          "i see two figures fighting to reach one another
           a man and a woman
           the man has a beard..."

                                                  (that's
                                                   paul!)
sssssshhhhh
          "the woman is young and...well endowed"
                                                  POOKIE!

          "i can't go on unless it's perfectly quiet"
                                                  sssssshhhhh
 sssssshhhhhhhhhh
                                        hey quiet!
(sssshhhhhh)
          "the woman is in the arms of a man..."
                                                  (incest!)

          "the arms of another man a dark man
           this man is much older than she"
                                        "who?"
   bbbbzzzzzz
                    i wonder if it could be

                                                  "she had
                                                   a crush on"
   how about that spanish count
                              there was that guy in rio
       wuzhiz name
bbbbbzzzzzzzzzzzzzzzzzzzzzzzzzzzzzzzzzz
                                                  ...oh wow!

          "i have lost the picture
           there is too much interference here"
sssssshhhhhhh
                                                  SHADDUP!

  "HEY QUIET!"
          "it is no use my friends the image fades
           the ball has ghosted up i'm afraid my flowers
           i'm afraid this reading is over my dear ones
           my secretary will be happy to accept your
           contributions and for those of you here
           who wish to purchase my meditation necklace
           or my horoscope chart or my handwriting
           analysis booklet or other items of interest
           a convenient booth has been set up in the lobby"
(will there be
 another reading
 today swami)
          "i will call on the divine spirits at my evening
           vespers service
                         contributions for this special service will
           be $5.00 at the door
                         i must return and meditate now..."

(eduardo)

                                                 (si *el presidente*)

(ze sweetmeats have presented us
 with a most welcome diversionary
 move)

                                                 (as marx is our father señor)

(now is ze time for us to make
 ourselves ze move)

                                                 (you have a plan major?)

(eef ze CIA is made to believe ze
 sweetmeats are their own agents
 they will pay mucho dinero to have
 them back no?)

                                                 (but señor
                                                 ze sweetmeats no do work for ze CIA)

(of course not you fool
 but ze CIA no never need to know
 dot)

                                                 (i do no understand)

(we work for ze CIA no?)

                                                 (dot is so *el bravo* i tink?)

(we can say ze sweetmeats were
 working for us no?)

                                                 (are they?)

(of course not you fool
 but ze CIA will buy practically
 anything)

                                     *and speaking about buying anything
                                     here is brentin strong
                                     your vietnam correspondent-at-large
                                     with a special report:*

"it looks like daylight
 but what you are seeing is the light from
 hundreds of flares illuminating the town
 of fuc hue located squarely in the middle
 of the strategically important ying yang
 valley
       the communists control this town by
 virtue of their prolonged terrorist campaign
 of bombing which earlier this year cost the
 inhabitants of this small village their mayor
 and police clief
                  estimates are that a battalion
 of the enemy lay waiting beneath bunkers dug
 deep in the hillsides surrounding fuc hue
                            since
 three o'clock yesterday afternoon
 allied planes have dropped hundreds of tons
 of explosives on this town to 'soften up' the
 enemy's positions
                now it is time for the americans
 to advance
          on my right is captain john quigley of
 the 348th light cavalry division
                        his unit is
 selected to be among the first to make the final
 assualt at daybreak
                can you tell me how you feel
 at this moment captain"

"we have a job to do
and i'm gonna see that
it gets done"

"how do your men feel about being in the forward
assault line"

"this isn't the first
time we're taking the
advance position
                    at pleiku
we were in the front
ranks when we attacked"

"so you know what to expect"

"i figure between 50-60
per cent casualties"

"and how many for your own men"

"that *was* the figure
for my own men!"

*this flow chart for making chocolate
fudge (shown here greatly reduced) is
typical of over one hundred illustrations
used to clarify important points*
                              in graphical determination
                              of truss deflection and moment
                              distribution

"as we join the russell smith family
we hear pop smith (russell's father)
muttering outside the kitchen..."

                              can't find a thing in thish
                              house
                                    makes me kinda mad
                              yesherday i wush lookin for
                              a hammer an it took me all
                              afternoon

(did you use your head?) hi!

                              well hello there linda
                              what'cha makin?

fudge

                              fudge huh
                              your grandma makes good fudge

i know
grandma's teaching me

                              back in the old days
                              all young girls hadta know
                              how to make fudge

(here we go again)

                              they had a song back then...
                              *can she make some chocolate
                              fudge billy boy billy boy...
                              can she make some chocolate
                              fudge charmin billy...*

can she bake a cherry pie
grandpa

                              she weren't much good at
                              that

i mean
that's how the song went

                              oh yeah?
                              what song?

aw never mind

                              you kids know everything
                              these days

                                    here
                                    want a lick?

                                                        why i think i would linda
                                                        thank you kindly

DAD! WHERE ARE YOU?

                                                        IN THE KITCHEN MOM mmmmmm
                                                        that's awfully good linda
                                    thank you

        russell wants to know
        if you found the hammer
                                                        NO!
        he says it might be in
        louis's room

                                                        all right
                                                        i'll look there after lunch
        what?
                                                        i said
                                                        I'LL LOOK AFTER LUNCH

        linda
        are you still stirring
                                    i've been stirring
                                    for a half hour
                                    already
        it still looks lumpy
                                    (shit)
                                                        don't look too bad
        hasta be smooth
                                    grandma
                                    can't i use the...
        what say?
                                    CAN'T I USE THE
                                    ELECTRIC MIXER?

        the electric mixer?
        goodness no!
                                    but i've been in this
                                    d....this kitchen for
                                    an hour already
                                                        in the old days the women
                                                        stayed in the kitchen most
                                                        of the day
                                    (oh god!)

        (hasta be smooth)
        stir child stir!
                                    grandma i think
                                    i hear someone at
                                    the front door
        eh?
                                    i hear SOMEONE AT
                                    THE FRONT DOOR
        i don't hear anyone...
                                                        i'll go see
        now fold in the nuts
                                    fold?
        here give me that bowl
        you fold in the nuts
        like this
        see?
                                    (toss in nuts)
        now stir that all
        together for awhile
                                    i'm going stir crazy!
        that's better

                                                      nope lin
                                                      t'aint a soul there
now spoon it out on
this here tray
                              grandma...

use the knife to get
it off the spoon child
                              grandma
                              can't i please...

                                                                    rrrrrrrrrriiiiiiii
iiiiiiiiiiinnnnnnnnggggg
                              THE PHONE!
                              DON't YOU HEAR THE PHONE?
i don't hear the...
                                                      i'll get it
                              no!!!
                              it's for me (please god!)
                                                      "hello"

    "lin?"
                                                      "bud?"

    "yeah
     get your work done?"
                                                      "just about
                                                       grandma's teaching me
                                                       to make fudge"

                                                      "yeah je-sus"

    "aren't you lucky"
                                                      "danny and i made a date
    "you decided about tonight yet?"   already sort of"

    "danny!
     you're not going to the bust with
     that creep are you?"
                                                      "i don't know...i'll see"

    "come down to the sur with us"
                                                      "the sur!
                                                       i thought you were going
                                                       to the dance"

    "changed my mind
     everyone is going down there tonight
     should be freaky
                    whaddya say?"
                                                      "can't bud
                                                       i gotta be in by twelve"

    "no sweat"
                                                      "my folks can't find out"
    "naw"
                                                      "i don't think..."
    "got some fantastic stuff"
                                                      "do you?
                                                       really bud?"

    "panamanian"
                                                      "oh wow!"
    "and mitch copped some acid"
                                                      "shazam!"
    "well waddya say"
                                                      "well...okay"
    "what time can you get out?"
                                                      "no earlier than six"

"make it five-thirty
hey
did you hear the latest news
about the sweetmeats?"

"i've been making fudge
all morning"

"their manager vogel you know
the creep who used to book their act ...
anyhow he goes up to the stonehouse to
talk with them but the front door is
locked so then a voice from inside says
everything is cool and they want him to
get things together for a concert"

"the kidnappers said that?"

"that's the freaky part
vogel swears the voice he heard
sounded just like paul's!"

PART TWO

did you take your break america?
                              did you
did you raid the icebox
take a shit
buy popcorn america?
                                   did you spend a pleasant hiatus
                                   hating every high of it
                      america

                                                      spilling pillboxes
                                                      piled with bodies

                        america in the noon-day sun
                        madder than mad dogs
                                        tearing ass off the asphalt
        getting bombed on three-point-two
                                   stepping into main street
                                   that saturday
             wearing their best
             pillsbury sack dresses
                              a fine spring day
                              (rain showers in the ozarks and rockies)
        god was either smiling on us
        or congress was still in session
                                        there was law and order
                                        and sugarplums
                                                    (plied with pills)
                                        spilling out
                                        gutless bellies
      there was war and lard
                      (or guns and butter spilling out)
                                                   there was good times
                                                   for me and you
good times
                   the best of times
                                        andy griffith
                                        red skelton
                                        jackie gleason
                                        reader's digest
                                        lawrence welk
       keeping them happy
       keeping their minds off their minds
                                        jack and the beanstalk
                                        dean martin
                                        andy griffith
                                        bob hope comedy special
     a great line-up for a great season
     seasoned with schmaltz
                              "you could have knocked me over
                              with a fedder"
            the pushing of buttons
            turning of dials
            meshing of wheels gears spindles spangles
                                        bright shining things
turning over and over in that fine may day
                                   spinning
                                   spilling
        over and over
        high on vitamin d-e-f-g-

                                   out of control ...
      stuart
      basically nice psychotic killer
      is stopped at the roadblock by
      one of ochre's men

"but i have to..."

"can't get through buddy"

"can't you see them line of
  cars
      that's backed up traffic"

"how far is..."

"fifteen miles"

"fifteen miles to
  big sur?"

"that's right buddy
  traffic's backed up for
  fifteen miles"

while at that very moment
louis smith is piling into mitch frankle's car
and together with brenda quigley and carol richards
the four of them bomb down 1st avenue
                            twowheel it into elm street
and head out towards the sur
                  "did you tell your parents?"

                                              "naw"

            "me neither
              they'd never let me go"

                                              "cool it"

            "we'll be back before dinner
              won't we lou?"

                                              "any beer?"

AUDIO

...NOT just *any* beer...good

Crass Beer. The beer prohibition

couldn't stop.

carmella karma is horrified that beer
ads are being heard and seen by millions
of "children under 18" and if she had
her way:

"...i would ban all advertising
 of beer and cigarettes wherever
 such advertising now appears"

(including the novel
the sweetmeat saga)

VIDEO

OPEN ON CU OF RAT CAGE FOCUSING
ON RAT AS HE RUNS BACK AND FORTH.

AUDIO

(Anncr. V.O.) There has been a lot

of talk recently about cigarette

smoking and cancer...

CUT TO MCU OF ANNOUNCER.

...let's get the facts straight...

MOVE IN AS ANNOUNCER TAKES PUFF
INHALES AND SLOWLY BLOWS THE SMOKE
THROUGH HIS NOSE.

                                        ...Grasslands deliver on flavor.

                                        That's the whole story. The only

                                        story that's backed up by millions

                                        of satisfied smokers.

CUT BACK TO RAT CAGE.

                                        So next time someone mentions ciga-

                                        rette smoking causing cancer tell

                                        him...

DISS TO GRASSLANDS PACK.

                                        to try Grasslands. Regular or king.
          cccccchhhhhhhhuuuuuuuuuhhccccchhhh
ccccccccchhuuuuuuuccccchhhhccccchhh
                              placing their quarters in vending machine coffers
   (hash ways had not as yet
    replaced ashtrays)
                              placing their loved-ones in vending machine coffins
   (coughing even now above
    the grave)
                              placing their hope and faith in god
   (ironically a non-smoker)
                                         cccchhhhhhhuuuuuuuuuuuuucccccccchhhhhh
          yellowed fingers fidgeting open a present
          fumbling over the tinsel
                         (the ritual of making fire
                          the pyrotechnics of the fire-keeper)
      man
      in utter control
      goes up in a puff of smoke

                 AUDIO

...so for getting out those

troublesome nicotine stains

get NEW -- the modern detergent

as kind to your clothes as it is

to your hands.

                                        oooooooooooooooo
                                        wait till i get my hands
                                        on stuart exclaims dr.
                                        mountmother

           (who at that very moment has abandoned
            his car and is making his way through
            the heavy underbrush)

                                        when he gets it into his
                                        head that he must kill...
                                        well there's really no
                                        stopping him ooooooooooooo

           woody wilson has made his way to u.s. #1
           and is frantically trying to get to
           general ochre's headquarters

but i must see him

                            not a chance

we're being invaded!

                            won't work buddy
                            i've heard that
                            one before

pearl harbor!

                            heard that one
                            in my cradle

i tell you
i saw a submarine!

("10 degrees starboard")

                                ("10 degrees starboard sir")

("open diving hatch")

                                ("diving hatch open sir")

("prepare for depressurization")

                                ("depressurization")

who could possibly be coming in by sub?

                            if you guessed timothy queen
                            you got another thing coming

for if you remember correctly
timothy queen had flown in on
friday night and had managed
to set up camp (conveniently
enough) less than 20 yards from
the press tent at base level

                        "oh for criminy sake
                        didn't we bring any #5 pancake!"

   (the fields surrounding
    parnassus mountain where the sweetmeats were believed to be
    looked like a refugee settlement camp on the outskirts of gaza)

mah
fallow
amuricuns

           one moment while we get the latest from brentin strong
           our war-correspondent-at-large

                        "there is something about war...
                        something that gets in your
                        blood and guts
                                it's that kind
                        of a war out here
                                something that
                        keeps sending you forward to
                        the front lines
                              but something also
                        that keeps you wanting to be home"

(what was this love-hate relationship
 we had with the war in vietnam

                  we both wanted it to go endlessly on
                  and wanted it to stop

                          it had been so much a part
                          of our lives

that to end it would be like killing a loved one)

                          a child with an irritating
                          voice calls repeatedly to
                          his mother for more sausages

read zero azimuth
on the jam shammer

               mom-my
                  mom-myyyyyyy

(you haven't seen my love
oh no ohhhhh i pray for)
       a frustrated housewife makes a
       telephone call
$40 BILLION HOTEL MOBILE WELFARE
      "...all circuits are busy..."
 six table gymnasium for
 transferred night derelicts
         (back to the story please)
circuits are busy
    (back)
           several startled
           onlookers learn
  to join the sound of a nation thinking
you
and
me
 wait and see
   and the world will be a better
         (oh yeah)
 take a
 trip
        circuits are getting jammed
 kick out
   and the world
        circuits
 "all circuses are go"
        circuits
 "integrated circuses"
     1234567890
       check for bugs
(someone may be listening)
    this is a watchbug watching a recording
    this is a watchbug watching you!
 give them bread and
 circuits
         bread?
         let them drink coke!
  "monday monday
  so good to me"
      circuits clearing up
circuitous eccentrics
        "... hello?"
 "this is chief broken wind"
        "who?"
 "how"
        "how who"
 "white man speak with speech impediment"
       major
       major macho sir
  si
       then what you are saying is
       that the CIA is really behind
       the sweetmeat abduction?
  si
 as breshnev is my brother
 dot is no baloney
    and within three minutes the fbi was calling
    the state department to confirm or deny

setting in motion
the magnificent square wheels of governmental bureaucracy
                                        which has as its motto:
            "make a fast buck
             then pass the buck fast!"
                                    hot potatoes
                                    on capital hill
the hurried handshake
and the harried snakeinthegrass
                                        "livin' it up on the hill"
                howde do
                howde hi
                        gladtomeetyou
the gladhand
and the handmedown problems from the last administration
                                        "nice baby you got
                                         there miss...
                                            eh madam"
        ...howde do
        ...me to
        ...don't say
        ...beautiful day
                        senator
                        just one more
     thank you thank you thank
                            washington
                            that *seat of government*
        sitting on its mason-dixon
                            smug in that sticky complacency
                            of barbeque sauce and bourbon
      of bean soup
      and oldlady gossip
                        gabbing its head off that saturday aft
"...the sweetmeats..."
                    "has the senator heard?
                     the sweetmeats are agents for the CIA..."
"i thought the CIA
 abducted *them*..."
                    "well one way or another
                     the CIA has something to do with it..."
                                            and now
                                            friends
(you guessed it)
                        a commercial
(but remember
 if you want to play the game
 you have to abide by the rules)
                        <u>AUDIO</u>

            "...write YUM Kipper Herrings, Box 5089

            Fulton Fish Market, New York City, N.Y.

            10003. So until tomorrow, this is Cantor

            Rabinowitz saying, have a significant

            sabbath and I hope to be herring from ya."

ethnic visual phaseout

                                        excuse me
                                        but does that term supersede
                                        mnemonic proprietary turnover

only so far as *visceral communication
paradigms* are concerned

                                        oh yes
                                        of course

     "we're ready for your
      TVA colonel dipper"

                                            "TVA?!"

     "thirty seconds colonel..."

                                            "TVA?! are we back in
                                             tennessee already"

     "TVA colonel
      it stands for television appearance"

                                            "television appearance!
                                             are you crazy
                                             i can't get my damn fly
                                             zippered"

     "sorry colonel ground control says
      we're pre-programmed for a 3PM TVA"

                                            "i'm hanging out all over
                                             the place and ground control
                                             is pre-programmed
                                                      a fine mess"

CBS

                              ARCAT
                                                            DDT
            PAL
     CORE
                              SNCC
                                                      ABM
                                   SANE
PLSS
          NCAA
                                                      STP
               KKK
                                   NFL
       NLF
                                            "...over and out"

          AUDIO

     "...when I get upset at blastoff
                                                    VIDEO

        time. Just before the countdown   ASTRONAUT BRINGS BOTTLE TO
                                                 CAMERA. FOCUS ON BOTTLE
     I take LET DOWN, the little blue   ON WORDS *LET DOWN*.

        pill that takes the edge off things."

                                            pookie took pills they said
she was either up or down
                          tripping on her weight tablets
                          or down on a tantrum of disillusionment
her mind both positive and
negative
          ions dissolving in acid

                                            "she was good i tell you"
                          torn between dream
                          and reality
                                            "...wonderful child"
                          until dream and reality
                          fused in frustration

and paul
                                        "wonderful boy..."
turning his amp full blast and freaking on a D+ chord
                                        "eating his oatmeal"
haunted by the ghosts of childhood
the blowing of kisses
the endless limos waiting
the bundling up and rushing past of stagedoor johnnies
the final wave
                swept up sleeping to connecticut
                                                (no! no!)
                                        "never cried"
    what's the latest
                                "they're alive"
    who says
                                "it must came over the news"
alive!
ALIVE!
                (are they in danger)
                                        (swami sahalami sees great
                                         danger)
                (what kind of danger swami)
                                        (i see many guns
                                         many bullets and gasmasks
                                         there is a man with a mike)
                (a microphone swami)
                                        (a microphone yes
                                         he is saying
                                         ying yang valley)
"...thirty miles north of saigon
                                this is brentin
strong your vietnam correspondent
                                with me is pfc raymond kelly of bangor maine
pfc kelly
can you tell me what's happening"
                                        "well
                                         over there is the enemy
                                         and we're over here
                                         and it's our job to wipe them out"
"and how does your outfit intend to do that"
                                        "uh
                                         first we're going to soften them
                                         up with napalm"
"that's napalm over there in those trucks"
                                        "uh right
                                         shoots outa that gun on top"
    (louis smith is pressing his gun
     against brenda quigley's thigh)
                                (don't lou not here in the car
        c'mon brenda
                                lou cut it out
                                or i'll take my leg off yours
        have another toke
                                all you ever want to do is smoke
                                or dry-hump me in the back seat
    so what's wrong with that
                                there's a time and a place for everything
    well..
                                just don't go so fast that's all

well do you want to get
hot or not

                              i do lou but...

so let me touch you

                       go slow lou...please...)

oooooooooooooooo
says dr. mountmother to himself
the trouble with today's *wunderkinder*
is that they are obsessed with sex
sex sex sex sex sex sex
and sex leads to violence
sex and violence violence and sex
they go together like needles and haystacks
                                   "i recall stuart told me once
                                    how aroused he got watching
                                    huntley-brinkley each night"

      (linda smith is presently thinking
       filthy thoughts about various positions
       to do with bud that evening
                              while cracking walnuts)
    bbbbbbrrrrrrrooooooooommmmmmmm
    bbbbbbbbbbbrrrrrrooooooommmmmmmmm
                          "road's blocked marvin"
                                             "you mean there
                                              are cars from
                                              here to the
                                              stonehouse!"
                          "all blocked marvin"
                                             "we'll go through
                                              the woods"
     so saying
     marvin tempest (in a tea of pot) heads his scrambler
     into the woods and promptly gets mired in the underbrush
                                        brrrrmmm brum
            marvin tempest issues a chain of epithets
            unprintable even here
                          and heads back to the road
                                             "we'll make a
                                              road through their
                                              lawns"
     and so saying
     downshifts through the daisies and dafs
     lining innumerable homeowners yards
                          the muffler roughers right behind
it was the nightmare of our minds
come true

                              the terror of the unknown
                              fiend-sadist-killer-pervert-hippie
                              stalking the city streets
generally described as a negro addict
                              a nat turner-type
                              with king-kong flashbacks
a large hulking animal
wounded and vicious

                              burning and looting and raping
                              and...

the destroyer of dreams
worst of all

                              destroyer of what we have come
                              to know as 'the american way of
                              life'

the american way of dreams

                                        one will get you two
                                        two will get you four
                                        four will get you eight
                                        eight will get you half a buck
"let the nigger do it"
                            the american way of dreams
                            flowing from spacious skies
"with liberty and justice"
                                        libation
                                        and just ice
amber waves of grain distilling
thy good with
get a liddle drunk
an' you land in jail
                    from stephan fetchit to the kingfish
                                            christening in
                                            a new era of hatred
                                            against that which we
                                            feared most
ourselves
                    "what ever happened to the peaceful fifties?"
        remember
                                        eisenhower's peaceful fifties
        patti page and vaughn monroe
        rock hudson and doris day
                        28 flavors of contentment
                                            two cars in every garage
                                            a chicken in every pot
    (and a pot was either something you cooked in
     or placed beneath a sick bed)
                                            a 24-inch teevee set
                                            to watch the colgate
                                            comedy hour on
        or toast of the town
        or the show of shows
                            or the sweetmeat family hour
                            every wednesday night
                                        "or was it tuesday night"

32 SOUND: BUS STOPS

33 SOUND: ALL SOUNDS OUT

34 POOKIE: (WIDE_EYED) So this is Paris! It's just like I

                thought it would be. Just like in the song.

35 DAD: Do you remember the song honey?

36 POOKIE: I think so...

37 MUSIC: "I LOVE PARIS INTRO UP: SWELL AND HOLD BKG.

39 POOKIE: Maybe you can help me with the words.

39 DAD: I'll sure try honey...

40 MUSIC: "I LOVE PARIS" DUO OF POOKIE AND DAD

                                            "them kids could
                                             do anything"

```
        what went wrong
                                    musta been the accident
        such well-behaved kids
                                                    "never cried or
                                                    nothing"
        a new generation of oatmeal-eating
        clean-fun-loving respectful kids
                                                    "said their prayers"
        the kind of kids we wish we had
                            100% sugarplums
                            dancing their way into our hearts
tippity tip
tippity tap
                dancing their way from their beautiful middle-class set
                of a living-room fun-room kitchen and dining-room
        into the
        dreary beer-stenched surroundings we were trapped in
                                            the sweetmeats
                                            were everyone
                                            we could have been
                                            or should have been
or would ever want to be
                    (until that terrible tragedy)
                                            but let's see if we
                                            can corner max vogel
        "there are just a few questions we'd like
        to ask you mr vogel"
                                        "i've said everything i want
                                        to say to the press"
        "...did you find..."
                                        "it's all in my statement"
        "could you please..."
                                        "they're re-playing my statement
                                        over in the press tent right
                                        now boys
                                            i have nothing more
                                        to say"
and now readers ...
the never-before-published transcript
of max vogel's statement   (official authorized version)
                                            (sssssssshhhhhhh)
        As you know, I was very close to Fay and Sam and, of
        course, the twins. When...they passed away...the courts
        appointed me their legal guardian. I want you should
        know how that tragedy affected those kids. I was with them
        every step of the way.  For weeks they were in shock.

        I'm not going to play amateur psychologist here.  I
        don't know what's been happening to them in the past few
        years.  I've tried to be understanding as a second father,
        but since they've been sixteen or so, I've only acted in
        a professional capacity with them.  I want you should
        know that I've never condoned the more sensational
        aspects of some of the things they've done lately.
        Actually, they've never keep me informed of anything they
        later do.  Not for several years.

        But I want you should know this much:  this is no press agent's
        stunt.  There's absolutely no reason why the Sweetmeats
        need this kind of publicity.  The twins are financially
```

set-up for the rest of their lives. Their income last
year set a record. And they certainly are more popular
today than they have ever been. And I think I would have
... I certainly would have been informed of this beforehand.

And I don't think they've been kidnapped. For one thing,
no ransom demands have been made. For another, all the
kids I've talked with seem to think they're in no danger.
In fact, if anything -- all the kids I've met are rather
unconcerned. They seem to be gathered here for some kind
of underground event, some kind of rock festival maybe.

There's thousands of kids up there, perhaps hundreds of
thousands, and it was very difficult getting through. But
I finally managed to reach the stonehouse and when I talked
to Paul through the front door he said, "Uncle Max" (that's
what's he's been calling me since he was a baby) "I want
that you should tell everyone we're okay, and I want that
you should set things up so we can do our gig here."

I intend to do that. I intend to look out for their
interests, but I want you should realize just
how much these two kids have been exploited in the past
few years. And I'm going to put an end to that sort of
thing right here and now. I'm still their legal guardian
and until they're officially 21, I'm responsible for their
actions. I want to remind everyone of that. I'm only
looking out for their interests. The commission I draw as
their manager has nothing to do with anything. I think of
those kids as if they were my own -- my own life and blood
-- and if they're being taken advantage of by unscrupulous
promoters or con-artists I'll make certain that who's
ever behind this is prosecuted to the full extent of the law.
Thank you.
            maxie vogel slips off
            his lavaliere mike
            and beats it out of the press area
                                    into a noonday nightmare
                                    that would scare the
                                    living daylights out of bosch
the fields on either side of the highway
were crammed-packed with cars facing in every direction
                                    and beyond that
roads leading to the highway were backed up for 15 miles
                                    and beyond that
                                            thousands
                                            perhaps
                                            hundreds of
thousands
of people were making their way slowly along the rutted dirt roads that wound
within the valleys
            a pilgrimage mostly made up of the young
                                    of all those who had
                                    grown up with
                                    the sweetmeats
thousands
of voices singing the lovetunes of their day
                              (the melodies both familiar and
                               strange
                                    the lyrics rich in mystery
                                    and understanding)

thousands in their used-war clothing
some still with the ghosts of hashmarks on their sleeves
                                        thousands in
                                        sandals and headbands
                                        in bellbottomed
                                        jeans
        in bush hats and lovebeads
                                in bandannas and see-throughs
        in wide belts and work boots
                                in eisenhower jackets and nehru
                                collars
        in torn levis and dusty loafers
                                in barechest and sweated shirt
they came
walking in the solemn stateliness of being stoned
                                        their eyes glazed with the
                                        happiness of the event
            from everywhere they were
            streaming in
                    (sunbeams traveling the shafts of light
                     filtering through the trees)
                                        all colors of the
                                        rainbow
            blacks and browns and reds and whites
            and yellows
                    kinky hair
                    processed hair
                    straight hair
                    braided hair
                            shoulder length
                            and crew-cut
frosted and teased and permanented
                                        flat noses
                                        and aquiline
        blue eyes
        black eyes
        green eyes
        hazel eyes
                                absorbing all colors of
                                the rainbow
                                        eminating all
                                vibrations of pure light
truly
beauty was in the eye of the beholder
                            and there was beauty
                                    everywhere

music fade out

"sonny swingle bringing it to you this saturday noon
you crazy sex-ridden fools you wwwwhhhooooo---eeeee
and we'll be right back to spin a galaxy of forgotten
stars right after the news at noon..."

(he glances up to see a frantic
clyde rawlins holding up a card
on which is scribbled SKINNER)

"but first for all you zapped-out little
sweetmeat fanciers
direct from where all
the action is down there on the sur
here
is KCUF's man-on-the-scene jim skinner
with an exclusive sweetmeat report who-eee
come in jim..."

(static)

...scene here is one of total confusion hundreds
of national guardsmen have descended on this small
sleepy town buried deep in the lucia mountains
they
have been joined by state police troopers and various
local vigilante groups made up of residents in the
area
thousands upon thousands of
young people have walked as
many as 15 miles to the site
all roads leading to big sur have been either closed
by abandoned automobiles lining either side of the
big highway here
or by roadblocks set up by the state
police
nevertheless
thousands of sightseers are making
their way through the woods and fields
as for the
sweetmeats they are reported safe still locked up in
the stonehouse high atop parnassus mountain

(three o'clock new york time
and hy frisbee is pulling his
hair out getting things together
for the 6 pm seymore savage show)

(savage meanwhile is having his troubles on
his interview tapes for his 10:00 special
one example:)

"...and your name sir"

"stuart"

"come closer to the mike"

"stuart"

"now mr stuart why did you
come to big sur today"

"the sweetmeats are here"

"...and you wanted to
be part of the scene..."

"no...i'm here to kill them"

"..."

"you know
like blast them with a
high-powered rifle"

"CUT!"

but before we find out who has
just waded ashore from a sub
waiting a mile off the coastline

you guessed it again
friends

a word from DIGITDOUCHET

OPEN ON A BATTLEFIELD SHOT TAKEN
FROM A HELICOPTER. ZOOM IN ON
SANDBAGGED BUNKER. CROSS DISS
TO INTERIOR WHERE OFFICER IS
STANDING BEFORE A WAR MAP IN
FRONT OF SEATED TROOPS. MOVE
IN ON OFFICER.

AUDIO

(SFX OF ARTILLARY, BOMBS ETC)

OFFICER

War is a dirty business, men,

but good grooming is essential.

That means on the field as well

as off, I want you men to clean

up regularly. That's an order!

CUT TO MCU OF SERGEANT.

SERGEANT

But sometimes that's impossible.

sometimes there's not even any

drinking water!

CUT TO MS OF OFFICER.

OFFICER

The Army has thought of that. You

men will be issued a daily ration

ON WORD *RATION* OFFICER TEARS OFF
WAR MAP TO REVEAL SCREEN WITH
BLOWUP OF DIGITDOUCHET PACKET.

of Digitdouchet towelettes. No

water needed. New aluminum-foil-

wrap Digitdouchet keeps moisture

in, germs out. Watch this film.

DIGITDOUCHET PACKET DISSOLVES
AS TRAINING FILM FLICKERS ON.
FILM SHOWS SOLDIER IN FOXHOLE
USING HIS STEEL POT FOR WASHING.

NARRATOR (VO ON FILM)

This is man is putting himself in

double jeopardy. He is using his

steel helmet to wash in...and he

is wasting valuable drinking water

in the process...

PAN TO ADJOINING FOX HOLE.

(flick the dial to
an adjoining channel)

...want a beer that swings with   MOVE IN ON GERDA LOINS AS SHE
                                                   BEGINS TO POUR BEER. PAN DOWN
                                                 AND FOCUS ON GLASS OF BEER AS

true-brew flavor, ask for CRASS.   HEAD OVERFLOWS RIM.

Remember, CRASS has class.
                     (fadeout to the back stop view of our national
    pasttime)
                      "we're in the bottom of the third
                      with the mets out in front by a
                      score of four to one"
                                                        those very words are
                                                        enough to hook any red
                                                        blooded american man within
                                                        a radius of 100 miles
                                                        from new york city
     to stop whatever he's doing and watch the game
                                                                 baseball
                      that national nine inning outing
                                                          baseball
                      two and a half hours of uninterrupted
                      base boredom
             running
             catching
                                                           pitching
                                                             bunting
                      bringing in the warm-up pitcher
                      bringing out the warm-up jacket
checking the sign
signing the check
                                                        trotting down to first base
                                                        flipping up his visor
        "the count on grospekski is two balls
        and no strikes"
                                              taking a pitch and calling a
                                            strike
      one entire generation had as its
      heroes
        baseball players
                                                  gehrig
                                                  ruth
                                                  hubbell
                                                  fox
               depression brought out the best in baseball
for forty cents
you could sit in
the bleachers and watch king kong keller connect
                                                there was a civic pride in
                                   a baseball city
                                        and a mystical familylike
                                        solidarity of white & poor
                                        even in AAA towns
      that brought out the best chauvinistic
      qualities
                      the best racist
      qualities
                      the best carnivorous underdog
      qualities in us
           all

"murder the ump"
"get that nigger robinson"

"kill 'em"
bbbbbbbboooooooooooooooooooooooo
"...bum"
that carried the impact of the war
in a claw-mitt and a beer belly

terwilliger to
ramazzotti to
cavarretta

into the fifties
and the age of the negro player
and the age of the baseball scholarship
and the age of the club that would move if
attendance didn't
pick up
the poor white city slob had had it
and so had baseball
"yeah yeah yeah
so says you you fucking egghead
...but millions of us still like to pop
open a beer and watch the yankees play the indians"

kill them!

watch the yankees slaughter 'em

the national pastime
for a hundred years
"this WAGH-TV new york"

"yes it is sir"

"connect me with seymore savage
show"

"surely"

(character hexadecimal)
"seymore savage show"

"this chief broken wind
me want to talk with savage"

"i'm sorry sir
mr savage is in california"

"this no buffalo bullshit you give
me is it?"

"no sir
he's doing a special from big sur
on the sweetmeats"

"that good
me will see him personally"

but i must see him personally

listen buddy
you know how many people
a day want to see general
ochre
a thousand
maybe even 10 thousand

i tell you i saw a russian
sub out there

nobody gets through
thems my orders

(at that very moment
marvin tempest roars up
the muffler roughers right behind)

                                                    halt!

rrrrrrhhhhhhoooooooommmmmmmmmmmmmmm
                                    "marvin!"
"hey woody baby
 what'cha doin' here"
                                        "they won't let
                                         me get through"
"hop on
 we'll take u.s. lawnway
 number 1"
                            linda smith is crossing her front lawn
                              where an eager bud thompson is gunning
                                his ten-year-old chevy
                                                    (i'm taking off for
                                                     the sur now)
                        (but you said around
                         six o'clock bud)
                                                    (the roads are all jammed
                                                     up)
                        (can we get there)
                                                    (i know a back way
                                                     are you coming with me)
                        (i got to tell my folks
                         something)
                                                    (tell them you're putting
                                                     up decorations for the
                                                     computer bust)
                        (okay but it'll take awhile
                         wait here)
                                                    (move your ass)
stuart has somehow managed to steal
press credentials and follows max
vogel out of the press tent
                        "...mr vogel"
"i've nothing more to say"
                        "i can help uou"
"who are you"
                        "my name is stuart
                         creedmore daily examiner"
"what do you want"
                        "i have a great interest in
                         the sweetmeats"
"so..."
                        "i'd like to do an exclusive
                         story on you"
"exclusive eh
 it might cost you plenty"
                        "my paper is willing to foot
                         the bill"
"five thousand now and
 five thousand when it's
 finished"
                        "that sounds reasonable"
                                            (and with that
                                             stuart peels off
                                             five one thousand $ bills
                                             from a bankroll that would
                                             make billy graham blush)
"eh (says vogel gasping)
 that's five thousand
 plus expenses of course"

"only if i can see them
alone for a minute'
"you're on"

manny makemore watches as
the finishing touches on the
pontoons converts his piper cub
into a sea-plane

*"pearl
have you tried meyer again"*

"he's not at home boss"

*"get me someone there
i don't care who it is
i have to get through"*

mayor meyer was indeed not at home

he was with about 30 other big sur
homeowners planning strategy down at
the firehouse

"we simply can't allow this
to happen"

"order has broken down"

"you should have seen what
my flower beds look like!"

"...cars parked on my lawn"

"...had the audacity to urinate on my rose bushes"

order

"complete strangers..."

point

"...went to sleep on
my lawn..."

"all the litter all around

it seemed like four or five cases of beer cans
at least"

quiet please

"...i swear..."

"... defecated right on the side
of the road..."

please

"...clearly posted
lands"

quiet please

"this young couple came in the kitchen
and asked us for a glass of water..."

"i think they were
high on marijuana"

let mayor meyer speak

point of order

"...then the hairiest of them
just smiled and said 'peace'"

sssssssshhhhhhhhhhhh

"...police"

"ssssssssshhhhhhhhhhhhhh"

"may i just say a couple of words

thank you
now friends i know we have a difficult situation here
and i'm just as concerned as all of you are

this morning when i woke up
and saw that incredible scene outside
I was speechless..."

the very words he used with seymore savage
when savage interviewed the mayor a half
hour later

           "and saw that incredible scene outside
            i was speechless"

(...simply speechless linda)

                  (aw mom
                  grandma and pop can see me
                  at the dance)

(they drove all the way down from idaho
to see you and you simply run off like
that
    i simply don't understand)

                  (i gotta do the decorations
                  mom)

(but you know grandmother and grandfather
were going to be here this weekend
                    you
could have changed your plans i think)

                  (sorry mom
                  gotta go)
                    sfx front door slam

"the sound you hear in the background is the
unloading of supply trucks of the 69th national
guard division
           the entire division is here at
big sur today
           more than 600 men strong
                    and to
house and feed a contingent that large requires
extraordinary logistics in an area this small
                      we
are surrounded by a sea of parked and abandoned
automobiles that have blocked all access routes
leading in and out of big sur since dawn this
morning
      these supply trucks were the last vehicles
to get through last night and it took them about
seven hours to get here from fort ord
                 just thirty
miles away
       the soldiers are busy setting barbedwire
and clearing the area
            to my right is a hastily
cleared helicopter landing site which has been
in constant use this morning and to my left is
the bivouac area for the guardsmen including
a first aid tent
         communications tent
             mess hall
latrines and the ubiquitous px
          this is pauline
farnsworth wagh radio news"
         how's that hy?

                  how about the (mumble)

the connection is bad

                ...sweetmeats pauline

      no word hy
      their manager is going
      to make another attempt
      to talk to them

              when

any minute now

...want you to go with
him when he goes

me?

have savage go with you

but hy...

...buts about it
i want live pictures
from the top

the van will never make
it
  it's too steep

then do a remote...want
live video to spark up
10:00 special

that's about sunset here

good...be enough light
...sure you use color

but hy
the color cameras weigh

...goddam what they
weigh i need color

AUDIO

(ANNOUNCER) Just watch those amber

waves of grain bubble into that cool

sparkling head. It's what makes

CRASS beer so taste-tempting, so

refreshingly different. Now, here

again, is Reverend Buttermilk, and

his radio gospel message for today.

"we hear a lot of talk today about a so-called
 'generation gap' and by gosh that's an apt description of it
                now what do they mean by a generation
gap
   (we certainly didn't have that phrase around when
i was growing into adulthood)
                        they mean by a genera-
tion gap the *void between*
                        that critical area
                        that critical time between
generations when misunderstandings arise
                misunderstandings and doubts about
the viability and validity of the other's generation
now what do i mean about viability and validity
                                        viability
or to translate it another way
                        'why was i born'
why was i born into such a troubled age
why couldn't i have been born in such and such a time
when conditions were better and things were great
                                                youth
today questions why they were born into the nuclear age

why they're called 'war babies'
                              imagine having to carry
that millstone about *your* neck for the rest of *your* lives
war babies!
          they actually admonish their parents for
conceiving them as if their parents and *not god* had
decided the matter
                  yes friends
                  today's youth are quick to blame their
parents for everything
                        even giving them life
                                      but very few
of them *come to god* with their complaints.

<table>
<tr><td></td><td>AUDIO</td></tr>
</table>

	AUDIO
	WOMAN CRYING
VIDEO	
TRUCK WITH WOMAN CARRYING WASH	Oh dear...oh dear...
BASKET INTO LAUNDROMAT. MS OF	
WOMAN AS SHE PLACES BASKET DOWN	i don't know what to do...
IN FRONT OF MACHINE AND HOLDS	
OUT HER HANDS BEFORE HER.	my clothes are so dirty...
	and my hands are too...
	2nd WOMAN
SECOND WOMAN SLIDES IN ON RIGHT	
WHILE CAMERA CLOSES IN ON A TWO-	Don't fret or frown...
SHOT.	
	no need to feel blue...
	everything is clean again...
ON WORD *YOU* SECOND WOMAN HOLDS UP	when you use NEW!
BOX OF NEW. ZOOM IN TO BOX.	
	1st WOMAN
FIRST WOMAN	But NEW's a detergent ...
	it simply won't do...
	too rough on my hands...
	it smells bad too...
	2nd WOMAN
	That was before...
	the chemists got through...
	there's a whole 'nother story...
	in new-formula NEW
	1st WOMAN

(for getting this far through the commercial
 you're rewarded by finding out that the man
 in the wetsuit who has just waded ashore on
 the rugged big sur coastline is none other than forest jagoff)

mah felluh
amuricuns

"now what do we mean by validity
                              by validity
we ask ourselves 'does our life have meaning'
                                        or
to put it another way
                    we like to tell ourselves
                    we were placed on this earth
for some important reason
                        but have we found that reason
my friends
          it's one of the big questions youth asks me
these days
          just the other day i was approached on the street
by a hippie
          he was high on something
          he needed a haircut and a bath
          i don't suppose he had a job or wanted one
          his clothes were torn and dirty
                                        a few years back
we'd call this fellow a bum or a tramp but today we make it
sound socially acceptable
                        we call them hippies or yippies or
zippies or something
                    well anyway this young person asked me
if i had a dime and i asked him right back if he was going
to use that dime to find out the reason he was placed on this
earth
      well my friends
      he was dumbstruck
he hadn't any notion of what i was talking about"
                                        a long-precision floating
                                        point constant is specified
                                        as a decimal fraction
(mantissa to you)
                    and an optional decimal exponent
                                        the constant will be aligned
                                        at a double-word boundary in
                                        the proper machine format for
                                        use in floating point operand

          the function of a flush tank
                    a typing pool
                    a rudimentary tail
                    a useless addition
                    none of these
                              (hundreds of thousands of high school
                              juniors were taking their SAT's that
                              morning in hopes of getting into the
                              college of their choice)
          while millions of parents
          were sitting home biting their nails
                              wondering if little johnny would
                              pay off on their lifelong dream
        (and their nightmare of scrimping
        and saving for a year's tuition)
the pressure was on
                    a flush tank
                    a typing pool

120

                                        Relocatable Expressions:
                                        R+2
                                        R-8*A
                                        R-R+R
                                        *-X'FB2'
                                        R-A
                                        2048

one of these statements is false
one of these statements are false
                              "only one of the above statements is true"
    (find the ten mistakes in
     this drawing)
                              the cow has no tail
                              the farmer is wearing a football helmet
                              the chicken has laid a square egg
"square egg or cubed egg
 is an acceptable answer"
                              the cow has a rudimentary tail
"the tail is used to swat
 flys"
                                        "i'll kill that kid if he doesn't
                                        pass"
"all he does is listen to records all day
 when he could be studying"
                    "i don't know what's gotten into him"
    a useless addition
                                        "once again"
    a useless addition
                                        "do you have it now"
  "a useless addition"
                                        what's a mantissa?
  (a typing pool?)
                    i didn't save for fifteen long years to
                    see my daughter become a secretary
and you know what this kid
says to me?
          "plumbers make more money than college professors"
                                        out of a possible
                                        800
        "that kid of mine got 285"
                              just on the verbal part alone
no kidding!
                    ("if he didn't go out so much he
                    could be top-ten material")
    oh
    he's college material all right
                              "a piece off the same bolt"
i didn't throw in a thousand to the
alumni fund last year for nothing you know
                              "chip off the old block
                              just like his dad"
    (when to apply)
                apply as early as possible
                                        ...only he applied
                                        himself
    (list your hobbies)
                "getting stoned"
                              college professors have just as
                              many pipes as plumbers

have just as many pipes
have fewer pipes
have more pipes
cannot tell from information given

<u>AUDIO</u>

ANNOUNCER (VO)

<u>VIDEO</u>

SPLIT SCREEN TO TWO SETS OF
HANDS SPRINKLING ON DIGIT-
DOUCHET, RINSING UNDER TAP,
THEN HELD TURNED-UP BEFORE
CAMERA. FREEZE EACH FRAME.

These two sets of hands have both

had a thirty-second wash-up with

new Digitdouchet. See how both

sets of hands are sparkling clean?

Would you believe that one set of

ON WORD *COLLEGE* TILT UP L. FRAME
TO REVEAL MAN IN A MORTARBOARD.
ON WORD *PLUMBER* TILT UP R. FRAME
TO REVEAL MAN IN A WORKMAN'S CAP.

hands belongs to a college professor

and the other to a plumber?

CUT TO MLS OF ANIMATED SPLIT
SCREEN WHERE BOTH MEN ARE DRYING
THEIR HANDS BEFORE WASHBASINS.

No matter what *your* line of work

your hands *do* get dirty. That's

why it's so important...

("i always had dirty hands as a child and
 my mother would always say 'stuart
                             see how
 nice the sweetmeats always look
                          they wash
 their hands before every meal
                       and after
 they go make peepeedoody'
                  and i wanted to
 be as clean as them after awhile
                          i had to
 get rid of the shame of my large dirty hands")
                                    i mean
                                    i've never seen so many filthy kids
                                    in my life
"absolutely no self-respecting citizen..."
                              "these kids had absolutely no
                               respect for themselves"

        filthy
              (they live in filth)
take a bath
you bum!
                  we read all of the pamphlets on toilet training
...communist
   conspiracy
                                      subversion through filth
                                      and sickness

      hair all over the place
                          unwashed
                          uncombed
   "full of god-knows-what"
                   "i mean don't those kids learn hygiene
                    in school anymore?"

now they call it sex education
                                        (they learn how to screw
                                but not to scrub)
                                                    after every feel
they report that VD is on the rise
                                (now we put toilet paper on every strange
                                seat before we sit down)
        filthy dirty hippies!
                                *"...and saw that incredible scene outside
                                i was speechless"*
"tell us what you saw
 mr meyer"

                                *"there must have been a hundred or more
                                of these hippies camped on my front lawn
                                and there was garbage everywhere
                                                        it looked
                                like dresden in may"*
"what did you do then
 mayor"

                                *"i told them to get off my property of course
                                i told them they were on private property
                                and they were trespassing and if they didn't go
                                immediately i'd call the state police"*
"go on"

                                *"then one shouted that the area had been liberated
                                and they all broke into cheers"*

no friends
            that wasn't cigarette smoke
            winding tendril-like into the springtimearly afternoon haze
            rising gently to the top of mt. parnassus
no friends
            that weren't no good grasslands cigarette smoke
            with the cool clean smell of springtimearly freshness
            drifting smog-like over the heads of those assembled
                                                            that
my friends
            was the greatest corrupter of our young people
            since comic books and coca-cola
                                            *negro jazz musicians
                                            brought it to the
                                            underground in the
                                            twenties*
        you mean...that what was called a reefer!
                                        the very same
        and here all along i thought a reefer was
        a turkish cigarette

                                        (could make an
                                         interesting cocktail)
        characteristic personality changes among
impressionable young persons from the regular
use of marijuana include apathy
                          loss of effectiveness
                                        and diminished capacity
or unwillingness to carry out long-term plans
                              endure frustrations
                                              concentrate
for long periods
              follow routines
                    or successfully master new material
                                                (how are
                                                you doing
                                                friends?)

        jack kerouac
        and allen ginsberg
        in the early fifties did it in the open
                                  let's do it
            let's fall out
                      "fall out in the fifties gave way
                       to the drop out in the sixties"
zig-zag papers reported a 16%
rise in sales for 1962
                              but surprisingly
                              the tobacco industry noted no gains
                              in cut tobacco consumption

marijuana was miraculously
transformed into *pot*
                              and some wag of a tobacco industry
                              executive copyrighted the word

and the word became against the law
                              and the law and the liquor and tobacco
                              lobbies in washington
and 100,000 frustrated parents
                              and every minister and rabbi this
                              side of the promised land
contacted every law enforcement
official living or dead
                    to ban this noxious weed forever and ever
                    till lung cancer or the dt's death do us part
and prohibition was
upon us again
                                        whoooppp-eeeeeeeeee
            let's do it
            let's fall out
                          "...to hear timothy leary and
                           richard alpert do a psychedelic
                           celebration presented by the
                           league for spiritual discovery..."
          meditation mudras
          consciousness cakras
                      lighting by rudi stern
                                        (tickets by globe)
        N E W S   O N   T H E   H O U R

RESIGNATION CHAIRMAN OF THE MOTORS AND MATERIALS
SPACE EDUCATION OF THOUSANDS OF CAMPUS RIOTS ON
MAY FIFTEENTH OFFENSIVE AT FUC HUE IN VIETNAMESE
TALKS IN LONDON RAP BROWN EAST OF THE SWEETMEATS

WHILE HUNDREDS OF NATIONAL GUARDSMEN IN BORDER
DISPUTE AT WASHINGTON AIRPORT EGYPTIAN ATTACK

"more news in a moment"

AUDIO

Now! A modern detergent that's

as kind to your dishes as it is

to your clothes -- NEW, the one

washday wonder that gets your whole

house clean.

"...stonehouse atop mt. parnassus

max vogel and
several members of the press have begun the
long trek to the mountain's top

if they do not
return in two hour's time then the national
guard has been instructed to move out

this is
jim skinner reporting from big sur california
for KCUF monterey"

METS LOSING HIGH TODAY IN THE
UPPER SEVENTIES
LOW TONIGHT RAIN NEWS NEXT AT FOUR O'CLOCK

"pash the pepper pleash"
(grandpop smith is having trouble
with his uppers)

"here dad"

"thank ya kindly
mighty good squash meg"

"whadhe say..."

"he said he likes the
squash mother"

"oh yes...yes..."

"where linda and louish"

"linda is putting up
decorations for the
computer bust"

"the what-what?"

"whadshe say russell"

"she..."

"THE COMPUTER BUST"

"what in god's country
is that"

"it's where the boys
and girls get paired
by computer"

"...pewter?"

"i git it...
machines match 'em up"

"um"

"...don't understand"

"machines do the
matching mother"

"machines!"

"mother"

"i don't want no machine
bothering my linda!"

                                        (chief broken wind has traded his pontiac
                                         in for a horse and has made his way on
                                         back trails to the base of mt. parnassus)
        ("me looking for
          seymore savage")
                                          ("just wait behind that barrier chief")
        ("me no wait")
                                          ("he left for the top of the mountain
                                            about ten minutes ago
                                                                you're too late")
        ("me on CPT
          still early yet")
                                        as just then a piper cub with pontoons
                                        buzzes them overhead
        ("um lookum there
          large silver bird with
          elephantiasis")
                                        manny makemore looks out over the
                                        acres upon acres of humanity
                                        rubs his hands together
                                        and automatically
                                        slaps his wallet

"there's gold in them thar ills"
                                        manny makemore
                                        product of the age of the product

was the apple of his father's eye
down on orchard street where he was
blessed into being January 19, 1920
                                        manny makemore
                                        who sold papers when he was eight
                                        who sold brushes during the depression
                                        who sold half his company's "C" rations
                                        during the war
(who would sell his mother even today
 if he could get his price)
                                            who took basic marketing at nyu
                                            night school with his g.i. bill
        and opened the first laundromat
        in the kingsbridge section of the bronx
                                                        another one on
                                                        tremont avenue
   and one on bedford street in brooklyn
                                        one on continental avenue in
                                        forest hills
who was grossing over a grand a week
late in '48
            when he had the good fortune
            of marrying sadie liebowitz
                                          (who was also taking basic marketing at nyu)
        to whom this day he attributes
        his success
                                        because it was sadie who knew someone
                                        who knew someone who knew someone
                                        who knew fay sweetmeat
   because it was sadie who pointed out
   to manny the war-baby boom
                            because it was sadie who convinced manny to
                            sell his laundromats to bendix
                                                    and to put his
                                                    money in a dying
                                                    chicago toy
                                                    manufacturer

and it was sadie who set up the deal
for manny to produce the original pookie and paul dolls

                                        pookie and paul
                                        dollhouses
pookie and paul
bridal outfits
                pookie and paul
                coloring books
                        pookie and paul teapot spout cleaner
                        pookie and paul pail and mop handle
                        pookie and paul blower & barbeque (portable)
                        pookie and paul golf cart umbrella attachment
                        pookie and paul furniture wax rags
                        pookie and paul shaft safety lock
                        pookie and paul trailer dolly
                        pookie and paul dental floss applicator
                        pookie and paul recording pill dispenser
                        pookie and paul self service table
                        pookie and paul hip thigh crutch
                        pookie and paul anti-backlash fishing reel
                        pookie and paul drain guard
                        pookie and paul electric door jamb
but that was only a beginning
                        for just before sam and fay sweetmeat
                        had that tragic accident
(thinking only of their children)
they formed a corporation with makemore
called Sweetmeat Enterprises
                                which gave makemore exclusive
                                promotional rights on anything
                                and everything the sweetmeats
                                put pen to paper with
                                (might not be grammatical but it
                                sure was profitable)
    "those kids was millionaires
     before they was ten"
                                "yeah
                                 but they blew millions too"
millions of kisses
                                        they stayed at the plaza
thousands of knishes
                (pookie and paul frozen knish-knoshers)
                                                they were
                                                beginning
                                                to go stale
            after sam and fay died in that terrible accident
                                                "it was like
                                                a member of
                                                the family"
    and the twins were thrown clear
                                        miraculously
                that was back in '55
                                                went into seclusion
"that's right
 they went into seclusion that time too"
                                while the offers for adoption
                                climbed into the hundreds
        and the mail was so heavy
        it was brought in on a fork-lift truck
                                        but it was never the same

oh sure
they had our sympathy in their comeback try

they were damn popular too
but it wasn't the same
they were beginning to go stale
(they had all the
bread they could
ever want)

beginning to get on our nerves
"i mean
we could only feel sorry for them just so long"

"...had it made in
the shade with a
spade"

if i give my love to you
i must be sure
if i trust in you oh please
i love you too
so i hope you see that i
would love to love you
and that she will
love you too

("i stopped collecting their records")
a generation of sweetmeat-
reared war-babies suddenly
deserted them

their tv series was dropped
"i don't know
i just didn't dig them as much"

"it was if they were
always playing to our
sympathy you know"

they didn't even use
electric guitars

"they were just so square"
so eisenhowerish
the kind of thing dick nixon would get
"a big bang out of"

just didn't make the scene
playing to our sympathies
with nonelectrical guitars

"i mean all axes in those days
were wired"

singing horseshit numbers
like 'on top of old smokey'
and 'green grow the rushes ho'

foxtrotting through the
age of the lindy

lindying through the
age of the cha-cha
mambo samba mumbo jumbo

cha-cha-cha

elvis and the everly brothers

cha-chaing through the
age of rock

by 1960 they had all but disappeared

15-year-old wash-ups
billboard and cashbox hadn't listed
either a single or an album of theirs
in over a year

                                        (and their sweetmeat family christmas
                                        carol album was for ten years a best
                                        seller every december)
        and then suddenly they dropped
dropped

                                                        dropped out
dropped out of sight
                        "oh they was all right and all"
they just didn't make
public appearances anymore
                        "they made one final cross country tour
                         and then they dropped out"
        i remember that tour
                        "thirty cities in thirty days"
a disaster
                                        (they drew bigger crowds than
                                         kennedy or nixon that year)
bullshit
they pulled quarter-filled houses
wherever they went
                                        (thirty of our largest cities
                                         from new york to spokane)
bullshit
the largest was clarksburg west virginia
                                        (traveling in three huge vans...)
two broken down caddies
and a beat-up chevy station wagon
                                        (in which max vogel...)
chewed out his fingernails
                                "all right
                                ALL RIGHT!
                                we all tell white lies about those days..."
    "what could i tell my kids...
     that pookie and paul never existed?"
                                        "why!
                                         my kids were brought up on the
                                         sweetmeats"
                we lied to them because
                we lied to ourselves
                                                the sweetmeats were
                                                our ideals
                                                        we couldn't
                                                destroy the myth
    "what could i tell my kids..."
                                "the sweetmeats were abroad i told mine"
i said that the sweetmeats
were doing a film
                                        (curiously they made three films
                                         in that time)
        six years ago...
                                the sweetmeat caravan and the death of a
                                dream
marvin tempest and woody wilson
have managed to penetrate general
ochre's defense perimeter
                        and presently stand before the general's tent
                        waiting permission to see him
(marvin's 5-speed 27@7200
 yamaha big bear scrambler
 idling in the background)
                        rrrrrrrrrrrrrrrrrrrrrrrrrrrrrrhhhhhhhhhhhooooooooommmmmmmmmmmmm
what's that racket!

                                        a motorcycle sir

shut that damn thing off!

                                          yessir
                                                (private exits)

*(can't get any peace around here
 where the hell is that bottle)*

                                          sir
                                              (private slouches in)

what is it private

                                        two people want to see you sir

*i'm only speaking to members of
the press*

                                          i told them that sir but...
                        (tempest and wilson
                             stride in)

what's the meaning of...

                                      "relax pop"
                                                      "cool it"

who...

                                      "my name's tempest"
                                                      "woody wilson"

what do you...you people want

                                      "that stonehouse is on
                                       roughers turf"

make sense man

                                      "the stonehouse where
                                       the sweetmeats are...
                                       that's on private
                                       property"

*private property bull!
i've just nationalized the
entire area*

                                                      "nationalized?"

*federalized...whatever you
call it*

                                      "that's illegal"

*i'm not concerned with legality
or illegality
            i'm concerned with
law and order*

                                                      "maybe the fact
                                                       that there are
                                                       russian subs in
                                                       the area would
                                                       concern you"

                                                      "right off the
                                                       coast"

RUSSIAN SUBS!

*my god...
then it really is a commie plot!*
                              (with me is general ochre leader of the
                               fighting 69th national guard battalion
                               what is the latest general)

       (well pauline
        it looks bigger than any
        of us thought)

                              (can you tell us what you mean)

(i'm not at liberty to say
 anything yet...
                    but if those
 ruskies think they can move
 right in and subvert our
 youth they got another thing
 coming)
                                        (do you mean that the russians...)
(i mean i think the sweetmeats
 are *unwilling tools* of those
 monsters
         possibly through
 hypnosis)
                                        (and what...)
(that's all i can say now)
                                        (this is pauline farnsworth
                                         big sur california)
"and this is sonny swingle with all
the heavies from hit-land kcuf
monterey
        heyyyyyy
                how about that report
 from big sur?
                whhoooo-eeeeee
                                really
grosses me out but i don't adam and
eve it you little pill-poppers you
                                so
here for judy and george and sandy and
ralph and randy s who loves barbara
                                a
glowing golden goodie from contemporary
kcuf top-forty fantastics
                        barry sadler's
ballad of the green berets

                                                (music cue)

        "charles victor is making his way to the
         microphone
                    he is flanked to either side
         by his mother and his father
                                    now the ap-
         plause from all those assembled here
         drowns out the army band
                                    private victor
         acknowledges the applause
                                    now he gestures
         for his mother and father to sit down
                                                he
         is smiling
                    he is still waving
                    a big grin crosses his face as
         he sees someone he knows in the audience
                    the audience is still applauding
         private victor waves to the press corps
                                                he
         asks again that everyone be seated
                                    and now
         private victor will speak"

                              thank you
                              thank you
                              i'm really glad to be back
                                        (he laughs
and the audience bursts into applause)
                              thank you
                              eh i'm not one for words really
                              but i'm really happy to be in the states
                              again and to be with my mother and dad
(applause)
                              so much has been written about hill 457
                              that i don't know if i can add anything
                              to what's been said eh
                                        but i consider
                              myself very lucky to be sole survivor of
                              that battle
(applause)
                              i never thought i'd ever make it
(applause and laughter)
                              i'd like to thank personally corporal
                              alvin finkleberg for finding me
                              and lt. stanley suture for doing such
                              a good job on me back in cam ranh bay
    "can you see mother?"
                                   "oh yes...yes peg...i can
                                    see very well..."
    "can you hear what he's saying?"
                                   "howszat?"
    "CAN YOU HEAR WHAT HE'S SAYING?"
                                   "some of it...yes..."
    "HE SAYS HE'S GLAD TO BE BACK"
                                   "oh yes...well i should imagine"
        ...so then our radioman got hit and we
        were pinned down on the other side of
        the clearing   (what's the count)
                                                (what's the count)
              (three balls and a strike)
                                        twenty million senior citizens
                                        are taking their afternoon nap
    perhaps another twenty million
    are t.v. tube-hopping
                              put down another twenty million
                              who are saturday moon-lighting
                              to make meat ends
                                        twice a week on
                              the family's foodlist
    twenty million are kids under
    twelve and they're raising all
    sorts of hell in back alleys and
    sandboxes from marthas vineyard to
    sausalito
                              twenty million work on saturday
                              as a general rule
        twenty million are gossiping
        on the phone or over backyard fences
                              twenty million female slaves
                              are spring cleaning
    twenty million are on the road
    taking the family for a spin
                                   twenty million are walking around
                                   with their hands in their pockets
                                   without anything much to do

which leaves twenty million
concerned americans (mostly in the
post-pubescent age bracket) biting their nails

over the sweetmeats

AUDIO

ANNOUNCER (VO)   VIDEO

Tense...nervous...upset? Almost   MOVE IN ON HARRIED MAN BEHIND DESK
                                        WITH A RAISED DOLLY SHOT. PAPERS
to the breaking point? LET DOWN   MARKED "BILL" SCATTERED ABOUT.
                                        ZOOM IN ON HAND HOLDING PENCIL. ON
lets you relax...takes your mind   WORD *POINT* MAN SNAPS PENCIL. FREEZE
                                        FRAME IN BLUR. SUPER WORDS *LET*
off those troubling day-to-day   *DOWN* CROSS DISS TO SYLVAN COUNTRY
                                        SCENE.
problems...takes it for a walk in

the country.   PAN TO TELESCOPIC SHOT OF MAN
                                        WALKING DOWN COUNTRY ROAD. SUPER
Let Down with its active ingredient   WORD *TETRAHYDROCANNABINAL*.

tetrahydrocannabinal works in the

bloodstream...rushing its medication

                                        ding-ding-ding-ding-ding
B U L L E T I N

0143
BIG SUR CALIFORNIA (UPI MAY 7)

REPORTS CONFIRM SIGHTING OF UNIDENTIFIED SUBMARINE OFF THE BIG

SUR COASTLINE. GENERAL OCHRE (PRON: OK-KUR) COMMANDING THE 69TH

NATIONAL GUARD BATTALION BELIEVES THE SUBMARINE TO BE OF RUSSIAN

ORIGIN AND HAS NOTIFIED THE JOINT CHIEFS OF STAFF, THE PENTAGON,

THE SECRETARY OF DEFENSE AND THE HEAD OF THE APPROPRIATIONS COM-

MITTEE.

                                        wouldn't you know it
those little buggers
the sweetmeats
                        spokesmen for the "new morality"
                                                kid cop-out artists
        "spies"
        "traitors"
                        ...part of a gigantic conspiracy to bring down
                        america from within
the sweetmeats and the
commies
                        pookie, paul and mao
                                        goddam sex education
                                        between church and state
        "yeah
         and how about prayers in public schools"
                                        destroying the moral fiber
                                        of the nation

            long-haired pot-smoking draft-dodging
      card-burning card-carrying son-of-a-bitch
                                    (and she was no better
                                    the little tramp)
remember when she publicly burned her
bra supporting the anti-war demonstrators
                                    her disgusting disrobing at the
                                    miss america pageant
          "how about her posing nude in
            foreplay magazine..."
                                    or paul whipping it out in dallas
show business activists
that's whut they was
                "in the thirties we would have blacklisted them"
                                                and yet...
      oh they had a great following if that's what you mean
                                    "i mean my kids
                                    were crazy for them"
          "if they were anywheres near chicago
            my kids would go an' hear 'em
                              and we lived in des moines!"
      bigger than the beatles
      or the stones
                bigger 'n peter paul and mary and presley put together
bigger than life
look and the saturday evening post
                              (do you feel dated over a reference
                              like that?)
          when they came out of
          seclusion three years ago
          they were all but forgotten
                        " ... i figured they were washed-up"

                    <u>AUDIO</u>

            ANNOUNCER (VO)   <u>VIDEO</u>

... matter what *your* line of work   CUT TO MLS OF ANIMATED SPLIT
                                             SCREEN WHERE BOTH MEN ARE DRYING
your hands *do* get dirty. That's   THEIR HANDS BEFORE WASHBASINS.

why it's so important to carry a

can of DIGITDOUCHET with you where-

ever you go. DIGITDOUCHET contains   ON WORD *GO* CUT TO CAN OF DIGIT-
                                             DOUCHET. POP ON, ONE AT A TIME
not one, but a combination of medi-   BENEATH, THREE HEXAGONAL "BEN-
                                             ZINE CARBON RINGS" MARKED *INGRE-*
ally-approved ingredients to...   *DIENT*.

      but that commercial is perfect there
      don't you see?
                                             cleanliness being next to
                                             godliness being next to
                                             the good book by bedside

            generations upon generations of
            americans gargling and douching
            their way into heaven
                                             cleanliness and the american
                                             way of life

short hair and shave once a day

"pardon me slip but your miss is
showing"

cleanliness and goodness follow
you the rest of your days and...

americans look and feel better
when they...

wear clothes

above all

"you could see she weren't wearing panties"

i see i see

"goddam little whore
didn't wear no undies"

no undie-wear

nothing to hide that little burger-patty

nothing to enclose
that snitchable
snatch

and a mini-skirt smaller than dick nixon's rug

(front rows to pookie and
paul's concerts were by
invitation only)

(you can take rows either way)

"an affront to the american
way of life"

filthy...unamerican...

"you can bet the army would take care of paul"

had that filthy habit...

"openly advocated smoking pot
to end the war"

morally filthy and degrading
to our *young people*

*or in the bell-like ring of
miss olivia pitt:*

"helene have you heard it just came over
the radio there are russian subs with missile
launchers off the coast of big sur...

well it can only mean one thing...
they're there because the sweetmeats requested their help...it's as
clear as day...and i've been saying so all along...

those filthy kids didn't

fool me for an instant

i was just saying to carmella the other day how peculiar
it was that the russian press hadn't mentioned anything about the sweetmeat
disappearance...not one word...well you can be sure...i know...and another
thing...you don't say...
well i'm going to call carmella right away bye"

*at&t started blowing
its plugs*

"all circuits are busy sir"

01000010
01000110
01001010
01110001

(operation code not a valid
mnemonic

as well as incorrect
separation character appears
in the operand field)

but it was too late

half the country believed the sweetmeats
were being brainwashed by the russians

and half the country
believed they were being brainwashed by their parents

"what the hell has happened
down there!"

           *...moment colonel...seem
be...trouble...signal*

"say again"

           moment...cap com...interference

"i'm not going to go through
with this TVA until i get
this suit problem licked"

           roger...check your acceler...

3840	3649	3850	2629	1934
3856	3665	3866	2645	1950
3872	3681	3882	2661	1966
3888	3679	3898	2677	1984

           ADCON2   DC   AL2(FIELD-256)

an explicit length not exceeding
four bytes may be specified

           unknown constants
           fly-by

37475769795837265978 37=55

           ...hold it...hold it...

      jam-shamming on the uncle ned

number please

      "unless analyzed anyone contributing"

ADCON1   DC   AL(AREA)

      FLYING-SPOT SCANNNERS

      (lines are bust)

    rrrriiiiinnnnnnnnnnngggggggggggg

           "hello?"

    "carmella?"

           "olive?"

"have you heard..."

"hello?"

           "hello?"

"is this ground control?"

    "well! of all the nerve"

           "olive
who's on the line
with you?"

    "on the line with me?!"

"this is colonel dipper
is this ground control?"

    "another one of those
obscene crackpots!"

           "it's getting worse
all the time"

"look ladies..."

    "you look here you...
pervert!"

"i can't help it if my fly
is stuck"

"oooohhhhhhh
i'm going to
faint"

"how did you get this
number anyhow
it's
unlisted you know"

"would you do me a favor and
call houston area code 713...."

"olive
call the police"

"you're absolutely right"

"but i'm really colonel dip..."

(click)

"colonel dipper frantically adjusts
his closed-circuit miniature tv and gets)

VIDEO

AUDIO

MS OF TECHNICIANS SCRUBBING DOWN
OUTSIDE OF SPACE CAPSULE WITH MOPS.
Where cleanliness counts the   PAN DOWN TO PAIL AND BOX OF NEW NEXT
most...where even the smallest   TO IT.
speck of dust could mean...

"you're going to have to do my
face over again
i'm sweating like
a pig"

"well for chrissake tim
i mean
you didn't bring *anything*
with you"

"lissen fuckface
i'm paying you to make me up
not to bring me down"

"this tent is a suanabath...
simply unbearable"

"it's almost two already"

(marvin tempest bursts in with
woody wilson as sidekick)

"well for criminy sake..."

hey is this here the press tent

"it all depends what you mean
by press"

i'm looking for seymore savage

"is that ass here?"

this ain't the press tent?

"no sweets
do we look like members of the
fourth estate"

*you look like a couple of three
dollar bills to me*

and bursting out of the tent again
they chance to see a parachute open
high above mt. parnassus
and a descending
figure frantically waving and kicking
like some bug caught in a spider's web

manny makemore hasn't even *seen* a
parachute since world war two
but that's manny all right

137

with a 16 mm zeiss moviecamera
and a wollensak tape recorder
strapped to his stomach
                         ("hhhhhhhhhhhhheeeeeeeeeeellllllllllllll111ppppppppppp
pppppppppppppppppp")

did you see what i see
says max vogel to stuart

                              it's landing on the
                              other side of the hill

somebody's trying to beat
me to the sweetmeats

                              i'll try to pick him off
                              with my rifle

your rifle!
that's what you have
in that case!?

                              it's not much really...

my god! put that thing away

                              i have to assemble the
                              mount

what newspaper did you say
you worked for

                              newspaper...?

look buddy
here's your five g's back
i think i'll make the rest
of the trip alone

                              you're not going anywhere
                              without me
                              says stuart pointing the
                              muzzle at max
                                        we're going
                              together all the way
                                        now

                    (i can't let this lunatic
                    reach the stonehouse) thinks
                    max
"a felleh of that description
 left with max vogel about a
 half-hour ago doctor"

                              "ooooooooooooooo
                               that must be stuart"

"the two of them were making
 their way to the stonehouse"

                              "ooooooooooooooo
                               how far is that"

"you can't miss it...
 just keep walking uphill
 but no one is supposed to
 cross these barricades"

                              "oooooooooooooooo i see
                               but what is preventing me
                               from going back ten feet and
                               cutting through the woods"

"beats me
 i'm just supposed to see that
 nobody crosses these barriers"

                              (while at that very moment
                               the now-famous submarine bulletin
                               had just interrupted the private
                               charlie victor press conference)
brought to you by princess gefiltefish
                              (not the bulletin
                                        the press conference)
                                                        and
back
at
the
russell
smith's
                                                  "my god meg
                                                   that's 30
                                                   miles away!"
                    "did he shay russian
                     submarines"
                                        "dad
                                         don't get excited"
"what..."
                    "WE'RE BEING INVADED!"
"we're...being..."
                    "INVADED...INVADED..."
"oh yes...yes of
 course...my my..."
                                                  "meg this is
                                                   serious"
                                        "oh where's louis
                                         and linda"
                    "i knew i'd live to shee
                     the day when those dog-
                     gone ruskies..."
                                        "we have to get
                                         louis and linda!"
                                                  "call the high
                                                   school"
                                        "where's louis"
                                                  "he said he
                                                   was mowing
                                                   grass"
"who's that on the
 television meg?"
                                        "that's miss
                                         gefiltefish 1966
                                         mom"
"whassay...?"
                                        "IT'S JUST AN AD!"
                    "A COMMERCIAL MOTHER
                     DON'T LET IT CONCERN
                     YOU NONE"
                                                  "i'm going to
                                                   check the
                                                   fallout shel-
                                                   ter"
                                        "wait russell
                                         let's get the news
                                         on the radio"

beep-beep-
beep-beep-beepedee-beep-beep-beep-beep-beepedee-beep-beep-beep-beep-beepedee-
beep-beep-beepedee-beep-beep-(fade)

"this is kcuf monterey news at two clyde rawlins
reporting
well as you've just heard it appears
as if submarines are off the coast of big sur
but whether they are from a foreign country or
not is still in doubt
and still in doubt is the
whereabouts of the sweetmeats who are believed
to be still held in the stonehouse high above
parnassus mountain
late word reaching kcuf says
that max vogel sweetmeat manager has not returned
to base camp yet
vogel was given two hours to
arrange for the release of the sweetmeats and
return before the national guard's 69th battalion
under the command of general ochre makes an
assault on the stonehouse
vogel has less than an
hour to go
it has been learned that the president
has been informed of these developments and is
keeping a watchful eye on these late-breaking
events
in other news
in vietnam today ground action
was heavy in..."

TURN OF EVENTS CARD

JACKIE offers to trade the secret

of the "Jackie look" for Russian

missile secrets
---GAINS PERSONAL IMAGE

shock upon shock
our conditioning

cards and newsbreaks flung free
in a wonderland of paranoias

we hadn't slept a wink since
mac the knife cut pumpkins open

and the secrets of our society made
known

it was always something
lurking there

something evil and dark and foreign

not out in the
open like say
an A or an H-bomb

something that attacked from within
eating out the guts of the jolly green giant
like some insidious parasite

to bomb
or not
to bomb

that was the question
whether we should have all-out confrontation
and by so doing disgorge this bloodsucking
serpent from our system

                                                        or work
                                                        through
                                                        the system
                                                        itself

                        countering its insidiousness with our own
                        with each plan more insane than the last
                        more evil and dark and foreign
                                            than anything the enemy
                                            could ever aspire to
and of these two choices
there was only one
                        we would enema ourselves and our neighbors
                        and purge the paranoia from our souls
                                                    but when...
when oh god
would it end!

                                            "take two"
(clack)

        16. EXT: IN THE WOODS--AFTERNOON

        SYLVIA leads EDUARDO to a clearing where she gestures that
        he sit. He wants to go on but she sits herself down and finally
        so does he. She wants to make love but EDUARDO is oblivious
        to it all.

                        SYLVIA

                I love these woods. It's so peaceful and
                comfortable here.

                        EDUARDO

                I suppose it's all right if you like a lot
                of trees.

                        SYLVIA

                Oh, it's more than the trees. It's a feeling...
                powerful and strong. Powerful and peaceful at
                the same time. Do you know what I mean? Like
                making love...

        SYLVIA lies back as the camera closes in. EDUARDO studies her
        face, then looks down her body. SYLVIA raises her knees and
        her dress falls above her thighs. She begins to pull EDUARDO
        towards her.

                        SYLVIA

                (in heat) Sometimes I think of you as a tree.
                I mean, how big you are and how straight and how
                strong. A rough tree...

                        EDUARDO (shaking her off)

                You must be nuts!

                        SYLVIA

                Your nuts...like a tree...

SYLVIA pulls him to the ground and falls on him. EDUARDO
struggles but SYLVIA overpowers him. She puts her forearm
over his neck while with her other hand, she manages to un-
do his belt and his fly. CU of her hand in his pants. She
is determined to rape him.

                    EDUARDO

          (terrified) No...no...

SYLVIA pulls off her panties and falls on top of EDUARDO.
He is still struggling.

                    SYLVIA

          But you must...you must...

TTTTTWWWWWWWWEEEEEEEEEEEEEEEEEEEEEEEEEEEDTTTTTTTTTTTTTTTTTTTTWWAWWWWWWWWEEEEE
                                              "HOLD IT"
what the hell is that!
                    ok ok
                                        "CUT CUT!"
                                              "ALL RIGHT ALL RIGHT"
cut cut cut   TTTTTTWWWWWWWWEEEEEEEEEEEEEEEEEEETTTTTTTTTTTTTT
                    "what the hell is this"
                                              "ALL RIGHT ALL RIGHT"
CAPTAIN FRANCONA steps into the clearing. His men
have completely surrounded the shooting location.

                    FRANCONA (billyclub in hand)

          "All right, what's going on here?"

                    RIC GLAND (on his feet at once)

          "Nothing officer...eh...we're making a movie."

                    FRANCONA

          "A movie huh? Just what *kind* of a movie."

                    GLAND

          "Uh...a movie with sociably redeeming qualities,
           sir...uh officer..."

                    FRANCONA (to gerda on the ground)

          "And what about you, miss. What was this guy
           trying to do to you?"

                    GERDA LOINS

          "My God! Who wrote this lousy script!"
okay
that's a take
cut to ochre speaking to david cohen leader of S.H.A.M.E.
just as the general tells cohen he is free to go...
                                        (thanks general)
                    (but just as soon as this
                     war is over i'm going to
                     hang you by the balls)
                                        (what do you mean war)

                    (you ought to know you
                     goddam commie
                                    they're from
                     your country)
                                                        (huh?)

                    (your goddam russian pals
                     have landed off the coast)
                                                        (russians have
                                                         landed?!)

                    (my boys will take care of 'em)
                                                        (my god *thinks david
                                                         cohen* it's the
                                                         REVOLUTION!)

                    (blast 'em sky high)
                                                        (holy mao!)

                    (okay wilson
                     let's go)
woody wilson and general
ochre head out in the general's jeep
for the place on the coastline where woody saw
the sub
        but outside the bivouac area they are suddenly
engulfed by a massive jam of cars and humanity
                                        "we'll never get through this
                                         mob"

   "we could by motorcycle
    general"
                                        "i don't have a motorcycle"

   "marvin tempest could take us
    he's a friend of mine"
                                        "it's not dignified for a
                                         general to..."

   "but some of the roughers have
    sidecars
            you could ride in one
    of them"
                                        "well..."
                                                (break into charlie
                                                 victor's press
                                                 conference)

        ...so by the fourth day we were all pretty tired
        and we were down in our rations and we had nothing
        to drink except a little rainwater
                            but we had these
        here FEEL UP pills that some dead three-rocker had
        on him and we took them pills to keep going

                                                (this unknowing plug
                                                 would some day be
                                                 charles victor's
                                                 testimonial for the
                                                 product)

though it was already well-known to louis smith
who at that moment was popping a FEEL UP into
brenda quigley's waiting wanting kissyface

                                        VIDEO

              AUDIO   MCU OF BOY DOCTOR PLACING PILL
                                        IN DOLL'S MOUTH. CUT TO ECU OF
          ANNOUNCER (VO)   DOLL'S FACE AS THERMOMETER IS
                                        INSERTED.
...takes her medicine just like

grownups do. And look! You can

even take her temperature.

PAN WITH THERMOMETER AS IT IS
WITHDRAWN AND PASSED BEFORE THE
EYES OF LITTLE GIRL IN NURSE'S
OUTFIT.

It really works!

You'll really have *fun* with this new

DIP TO DOCTOR'S KIT WITH IMPLE-
MENTS SPREAD BEFORE IT. GIRL

Pookie and Paul Doctor's set. You

POINTS TO VARIOUS ITEMS AS THEY
ARE MENTIONED.

get everything you need including a

nurse's cap and gown...thermometer...

DISS TO BEAUTY SHOT OF KIT. POP
ON LOCAL TAG TO END.

tongue depressers...eye mirror...pills

...even a hypodermic syringe! So get

your Mommy or Daddy to...

("get your pookie dolls")

pookie and paul dolls only $1.00 eaah

("sweetmeat dolls here")

pookie and paul detective sets
pookie and paul army sets
pookie and paul navy sets
pookie and paul marine sets
pookie and paul businessman sets (pookie acts as executive secretary)
pookie and paul moviestar sets
pookie and paul recording artist sets
pookie and paul maid and butler sets (dolls are painted sepia)
pookie and paul dreamhouse sets

("sweetmeat sets here")

"you mean this is the end
 of the line of cars bud?"

"i guess so lin"

("get your sweetmeat set")

"but we're miles from big
 sur"

"i figure about
 five miles"

("pookie dolls)

"unbelievable"

"hey miss
 you want a pookie doll"

"no thanks"

"hey
 how far to big
 sur mac"

"i donno
 maybe six seven miles
 hey everybody...
 get your pookie dolls"

"well
 do you feel like
 hiking lin?"

"sure why not"

("...only one dollar")

"i used to have a whole
 bunch of those sets"

"yeah me too
 what did you do with yours"

"i performed a search and
 destroy on them"

                              linda and bud join that

great pilgrimage of barefeet and beads

                              sunbeams streaming back to the
                              mudra source

   (pleasure gardens and guards at the
    city-gates symbolize the internal and
    external obstacles to enlightenment of
    spiritual growth)

                                        "okay okay
                                         keep it moving!"

(down the DNA canal)

              traveling down evolutionary memory chains
              through human, animal, cellular, molecular forms

(down the eightfold
 path)

                    "c'mon keep it moving!"

                                   multitudes of gotamas
                                   walking the rutted roads

      kicking up dust that mingled with the
      mirages of marijuana

                                   lines stretching several
                                   miles in all directions

wending tendril-like along the valley floor

                                   winding along the hillsides
                                   like some many-legged headless
                                   hydra
                                        dividing and then dividing
                                   again
                                        forming its own pathtrails
                                   through fields and forests
                                                    regrouping
                                   setting out again

surely and slowly to the stonehouse

                                        (hey
                                         any of you kids
                                         need-um peacepipes?)

                                        (how about-um
                                         pookie and paul
                                         bedrolls)

               (no thanks chief)

                                        (bedrolls made out of
                                         strong indian hemp)

               (no thanks)

chief broken wind gets off his horse
and blocks the path before a bunch
of kids

                                        (you have-um choice of
                                         either color
                                                    acapulco
                                         gold or veracruz
                                         vermilion)

   (no thanks chief)
                (we brought our own)

                                        (how about authentic
                                         indian-styled hookah)

             (hey just
              what kind of an indian are you)

                                        (ugh
                                         you think every indian
                                         must be stereotyped
                                         tonto-honcho type?)

(...no)

                                                        (want you to know i have
marketing degree from
u.c.l.a.)

     (...sorry chief)

                                                        (marketing these fine
mexican hemp mats now)

       (how much chief)

                                                        (table placemat size
twenty dollars)

  (wow! that's a lot for a placemat)

                                                        (bedroll size
nine hundred dollars)

                     (that's a lot)

                                                         (half a bedroll
five hundred)

     (too much)

                                                        (to you
only four hundred)

(we don't have anywheres near that amount)

                                                        (make-um you special
deal me make sweetmeats)

  (you deal with the sweetmeats!)

                                                        (me been dealing with
them for years)

(wow)

                          (wow)

                                                       (sell-um you quarter-share
in bedroll for one hundred
honest george's)

    (...and it's dynamite?)

                                                        (as millard fillmore is
my great white father i
swear)

   (well...)

           "...how about that you little sweetmeatniks
             pookie and paul doing *potluck*
                                   their newest and
             truest from kcuf one-oh-one on your radio dial
             and this is sonny swingle bringing you the top
             twenty of plenty right here at two-thirteen on
             this beautiful afternoon
                                 who-eeeeeeeeee and this
             one is from our storehouse of ever-heavy hits
             for artie and carol
                      louis and brenda q
                              fats domino and..."
mah felluh amuricuns

                    hey shouts mitch frankle
                    to louis smith and brenda quigley
                    on the backseat floor in mitch's 1960 olds
                    sonny swingle is doing your request
   but louis and brenda
   were by that time
   balling on the differential hump

                                        driving his stickshift
                                      into the four-on-floor giggley
                                      gearbox grooving beneath him
                  tearing ass as it were
                              while america
drifted through an anxious
may afternoon

                                        ear to transistor
                                        shoulder to the wheel
          nose to the grindstone
          lips to the wet of the whistle
                                   in bars and bordellos
       ballparks and billiard parlors
                        (less than an hour until general ochre
                         and his troops would be moving out)
       butchershops and bakeries
                                        NO WORD YET
         FROM SWEETMEAT MANAGER MAX VOGEL WHO LEFT FOR THE TOP
         OF THE MOUNTAIN MORE THAN AN HOUR AGO
                                        america was listening
                                        for the latest word
on wavelengths of many bands
                              headbands
                              wedding bands
                              bands of angels
                                        (in the mets' outfield)
backyard barbecues
hamming over burgers
                   humming the latest levittown lowdown
                                                  telling sad
                                                  tales for
                                                  a pint of
                                                  twister
          twirling a baton and
          batting a fungo
                          belting a home run
                          and running home for a belt
america
        was
        tuned in to the news
                                        tuned into the mainstream
                                        of middletown
mindless and maple-tree-lined
                        (*dick and jane* readers
                         in a poet's notes)
                                             that afternoon
                                             america was listening
        and perhaps even hearing
        for the first time
                        in a long time

as we join the russell smith family
in their little frame house on pleasant
street we hear pop smith's lumbering
footsteps as he climbs the stairs to
the second floor bedrooms

                                        (cue in footsteps)
            as he thinks to himself...
                                    "if those ruskies come we gotta
                                    pre-tect ourselves
                                                it's too bad
                                    'bout russell not ownin' a gun
                                                        i
                                    sure wish i remembered mine
                                                but if
                                    i could find that hammer i've been
                                    lookin' fer i could sure build us
                                    a nifty-lookin' fortification
                                    quick as a bull climbin' a cow"
pop smith goes into louis's room to
look for the hammer

                        "maybe louis got it"
and comes across it interestingly enough
on a shelf that supports louis's typewriter
                        where louis
                                    the promising poet he
                                    was then
                                                and the great
                                                poet he was to become
                                                had written

(*...Visions of sugarplums had long passed*
    And all other visions as well
                        and yet
    It was a time for vision
    A time when all was envisioned and little seen
    An envisionment of the war's end
    An envisionment of racial cool and working poor
    An envisionment of together generations
                        but
    The great society rolled mercilessly over corpses in Vietnam
    As we prepared for lucibird's nosejobed nuptuals
    And you pig politicians made resolutions
                        and revolutions
    Promising limited wars for everyone
    While the stock market spurted to new highs
                                    and blood spurted
                                    in paddyfields and
                                    pawnshops from newark
                                    to natrang
    And the protests were screamed among the young
    And hushed among the old...)
but
pop
smith isn't interested in the poem
                        what interests him far more
                        is why louis had wrapped an
                        old sock about the hammerhead
            and he thinks to himself...
                        "mustuv' been usin' the hammer as
                        a mallet..."
            and in that very moment sees
            a small vial hidden behind the
            typewriter

148

"looka here..."

a vial crammed full of crushed
morningglory seeds
        but pop smith wouldn't
know ololiuqui from nutmeg

                *"wonder if russell knows what these
                are..."*

and so decides to bring them
to his son who is feverishly
working on the fall-out shelter
and who had
at that very moment
flipped on the portable radio
in the readymade grave in the backyard
(attempting to tune-in on the emergency broadcast band)
but who had gotten network news at two-thirty instead

                                        (weeooooeeeeoooo)

    "...can't begin to describe the incredible scene
    about me
            police estimate that over one hundred
    thousand have converged on this small westcoast
    californian town and they are still flooding in
    for miles about
                where they are going is up that
    hill directly behind me
                    mt. parnassus
                        it's on top of
    this two thousand foot mountain where the sweetmeats
    are believed to be held and where max vogel
    sweetmeats' manager left for over an hour and a
    half ago
            if he does not return with the
    sweetmeats in the next half-hour
                        then general ochre
    and the fighting 69th national guard battalion has
    orders to move out and take the hill
                        general ochre
                        meanwhile
    is investigating reports of unidentified submarines
    in the area and a close surveillance is being kept...
    with me here is david cohen
                    student radical leader
    from berkeley
                can you tell us what is happening
    david?"

                                "well let me say
                                first that i am a
                                radical *student
                                leader* from berkeley
                                    not a *student
                                radical* leader..."

    "i'm sorry..."

                                "a typical masscom
                                trans take"

    "masscom transtake????"

                                "mass communications
                                transposition
                                mistake
                                    happens all
                                the time"

    "well what in your view is happening"

"well i think simply
that this is the
revolution"

"the revolution...?"

"i think everything
is together for it
and its happening"

"when you say 'the revolution' do you mean
that the power structure is..."

"i mean
like
the establishment
just doesn't make it
with us anymore"

"so you are revolting against the..."

"those facists who
burn villages rather
than build cities"

"by facists do you mean the militaryindust..."

"by facist savage
i mean you!"

"this is seymore savage WAGH news"

"is it much further
bud?"

"are you getting tired lin?"

"a little"

"you wanna rest?"

"just for a minute"

"okay" (they sit by the road)

"i wish there was something
to drink"

"me too"

"maybe one of those guys
will give us a drink of wine?"

"no harm asking..."

bud thompson
crosses the
road
     raps for
a moment
          then
returns with
the bottle

"they gave me the rest of
the bottle -- free!"

"groovy!"

"i never met them before"

"maybe we could give them some
grass"

"sure why not..."

thompson takes
out a couple
of joints from
his shirt
pocket and
brings it
across the
road
     the others
flash a V sign
back at linda

"beautiful people"

        "yeah really outasite"

"there must be about
a buck's worth of
wine here"

        "y'know bud
        i thought i was going to
        be uptight about coming here
        and instead..."

"i know
there are good vibes
all around"

        "i just hope my parents don't
        start worrying about me"

"didn't you tell them you'd
be down at the school?"

        "yeah
        but my mother might just double-
        check
          she's done that before"

RUSSELL RUSSELL
WHERE ARE YOU!?

        (in the fall-out shelter)

    RUSSELL!

        (i can hear you dammit
        i'm back here behind the
        bunks)

    russell...
linda's not down at the school
she never got there

        never mind that
        look what i found behind
        the canned lima beans

    it looks like...
a plastic bag full of weeds
that's all

        that's all?
        THAT'S ALL!
        you know what this
        stuff is?

    it looks like goldenrod
to me

        meg this is marijuana

    marijuana? oh russell
how could that get here?

        i don't know...
        but...remember last year
        louis used the shelter
        for his young republican
        meetings...

    you don't think louis...

        of course not
        but maybe one of his group

    the pincus boy
you know the tall kid with
with that dirty long hair

        or that little slutty bitch
        what's her name
        y'know with those short
        skirts and those seethrus

                    brenda quigley
                                             yeah that's her name
RUSSELL
YOU DOWN THERE?

                                             WE'RE COMING UP
          RUSSELL!
                                             what is it dad?
       i finally found the hammer
                                             good for you pop
       found it in Louis's room
                                             that's good pop
       right behind the typewriter
                                             okay pop...
       and i found these too...
       whut in tarnation are they
                                             let me see that vial
       looks like seeds
                                             they are seeds
                                             morningglory seeds
       whut would louis be doin'
       hammerin' em to a pulp?
                                             my god...i just read
                                             about this in readers' digest
          russell what is it?
                                             oh my god... my god...
       whut is it son?
                                             where is he?
                                             where is louis?

          he said he was cutting
          grass
                                             CUTTING GRASS!!!
                                             MY GOD MEG!
                                             OUR SON'S AN ADDICT!

          ding-ding-ding-ding-ding-
          ding-ding-ding-ding-ding-
B U L L
                                                  (hold it
                                                   hold it
                                                   you're going too
                                                   fast)
                                        (how about
                                         this then)
B   U   L   L   E   T   I   N
                                                  (much better
                                                   thanks)

1840
BIG SUR CALIFORNIA (UPI MAY 7)

INVESTIGATION BY GENERAL OCHRE OF THE 69TH NATIONAL GUARD

BATTALION STATIONED HERE REPORTS THAT A SINGLE SUBMARINE OF

UNKNOWN ORIGIN IS PATROLLING COASTAL WATERS OFF BIG SUR,

CALIFORNIA. THE COAST GUARD HAS BEEN ASKED TO SUPPLY IMME-

DIATE ASSISTANCE IN IDENTIFYING THE CRAFT.

    IN FURTHER DEVELOPMENTS, MAX VOGEL, SWEETMEAT MANAGER

HAS NOT YET RETURNED FROM A CLIMB TO THE TOP OF MT. PARNASSUS,

BELIEVED TO BE THE HIDING PLACE OF THE SWEETMEATS. SHOULD

VOGEL NOT RETURN BEFORE 3 O'CLOCK PACIFIC STANDARD TIME, THE

NATIONAL GUARD UNDER THE COMMAND OF GENERAL "CHICKENHAWK" OCHRE

WILL ADVANCE UP THE 2280-FT MOUNTAIN.

    UNCONFIRMED SIGHTINGS REPORT PARATROOPERS LANDING IN THE

AREA OF MT. PARNASSUS. WITNESSES SAY XXX

hey
what are you doing in that tree

"for chrissake can't you see
i'm stuck!"

i can see that
but what are you really doing
up there

"look...(says makemore pleadingly)
i'll give each of you kids five
bucks if you can help me down"

why don't you come down the
way you went up

"how would you each like a pookie
and paul pill dispenser"

i got one already
        me too

(at his wit's end) "...well what
the hell do you want!"

why don't you just be cool
about it and ask us nicely
you don't have to bribe us

"would you *please* help me get down
from this tree"

sure man
why didn't you say it like
that to begin with

(and with that the black kid and the white
kid shimmied up the tree while the two chicks
stayed below)

"stella
is robert over there"

"well no harriet
i thought my charles was
over at your place..."

"i can't find robert..."

"hello"

hello?

rrrrrrriiiiiinnnnngggggggg

"who's this"

"this is mabel
cartwright's mother..."

(is cynthia at home?)

hello?

is barry playing with...

... perhaps playing baseball?

rrrrrrriiiiiinnnnngggggggg
rrrrrrrriiiiiiiinnnnnnnnnggggggggg

who's calling

i can't find robert anywhere

"did he say you"

rrrrrriiiiiiinnnnnnnnngggggggggggggg

i don't know
one minute he was in the house
and the next minute he was gone

"i'm terribly worried..."

aggravation is all i get from that kid

(...supposed to be in the yard...)

"i bet that little bastard
went down to big sur"

rrrrrrrriiiinnnnnnnnngggggg

"hello"

"...hello?"

"is janet..."

"any day now i expect to get a
call and it will be the police
telling me to come down to the
station"

i get it all the time
these kids

"rrrrrrriiiiiiinnnnnngggggggggggggg"

...i'm just so upset
i could cry dear...

well
i'm going to call the police!

i mean
she said she'd only be gone
for fifteen minutes...

"...is howard working for you this
afternoon mr. burns?"

"i haven't seen howard
for about three years
mrs. crawley"

rrrrrriiiiinnnnnngggggggg

i've tried everything

rrriiiiii

(at my wit's end)

well i mean

nnnnnnggggggggggg

first he tells me

(...hello?)

and then

i'm going to call the police
stanley

he's not bagging at big apple
he's not at wendy's house
he's not playing basketball
he's not...

*(i mean i know that kid
of mine
if he says he's
at the movies...)*

oh what the hell
i said 'go if you really want to'
because he would anyway

...is ramona there...
oh she's with betty...
and where's betty...oh
they did?

*you bet they did
every kid who could*

from san jose to fresno to santa barbara

some coming as far
as hashbury and the strip

                              trekking into towns soon immortalized

        hamlets such as jamesburg
                    and tassajara
                    and lucia

                        a raggle-taggled army of deserters
                        moving silently uncomplainingly
                        along the dusty roads

in their own way as battlescarred and
shellshocked as any kid fighting in the nam

                                    and all
                                    ironically
                                    fighting to save
                                    our country

        (while the u.s. and mexico issued a joint communique
        on ways to reduce marijuana smuggling)
action
camera

<u>17. EXT: IN THE WOODS--SAME AFTERNOON</u>

SYLVIA and EDUARDO are busily putting together a lean-to.
She wants to make love to him even after he's disclosed his
impotency to her. His disability has aroused her even more.

                    SYLVIA
            (near tears) It doesn't matter. I loved
            you long before I knew.

                    EDUARDO
            But I knew long before you knew that it
            couldn't work out.

                    SYLVIA
            (suddenly angry) Why? Why! Why couldn't
            it work!

                    EDUARDO
            Because...because...you're a woman, see?
            And I'm...a man. It's only natural that we
            should...that is, you'd want me to perform
            as a man...and...

                    SYLVIA (approaching him)
            Darling...(forgiving) There are other things
            between a man and a woman besides sex. Do
            you play tennis?

EDUARDO puts down his pine branch and embraces SYLVIA.
Over her shoulder he notices a movement in the underbrush.
Then all at once, CHIEF BROKEN WIND in full headdress and
buckskin and riding a 22-hands high Morgan bursts in.

                    GERDA LOINS (turning)
            (screaming) EEEEEEEEEEEEEEeeeeeeeeeeeeeeee!

                    BROKEN WIND
            You no be frightened. Me come in peace.

                    RIC GLAND
            What the hell is going on here today.

>   LOINS
> Get that...that indian out of here!

>   WIND
> Who make-um that lean-to?

>   GLAND
> (indignent) I did. Why?

>   WIND
> It looks like you get-um your architectural
> degree in Dresden 1945.

>   LOINS
> Are you going to let some indian speak to
> you like that, Ric?

>   GLAND (to BROKEN WIND)
> You got any ideas about fixin' it?

>   WIND (taking book from saddlebag)
> It all in my book, "Enjoying Nature For Five
> Dollars a Day." You said you take one?

>   GLAND
> Yeah, okay. How much did you say it was?

>   WIND
> Five dollars.

>   GLAND (handing up the bill)
> (exasperated) Please...get off the set?

wwwwwooooooooo-eeeeeeeeeeee
a triple-header set for you
tripped-out little tin lids

>   and this is sonny swingle bringing it all your
>   way this beautiful saturday 83 sen-sa-tional de-
>   grees (chime)
>   and the chime time is now two-fifty-
>   two whhhhoooo----eeeeee
>   but before we give you
>   another blast from the past in KCUF's golden
>   memory segment
>   i want to talk to you a moment about
>   YUM kipper herrings...

ANNOUNCERS' COPY (60-secs)

You know, when the kids drop in these days, they expect a

little more than just cookies and milk. I mean that was a

groove fifteen years ago, right? Well, it doesn't rate in

today's now crowd. The groove today is for something together,

something *wild* and *refreshing*. And YUM Kipper Herrings fill

the bill. They take your taste-buds on a tantalizing trip

to tingle-ville. A way-out taste-treat that can't be beat.

And YUM Kipper Herrings are low in calories, high in energy

-- the perfect pick-me-up that doesn't fill-you-up. So the

next time the gang drops in, space them out with YUM kipper

herrings, In wine or sour cream. (END)

                wwwhhhoooooo---eeeeeee
                            gotta be 21 to eat those
                herrings in wine
                      ok-ay this is for loretta and
                gil and bonny and moe and rich and sandy down
                at the sur today
                      the sweetmeats and *half an hour*
                from the highway

just follow me down
to the end of town
there's a whole 'nother world
beyond the grey clouds
              don't need no directions
              just some recollections
              how it was before they knew
              you were not among them
                        but they weren't caring
                        too busy out comparing
                        their wasted wanting lives
                        you couldn't waste your time

half an hour
from the highway
i found you
half an hour
lost in space
your face
a fantasy forgetting
getting stoned
saying 'oh no no
nobody's home'...
              "for the last time mrs. ettinger
              nobody resembling your son's
              description has been turned over
              to us"
                                      ("please captain
                                      francona
                                          we're all
                                      terribly worried")

              "if we hear of anything we'll
              notify you"
                                    ("please...")
              "goodbye mrs. ettinger"
                        williams
              i don't want to take any more of
              these calls
but chief
headquarters says its
switchboards are jammed
              i don't want to have those
               calls transferred
                      i have enough
              on my hands as it is to worry
              about mrs. ettinger's kid or

anybody's kid...

        for chrissake
there must be a million kids
out here

        OK OK KEEP IT MOVING!
        KEEP IT MOVING!

"help
 help!"

                "whatthe..."

"officer
 help!"

                        (max vogel breaks through
                         the underbrush)

                "yeah?"

"listen officer (pant)
 my name is vogel
 i'm the sweetmeats'
 manager..."

                "yeah so what?"

"(pant) i just got loose
 from a nut who's gonna
 kill the sweetmeats...i
 was with him..."

                "yeah so what?"

"i have to get to general
 ochre before three o'clock"

                "yeah?"

"don't you understand...?
 i was supposed to see the
 sweetmeats but this nut
 tagged along with me so i
 had to lead him along a
 false trail see?"

                "yeah?"

"but i have to get back to
 general ochre before three
 o'clock or else they'll
 send the national guard up
 there..."

                "is that right"

"you have to call him for
 me..."

                "i don't have to do
                 nothing buddy"

"please...it's important!"

                "now just hold on for
                 a moment
                         lets have the
                 story again"

"my god
     there isn't time!"

                "i got all the time in
                 the world"

"look officer..."

                "francona"

"francona...
        my name is max
 vogel and i'm manager for
 the sweetmeats"

                "yeah so what"

158

                                                just this...
                                                that in less than four minutes
                                                general ochre would lead his
                                                men from their base camp at the
                                                bottom of mt. parnassus up the
                                                2280-ft mountain
yeah so what

                                                unless max vogel could get to
                                                him before then
yeah?

                                                you see vogel spent the entire
                                                time leading stuart on a goosechase
                                                and then managed to escape him
                                                by camouflaging himself as a
                                                bedroll alongside a crowded back
                                                road
yeah?

                                                but by the time he explained all
                                                this to captain francona it was
                                                almost three o'clock
yeah so what

                                                so francona put a call to general
                                                ochre but there was trouble
                                                making contact
                echchehchehch
                                 zzz-zzz--zz---zzz---
                                                                "...calling..."
        KNB856 calling
                                        ("wwwwwwWWWWWWwwwHHHHHhhhhoooo")
can you read me
can you read me
                                ....CQ CQ...........
                hundreds of kids
                have...
                                                                ...absolutely
                                                                fantastic scene...
        ddid-di-did-did-i-did-di-di-dit
                                blocked roads for miles
never anything like it
                        "...listen mrs. ettinger i have no word..."
        never any word
                                                        but there were many
                                                        informed sources
                and millions on the phone
                                        members of the press
                                        and members of the oppressed
        and all those waiting by their radios
        and televisions
                                        when the word got through
                                GLAND
                        (annoyed) Where the hell did all these
                        kids suddenly come from!
thousands
hundreds of thousands
a million or more
                who really knew?
                                                making their way slowly
                                                up mt. parnassus
                        "sorry vogel
                        i can't get through"

and then it was three o'clock
 just as the bulletin hit the wire services
(just as the bullet
 was hitting john quigley in the gut)

                                    ding-ding-ding-ding-ding

(my god! my god!)
            B U L L E T I N
                              1500
                              BIG SUR CALIFORNIA (AP MAY 7)

                              MEMBERS OF THE 69TH NATIONAL GUARD

BATTALION UNDER THE COMMAND   OF GENERAL OCHRE HAVE BEGUN MOVING

OUT FROM THEIR BASE CAMP FOR   BETTER VANTAGE POINTS HIGHER ON MT.

PARNASSUS. THERE HAS BEEN NO   WORD ON THE SWEETMEATS OR FROM MAX

VOGEL, SWEETMEAT MANAGER, SINCE   VOGEL LEFT FOR THE MOUNTAIN'S TOP

SEVERAL HOURS AGO.

PART THREE

a day had passed

                                           exactly a day

since you first heard the news america

                                           exactly a day
                                           to the very minute

and everything was happening
and nothing was happening

                               a day had passed and you knew no
                               more about anything
                                           except that something
                                         was happening

something and nothing
ambiguous growlings
anxiety
dread

                               an interruption from your boredom
             a trip to the paranoic
             icebox of your mind
                                         the note in your paycheck
                                         the hand in your pocket
        the knock on your door
        the tap on your shoulder
                       america
                       something was stirring all right
                       something that swept over the country
                       like a silent shadow
something both wondrously good and
horrendous

                                america was tuned into
                                the sweetmeats
        at the drop of a cocked hat
        ready to be asked the perennial question
                            "where were you when you heard
                             the news?"
        that would be asked by generations yet
        to be born
                and would be answered by generations yet to pass on
for even the
most disdainful
                now took an interest in the events from big sur
                                           and though
                                           you still
                                           puttered away
                                           through the
                                           afternoon
        though you still were putting burger patties on the charcoal
        grill or studying or having an egg cream or shovelling shit
though
        you were playing cards or hoeing your rock garden or watering
        the flowerbeds or shining shoes or driving buses or sacking
        groceries and/or villages
                                wherever you were
                               america
                               you were tuned into the sweetmeats
        for the final act was to be played
        and for that final act
                        your attention if not your presence was required
wwwwhhhhoooooo-eeeeeeeeee
that was the sweetmeats and
'just an hour from the highway'

all of you transistor freaks
out there
  and this is sonny
swingle bringing you all of the
sounds that abound underground
the nitty of the gritty
the latest of the greatest
    and how
about this latest word on the
sweetmeats that the national guard
is going up to get them
wwwwwwwhhhhh-eeeeeeeoooooooooo
just came over our KCUF teletype
about a minute ago
   we'll have a direct
report from the scene from jumpin' jim
skinner in a few moments

     (reverend buttermilk arrives at the
     TV station to tape his sunday
     evening vesper hour)

(he would remain there after the taping
 to partake in a live forum with the
 subject: *where is today's youth going?*)

     buttermilk was always asked
     to be a panelist

  last year he sat on a record 103 panels

     discussing every subject
     from pollution to birth control

  he was a guest speaker at an additional
  117 functions

   was slated to give the opening blessings
   at no less than 7 high school graduations that june

and to participate
in 3 college convocations
in the fall

     he attended 9 football games
     and close to 20 baseball and
     basketball games the year before

  performed 38 baptisms
    4 confirmations
   21 weddings
   12 funerals

     opened a grand union in fresno
  closed a whorehouse in san mateo

     saved some guy from killing himself
  wrote a weekly syndicated column

     set up a marriage counseling service
  edited a book on world brotherhood

     and advocated separation of the races

(anyhow before the taping begins
 it is this same reverend buttermilk
 who puts a long distance call through
 to swami sahalami in new york)

    "this is reverend buttermilk
    is this the swami?"

      ("it is")

    "i hope you remember me
    about three years ago you
    gave me that nuclear test-ban
    treaty scoop"

      ("it is
      acknowledged")

"i'd like to have a divine
inspiration from you again
swami"

("on the
sweetmeats?")

"why...yes..."

("intuition
rates on
this subject
very high")

"well intuition rates are
going up everywhere aren't
they swami ha ha ha...
how much"

("thousand
dollars a
question")

"holy cow!...i mean that's a
lot more than what i paid in
1963"

("wire money
with your
amex card")

"i need the answer before eight
o'clock tonight"

("i will call
you swami-
to-person
collect")

"i'll get the money order out
immediately"

("may mammon
take a liking
to you")

reverend buttermilk's question was
of course
will the sweetmeats be saved
and he meant it in the spiritual sense
but by the loaded nature of the question
he figured it might be possible to get
a beat on the sweetmeats' current physical
crisis as well

(actually pookie and paul had
touched on the spiritual question in September 1965's Foreplay Magazine interview)

Foreplay: There have been certain charges
from clergymen throughout the country that
you have started a kind of hedonistic cult
in this country. They seem to be saying that
you advocate salvation in pleasure.

Paul: We don't advocate anything.

Pookie: It's where your head is at.

Paul: Look. There are many ways to save
yourself. Nobody has a corner on the salvation market. It's doing your own thing, getting yourself together. And if your groove
is just getting satisfaction, getting physical
pleasure or whatever, then if you're doing it
you're saving yourself, dig?

Foreplay: Do you believe in heaven or hell?

Pookie: This is it, man.

Paul: I think you either make a heaven or hell for yourself here on earth.

Pookie: When we were growing up, that's all we ever got. If you're good you go to heaven and if you're bad you go to hell. But I didn't want to get stuck in heaven if I had to be goody-goody all day.

Foreplay: Then do you believe in God?

Paul: I think God is where your head is at. I think if you're a beautiful person you see a beautiful God, and if you're an evil person you see an evil God.

Pookie: Sometimes I see God when I'm tripping on acid. He's not a person. He's a warm white light, like sunlight. I just fly into the light and I'm totally embraced by it. And I'm totally in God and God in me.

Foreplay: You see God in acid then?

Pookie: Sometimes I see God in a beautiful sunset, too. Sometimes in cauliflower clouds.

Paul: I once saw God in a Persian rug. In the design.

```
                                                 strange words
                                                 you thought
                       until you read the computer print
                                                 out
LOOP
LINK
SINE
COSINE
PROGB
                                  and realized you couldn't speak the language
            and their world
            and your world
            were worlds
            apart
                       and all worlds were worlds apart
                       with a hundred tongues and a thousand meanings
the tower of babel
babbling away on molecules of misconnections
                                                 "hello sandy?"
                "what number do you want?"
                                                 "is this TR4-8967"
     this is a connection
                             (operator i tried to get)
                                                 i'm sorry sir
                                                 this is a
                                                 recording
            "hello operator i tried to get"
```

deposit five cents for another
five minutes sir

"...bad...nection...hear me..."

"I JUST PUT IN A GODDAM DIME"

hello
hello?

seems to be a little trouble

68784995867472658

hello?

(eee-ooo-ooo-eee)

mida yo tengo una

"do you know if freddie is there"

...seems to be some kind of vigil

they both walked out the door and
said they'd be home later tonight

("i had to lock brenda in her room")

hello?

"circuits are all busy sir"

*the function mapping each
rational number into its
reduced representative is a
1-1 denumerable set*

(a lilliputian butler takes
a napkin from the enormous
box he's carrying
and stuffs it into
the amazed diner's shoe)

"...read me..."

come in

(canned laughter)

*oh it's you
i thought it was desi*

luci (cries ethel mertz)
desi had a car accident

(canned laughter)

and the baby was with him

(canned laughter and music)

due to circumcisions
beyond our control

...hello?

communications breakdown
can't get through

("clyde clyde can you hear me?")

ball two strike two to grospekski

"clyde this is jim can you..."

(signal fade due to misreading
of polar coordinate read-out-dials)

...please...
...please...

("my daughter is lost!")

"calling KCUF monterey..."

"...read you jim..."

"better now?"

"loud and clear"

"i have david cohen with
an interview"

"we'll tape it
send it over"

(static)

"with me is david cohen leader
of S.H.A.M.E. -- students hindering
american military efforts
what do
you think of general ochre's
decision to take the mountain"

"ochre is employing the usual
military-industrial tactic of
takeover by brute force"

"do you think he will use
force to get to the sweetmeats"

"first of all he's never going
to make it to the top
there are
thousands and thousands of kids
up there already
they're not going
to stand aside and watch ochre
annihilate their...(fade)

"...the sweetmeats alive"

"sure i think they're alive
i
think they're planning strategy"

"strategy for what"

"i think this may finally be it!
i think this is the revolution!"

"revolution?
what kind of revolution?"

(static)
"...but...the basic structure..."

jagoff to
underwater one
can you read me

(static)
"...real power is...of..."

repeat
can you read me

underwater one...

grappling iron
is secure
i'm going up

stay low
there are all sorts
of craft in the area

you do the same
i'll signal you
when i get to the top

aye aye
over and out

scaling mountains was nothing new for forest jagoff
two years before
he had climbed everest
and a year before that mt. blanc

the man raced autos
skindived
skydived
sailed
jiujitsued
flew his own plane

                    played championship tennis
                    never lost in baccarat or polo
                    could prepare a 7-course dinner for 12
                    spoke french spanish german and russian
                    knew his wines and his cigars
                    played piano and composed
                    was an expert dancer
                    a charming host
                                              and a multi-multi-millionaire
                                              who had estates in cannes
                                              crete st. martins rio and pago-pago
          who had cornered the titanium market
          and who brought xerox at 12
                                              who owned innumerable corporations
                                              and sat on the boards of dozens more
          who ran a vast publishing and
          communications empire that virtually
          controlled the entire entertainment field
                                              and who had the great misfortune
                                              of falling in love with pookie
                                              when she posed in Foreplay
          forest jagoff seemingly had everything
          or could lay his hands on anything
                                                   but pookie
he made fantastic offers to her
from outright propositions to proposals of marriage
                                              she declined them
                                              all

he named a nightclub after her
a racehorse
his yacht
                                              "so what else is new"
                                              said pookie
              he sent her flowers daily
              a chrysoberyl alexandrite ring weighing 65.7 cts.
                                              "send the creep back
                                              his ring"
              he delivered a pheasant for christmas
              chocolate matzohs for passover
nothing
moved her
                                              "if he doesn't stop
                                              bugging me i'll
                                              get an injunction"

              and it was reported that he built a
              'pookie room' in his chicago mansion
              filled with floor-to-ceiling blowups
              of pookie's illustrious illustrative
              lust shots
                        (the first total beaver views
              ever found in an over-the-counter
              national magazine)
                                              "i did it for the
                                              women's liberation
                                              movement" said
                                              pookie in defense

              and now
              forest jagoff was acting out his fantasies
fantasies
shared by
millions of other losers

to capture the golden sunlight
in pookie's taillength tresses

to run fingertips about
her firm but adequate gluteus maximuses

to nibble on those
ample mammees

in short
(and in shorts)
to do what you should have done with your wife
and what you are not allowed to do with your daughter

but who
like jagoff
would never get the chance to do either/or except in fantasy

(fade of a
henry mancini
theme)

"OK KEEP IT MOVING"

"captain francona..."

"C'MON KEEP IT MOVING!"

"captain..."

"YEAH?"

"there's a lady here to
see you"

"huh?"

"she says that she has to
talk with you"

"okay WILLIAMS TAKE OVER"

"over here..."

"yeah what can i do for you ma'am?"

(captain i think my daughter is
here)

"yeah so what?"

(my husband and i are just
worried sick)

"yeah"

(her name is pamela fisher and
she's fourteen and she weighs...)

"lady...
there must be a couple of hundred
of thousand kids out here today..."

(but...)

"they all look like your daughter
even the boys"

(she's only fourteen officer...)

"i know lady..."

(she's just a child
i'm so worried
that something will happen to
her)

"i don't know how i can help you"

(is it true about the russian
submarines?)

dot is no russian sub
dot is a coo-ban sub

and what you're saying major
is that the cubans are working
with the CIA to...

no please
do no misquote me
i do before say dot ze pro-CIA
cuban revolutionary party has

formed a new coalition of anti-
castro elements
                              dot is what i say

                                        and they have hijacked the sub

si
                                        but they are pro-sweetmeat

i no can discuss dot at zis time

                                        thank you major macho

"doctor mountmother
 doctor mountmother
 can we have an interview
 from you"
                                        "i am always happy to grant interviews"

"you have done many psychological
 studies on today's youth
                    can you
 tell us what the psychological
 basis is for what is happening
 here today?"

                                        "ooooooooooooooooo
                                         basically it is what we call the croft
                                         syndrome"

"the croft syndrome?"

                                        "yes
                                         named for sam croft
                                                    the platoon sergeant
                                         in *the naked and the dead*"

"i'm not familiar with..."

                                        "you will remember that he exhibited an
                                         infantile fixation toward the maternal
                                         breast in his compulsion to climb a
                                         mountain"

"i don't recall..."

                                        "these kids are climbing the mountain to
                                         return to the womb"

"but the breast and the womb
 are two different things doctor"

                                        "ooooooooooooo
                                         well it is just a theory anyhow"

"thank you doctor mountmother"

                                                            thousands
                                                            of theories

          from bars in baton rouge
                            to beauty parlors in buena vista
          from delis in deer park
                            to garbage dumps in dallas
thousands of theories
and thousands of fears

                                        witness carmella karma

(hello lulibelle
 this is carmella...yes...well how are you...um...
 well i had a perfectly awful time getting a dial
 tone...i know it's just impossible...well certainly
 i think that's behind it...it's a conspiracy...
 i don't know who's behind it frankly but i'll tell
 you one thing
          i'm not ruling the chinese communists
 out...
     i saw a movie recently about how the chinese
 implant tiny radios in people and make them do any
 thing they want...uh huh...and then those people
 with radios were told to implant radios on other
 people...oh you saw that movie too...that's right
 it was called *Wireless Warlords*...um hum...)

*break-away for seymore savage
reporting from big sur*

CUT INTO THE SEYMORE SAVAGE SHOW

"now reporting directly from the scene..."

        three seconds

"here is seymore savage..."

        two seconds

        visual

"can you hear us seymore?"

        audio

        "yes i can hy"

"what is the situation"

        "we are in the vanguard of a forward
        reconnaissance team made up of able
        and baker batteries of the 69th
        national guard battalion under the
        command of general 'chickenhawk'
        ochre
        just a few minutes ago general
        ochre gave the command to advance
        up mt. parnassus directly behind me
        however as you can see
        the road is
        completely blocked by the thousands
        perhaps hundreds of thousands of
        young people who have flocked to
        the area
        it will be virtually im-
        possible to reach the summit of
        the mountain by this road and so
        some alternate route will have to be
        found"

"are there any other roads seymore"

        "only footpaths
        in fact this road becomes a footpath
        about half way up i'm told"

"what are the kids doing"

        "it appears that they've gotten a
        jump on the troops
        most of them
        started out last night and early
        this morning
        the area is completely
        saturated with them and its going
        to be difficult for ochre's men to
        make much headway"

"do you think some of the kids have
 reached the top"

        "i wouldn't be a bit surprised
        word
        has filtered down that the sweetmeats
        are alive and well
        standing with me
        is ric gland who was filming a scene
        from his new movie 'Lust Weekend'
        about a quarter way up mt. parnassus
        when...why don't you tell us in
        your own words what happened mr.
        gland"

"we were just finishing a scene
from our new picture for Pornopix
'Lust Weekend' starring myself with
gerda loins when about a hundred
or so hippies just came out of
the woods right on to the set"

                                              "what dill you say to them?"

"i was just very surprised...i
thought they were going to bust
up the equipment or steal it or
something"

                                              "what did they do?"

"they didn't do anything really
                            they
just stood around and laughed a
little
      i think they must have been
high on something
                    one of them was
passing a gallon of tokay"

                                        "well what did they say"

"well i heard one of them tell
another that 'everything was together and that it was still set
for that night'
              then the other one
said something like 'if i don't
crash by then'"

                                  "did they mention the sweetmeats"

"a couple of others did
                      they said
the sweetmeats were in 'good hands
with allstate'"

                                  "they believe them to be alive
                                  then"

"i'm sure they're alive
                      the kids
were saying that they could hear
the music coming from the stonehouse when the wind was blowing
in the right direction"

                                  "but you didn't hear the music"

"nothing"

                                  "well what happened then"

"the kids moved off the set and
continued up the mountain"

                                  "thank you mr. gland
                                  it seems then
that the sweetmeats are alive and
are indeed on the top of mt. parnassus and if they are preparing
for a concert tonight then they
can't be too bad off
                                this is seymore
savage
            big sur california"
                                        audio out
                                      visual out

"WAGH will be broadcasting a special on
the sweetmeats tonight at 10:00 EST"

<u>VIDEO</u>

OPEN IN DINGY HIPPIE PAD WITH
WALLS AND SCATTERED CANVASSES
SMEARED IN BLUE BY A RUNAWAY
ROLLER. PAN OVER TO SOBBING
GIRL SEATED ON A MATRESS.

<u>AUDIO</u>

HIPPIE GIRL (DV)

Oh dear...oh dear...

i don't know what to do...

my old man's a painter...

and his period is *blue*...

CUT TO FRONT DOOR AS IT OPENS
AND HIPPIE BOYFRIEND SLOUCHES
IN. HE CARRIES A BOX OF *NEW*
THAT HE CASUALLY TOSSES AT THE
GIRL.

(click!)
  disgusting simply disgusting says olivia pitt
  to herself
    first we get that lurid report from
  california
    next we get that absolutely filthy
  commercial
    i'm going to call the network...
        (but all the breadboards &
        circuses were busy)

(as were the headshops and murky ginmills
 as evening fell along the eastern coast)

      each to his own high
      each according to his right
      without regard to race
         creed
        or national
         origin

(miss loins
 miss loins
 can we have you by the microphones)

(honey
 you can have me anywhere)

              laughter in the press corps
(over here)

(how's this)
              *she takes a
reporter's hand mike and
puts it between her legs*

              more laughter and whistles
(miss loins)

(any of youse guys got
 a drink on 'em?)

(miss loins
 you've been here on parnassus mountain
 for several days making a film
 is that right?)

(the film is 'Lust Weekend'
 starring myself with ric
 gland in a minor supporting role)

(miss loins...)

(it's for Pornopix Pro-
 ductions and will be
 released...)

(miss loins...)

(...about a wetback grape
 picker and an industrial-
 ist's daughter he falls
 in love with...)

(...pregnant he is put in
 jail but...)

(about what happened on...?"

(um?)

(MISS LOINS!)

(what happened while you were shooting
 this afternoon?)

(well a whole bunch of
 filthy kids invaded the
 set)

(can you tell us again what they said about
 the sweetmeats)

(well i heard a couple
 of them say that the
 electricity in the stone
 house had been cut the
 night before...)

(but the sweetmeats had
 figured on that eventu-
 ality and had brought
 portable...what are those
 ...generators with them)

(yes...)

(one of the kids said 'so
 it's on' and the other
 kid said 'yes')

(andd what were the generators going
 to be used for)

(i don't know really...
 some kind of festival
 i thought i heard the
 words 'freakout festival')

(what was on)

(what does that mean 'freakout festival'?)

                                                (you got me...hey any of
                                                youse guys got a drink
                                                on 'em?)

                VIDEO

ECU OF PAUL DOLL FACE AS MINIATURE
GLASS OF WATER IS TIPPED AGAINST
ITS LIPS.

                                                "pppsssttt"

"pppppsssssssstttttttttt"
                                          "huh?"

"hey man
 what's the happenings?"
                                          "(choke)"

"don't get tight man
 just down it for us" (7 ethnic dukes surround him)
                                          "uh..." (woody wilson
                                          feels his adrenalin
                                          shoot out of the top
                                          of his head)

"sound it out man"
                                          "uh...i don't know
                                          anything brother"

"don't 'brother' us man"
                                          "look...i don't know
                                          nothing"

(sugar xxx steps forward and the
 splibs split)
                              "we saw you with the
                              general man"
                                            "no...really guys..."
                              "don't make us want
                              to burn you"
                                            "ochre's gone up the
                                          mountain to get to
                                          the sweetmeats"
                              "what kind of hardware
                              he carrying?"
                                            "i donno
                                          M-1's gas
                                          flame throwers..."
                              "tanks?"
                                            "no"
                              "half-tons?"
                                            "no"
                              "machine guns?"
                                          "maybe i don't know"
                              "mounted on jeeps?"
                                          "yeah i think so"
                              "motherfucker"

(the ethnic dukes ape guerrillas
 and steal back into the sanctity
 of the forest)
                                          cccllllluuummmmmpppppf
                "OOOOOWWWWWW!"
                                    "for chrissake pauline"
                 "this is ridiculous savage"
                                    "we're almost halfway up already"
                 "i'm not going any further...
                  i'm too *damn* tired"

"please pauline"

"climbing up this fucking
mountain with all this
equipment..."

"there's no other way to get
it up"

"why the hell do i have to
carry the camera?"

"i got my hands full with the
tape reels"

"this camera must weigh forty
pounds!"

"and you outweigh me by forty
pounds"

"that does it!
i'm not going a step further"

"so you're giving me an exclusive
on the story huh?"

"i'm not giving you my armpit
sweat!
c'mon faggot let's go!"

"that's the spirit pauline
i'll see you get a pulitzer for
this"

(speaking of faggots
timothy queen and
his entourage prepare for their ascent)

(are you bringing your rubbers tim?)

no
and i'm not bringing my electric
dildo either

(i mean your galoshes
it looks like rain)

hm
it is getting gray out

louis smith too
notices the overcast
conditions as he and brenda
quigley make their way from
mitch frankle's car

"it's a good thing i brought this
blanket" says louis

(jagoff jagoff
this is underwater one)

"jagoff here"

(wind is springing up
out here
the water's
roughing up)

"can you stay on top?"

(for the moment)

"that's the spirit pauline
i'll see you get a pulitzer for
this"

(fuck off savage)

that's not the spirit america
keep smiling

keep those cars and litters coming in

keep those sunshine smiles
turning sunshine dials

```
        keep the wheels of industry turning on
                                (keep turning on without the
                                 wheels of industry)
        keep the ten commandments and the
        twenty-three amendments
                                keep the clause in santa
                                and the cha in chanukah
cha-cha-cha
        keep the cherry pie and the billy boy
                                the cherry bomb and the
                                billy club
                the chubby boobie
                        and the bubbley clod
keep them all
smiling america

                        (a paid political announcement
                         from mah fellah amuricuns)
keep them all smiling
america

                        (a paid political announcement
                         from mah fellah amuricuns)


    "and now
     back to our commercial"
```

                              <u>AUDIO</u>

                         HIPPIE BOY (DV)

              (to girl) your come down's a drag...

              and this pad is, too...

              clean-up's a happening...

<u>VIDEO</u>   when you use NEW...

ECU ON BOX OF NEWS
            O N   T H E   H O U R
                                (from here to clity city
                                 and all points west)
VOGEL ESCAPES MAD KILLER SWEETMEATS AS THOUSANDS
WESTMORELAND PREDICTS REPRESENTATIVE AT FUC HUE
HAVE BEEN DEMONSTRATING IN RACIALLY-TORN BIRMING-
HAM UNEASY PEACE IN INVESTIGATION INFLATION OF
SUB-COMMITTEE BY REPUBLICAN DIRKSEN ASKS SENATE
ARMS IN VIETNAM DEBATE HIGH IN THE SEVENTIES LOW
TONIGHT IN THE NEXT NEWS SCORES
                        but first a word from FEEL UP

        <u>AUDIO</u>

    1ST SOLDIER (DV)   <u>VIDEO</u>

I don't know sarge...I feel so tired   OPEN ON MS OF SOLDIER IN BUNK
                                          WITH SERGEANT STANDING OVER HIM.
...I just don't want to fight today.   IT IS OBVIOUSLY A COMBAT ZONE
                                          FOR IN THE BACKGROUND ARE MUTED
        SERGEANT   EXPLOSIONS.

Suppose everybody decided to stay in   CUT TO CU OF SERGEANT

bed...where would we be then?

            SOLDIER   BACK TO MS OF BUNK AS SOLDIER
                                             TRIES TO PUT HIS COVERS OVER
I'm...just so tired of it all...

            SERGEANT (VO)   CUT TO SERGEANT'S HAND HOLDING
                                             PACKET OF *FEEL-UP'S*
Here...try one of these.

            SOLDIER

(peeking out) Aren't those habit   CUT TO CU OF SOLDIER

forming?

            SERGEANT (DV)
                                             CUT TO CU OF SERGEANT AND
Not if taken as directed. Millions   PULL BACK SOMEWHAT FOR A TWO-
                                             SHOT OF SERGEANT AND HAND-HELD
find they're just the thing for mid-   PACKET.

morning slump. Afternoon. Anytime

'the blues' take hold.

                                    ooooooooooooooo
                                    did i hear someone say that somebody
                                    escaped a mad killer?

        it just came over the
        radio buddy
                                    ooooooooooooooo
                                    that sounds like stuart
                                    what kind of mad killer was he?

        the radio said he told
        max vogel he was going to
        kill the sweetmeats
                                    ooooooooooooooo
                                    that's stuart all right
                                    did the radio say what the mad killer
                                    had as a weapon

        a rifle
                                    ooooooooooooooo
                                    that's most unlike him
                                    usually he just uses his hands
                                    ooooooooooooooo
                                    i must reach stuart immediately
        why don't you talk with captain
        francona
                he's the officer who
        found vogel
                                    where can i find captain francona
        he's standing right over there
        buddy
                right by the police car
                                    ooooooooooooooo thank you thank you
                                    captain
    yeah
                                    *my name is doctor milton mountmother
                                    and i*
    hol it
            "captain"
    yeah

                    "the wife of the assistant
                    D.A. is on the phone"
yeah so what
                    "she thinks their daughter
                    is here"
ok
i'll take it

                                                    (hello...?)

francona here

                                                    (oh captain!
                                                    i'm so worried
                                                                our
                                                    little penelope is
                                                    missing!)

(sigh) ok what
does she look like?

                                                    (she's fifteen and
                                                    is five-four and
                                                    weighs 120 pounds
                                                    and...)

does she have dark
long hair and is
she wearing jeans

                                                    (oh captain!
                                                    you found her!)

no lady
it's just that they
all look like that

                                                    (but captain...
                                                    penny is wearing a
                                                    buckskin jacket and
                                                    sandals...)

and sandals...

                                                    (then you *have* seen
                                                    her!)

lady...
that's exactly the
clothes my daughter's
wearing
            and she's some-
            where around here
            too!
                                        they were somewhere all right
                                        somewhere as darkness fell along
                                        the appalachian divide
            somewhere as twilight
            smothered out the faint sunglow
                                        behind the palisades
                                                                somewhere
as porchlights and buglights flicked on
                                    (the quiet tree-lined streets
                                    in warrington virginia
        a leaf-quilt patchwork
        against an indigo ohio sky)
                                                            birds were
                                                            silencing
(the crickets and katydos diding their thing)
                                        a waterfall of leaves
                                        a porch door slam
        dinner table diatribes
        television tantrums

somewhere

              that saturday night

  sons and daughters of ours
  failed to report in

        failed
        to let us know where they'd be!

failed us as responsible adults

        as flesh and blood

as the hope of america

                as all we could
                not be

as all what we were slaving "ten and twelve hours a day for"

                  as all we were
                  sitting up nights
                  worrying about

  oh they failed us all
        right
        (as we failed them)

                gave us heartburn and
                hangnails

indigestion
and aggravation

      "everytime the phone rang i thought i'd die..."

couldn't tell us
wouldn't tell us

        moody...ungrateful...selfish...

                and after all we
                did for them

  oh we weren't perfect...
  nobody's perfect

        but at least to have the common decency

at least to show a little respect

        to let us know where you'd be!

  (as if they could ever know
  where *you* were)

        to let us know...

  (as if they could understand)

        to let us...

  (as if they would let us let them!)

        "it's a phase
        that's all"

a phase

      a stage

        "i went through it my-
        self when i was an
        adolescent"

  they'll grow out of it
     grow tired of it

      it's merely a phase

"...out the back door"

      merely a stage when every young person

"and shouted an obscenity at me"

      merely a phrase when
            COCKSUCKER FASCIST

      merely a time

YOU FUCKING IMPOTENT SHIT

      merely a
         YOU GODDAM REACTIONARY RACIST

      merely

  and disappeared
  just
  like
  that

"i finally found you you little bitch"

　　　　　　　　　　　　　　　　　　　　"ric stop it
　　　　　　　　　　　　　　　　　　　　 people are watching"

"what the hell did you mean you were
 starring in 'Lust Weekend' with me in
 a minor supporting role!"

　　　　　　　　　　　　　　　　　　　　"please ric that hurts"

"we're through do you hear *through!*"

　　　　　　　　　　　　　　　　　　　　"we were through a long
　　　　　　　　　　　　　　　　　　　　 time ago"

"you're finished in movies
 i'll see to that"

　　　　　　　　　　　　　　　　　　　　"you've been finished
　　　　　　　　　　　　　　　　　　　　 for years
　　　　　　　　　　　　　　　　　　　　　　　　　people came to
　　　　　　　　　　　　　　　　　　　　 see me in 'Passion Pussy'
　　　　　　　　　　　　　　　　　　　　 not you!"

"they came to see your fat ass that's
 why they came"

　　　　　　　　　　　　　　　　　　　　"ric gland the great
　　　　　　　　　　　　　　　　　　　　 lover
　　　　　　　　　　　　　　　　　　　　　　　　 that's a laugh!"

(isn't that
 ric gland?)
　　　　　"i have millions of fans
　　　　　 tens of millions
　　　　　　　　　　　　　i was number one
　　　　　 male box office attraction in Cine-
　　　　　 Circle's poll last year"

　　　　　　　　　　　　　　　　　　　　"you're a loser"

(isn't that
 gerda loins
 with him?)
　　　　　"I'M a loser!
　　　　　 why you old shrivelled-up booze-bag"

　　　　　　　　　　　　　　　　　　　　"you diminished dip-
　　　　　　　　　　　　　　　　　　　　 stick!"

(let's ask
 them for
 autographs)
　　　　　"you dumpy dipsomaniac"

　　　　　　　　　　　　　　　　　　　　"you pusillanimous
　　　　　　　　　　　　　　　　　　　　 penis-puller!"

　　　　　"you..."
aan we have
your autograph
mr. gland
　　　　　"why sure honey..."
　　　　　　　　　　　　　　could you give us
　　　　　　　　　　　　　　your autograph
　　　　　　　　　　　　　　miss loins
　　　　　　　　　　　　　　　　　　　　"i'd be de-light-ed
　　　　　　　　　　　　　　　　　　　　 to dear..."

(you want-um genuine sweetmeat autograph?)
　　　　　　　　　　　　　　　　　　(you're out of your mind man
　　　　　　　　　　　　　　　　　　 i'm the sweetmeats' manager)

(no matter
 you want-um autograph?)
　　　　　　　　　　　　　　　　　　(i have hundreds of them)

(genuine)
　　　　　　　　　　　　　　　　　　(didn't you hear what i said
　　　　　　　　　　　　　　　　　　 i'm max vogel
　　　　　　　　　　　　　　　　　　 the sweetmeats' manager!)

(only twenty dollar)

                                        (i tell you...huummm...
                                        hey chief
                                                how much do you
                                        want for your horse?)

(indian never sell his horse)

                                        (yeah...
                                        i think i read that in a
                                        zane grey novel once)

(but this not my horse
 me get this from Avis Rent-A-Cur)

                                        (then...)

(me no can transfer rental agreement)

                                        (i'll give a hundred cash)

(me let you ride rumbleseat for two
 hundred cash)

                                        (that's highway robbery!)

(throw in 50 free miles)

                                        (i won't do it)

(me hear it long way to top of mountain)

                                        (i've made the trip once
                                        already)

(road very crowded)

                                        (i'll give you one-fifty)

(ugh)

                                        (one-seventy)

(one-eighty)

                                        (seventy-five tops)

(hand over money in cash
 you hop on behind me)

                                        (let's get going chief
                                        i've got to beat the
                                        others up there)

                                                68784827018968

        load complement negative

            reset location counter
ENTRY   LOOP
ENTRY   LINK
                                        zzzzzzzttt   zzzzzzzzttt
BILLION HOTEL MOBILE WELFARE
                            "shall be held responsible for"
    (hello hello)
                    height antenna azimuth reference pulse
                                            MTI STC PTC IAGC
    (can you hear me over)
                        jammer video target pulse reference azimuth
                antenna
                height
podunk center iowa here
                                    some interference on the line
    "CQ CQ this is K2085M"
                    "...trying to get a line sir"
                                            bee-boo-bee-bee
        (maybel?)
                    (an isomorphism of A onto B)
                                            aay-ooo-aay-aay
skunk hollow missouri here
                        "...things are really fouled up on..."
      "hullo
        KCUF just went off the air
        can you possibly tell me why"
                                            "sorry ma'am ..."

184

KCUF
KCUF come in

this is KCUF--rawlins here
what the hell are you
doing crossing into our
line!

this is swami sahalami calling

well get back into a ham
wavelength you fool!

it is written it is costly to eat
meat and a sin to eat ham

i mean...how the hell did
you get on our band?

i travel on psychic pulsebeats of
generative love

well that's great!
please get off our line
we've had to cut off our
transmission!

what is the latest status on the
sweetmeats

i will be more than glad to do so
but i first must know about the
sweetmeats

PLEASE GET OFF OUR LINE!

the latest report i've had
is that general ochre is
advancing...

i know that much

the sweetmeats are alive

is that positive?

my man on the scene
jim skinner says
he's heard music coming
from the stonehouse travel
down into the valley

this man you have there
jim skinner
what frequency is he on?

none of your business

i do not want to jam your signal
all night

(pause)...it's 1433kc

may mammon bless you
zzzzzzzzttt   zzzzzzzzttt

80684761058673

zero jammed azimuth

"try again sir..."
80684761058673

printout referred to relocatable-program
loader

"thank you..."

this is a recording
this is a recording
this is a recording of a recording

(hullo
mah felluh amuricuns
this is yaw presidunce)

"sorry
wrong number" (click)

for truly
the medium was the mess
that day

a breakdown in communications

                                        a jamming of phone lines
                                        worse than new year's eve 1960
                                        or during the cuban missile scare
                                        or when kennedy keeled over
                                        or when the sweetmeats first
                                            appeared on the major bowles'
                                            original amateur hour in 1949

there was no breakdown in communications
that night

                                        the sweetmeats won by a 20-1
                                        margin over all the other con-
                                        testants included together

                    (a champion corn shucker
                     a castilian *castrati* choir
                     a bird that did man-calls
                     a comedian cantor
                     a paraplegic pie-plate twirler
                     a rabbi who did imitations
                     a dog-cat-and-mouse act
                     a group of bell-ringing millionaires from liechtenstein
                     a paraplegic comedian)
and after that they
started their own
radio show in l950

                            singing and tap-dancing their way back
                            into the thirties

        (where we really wanted
         to be all along

                                poor but ignorant)

and then in l952
The Sweetmeat Family Hour
on television   * * * * * *
                             * APPLAUD *
                             * * * * * *

                                        where america's favorite
                                        family came into our living-
                                        rooms once a week

                and in the phosphorescent glow of
                blue-gray despair
                            showed us as we really were

                                                weak
                                                frustrated
                                                simpering
                                                middleclass clods

    (three million american women tried to buy curtains
     patterned exactly like those in fay sweetmeats' kitchen)

                                                believing the set
                                                to be a duplicate
                                                of fay's real
                                                home in greenwich

    (five million american male breadwinners purchased
     6-button blue blazers just like sam sweetmeat wore)

                                                working overtime
                                                to squeeze an ex-
                                                tra $30 from the
                                                budget

    (ten million american families with children wanted
     them to grow up in the same way pookie and paul did)

                                                respectful
                                                talented
                                                loveable
                                                beautiful

       (and twenty million american children grew up with
       what was later medically diagnosed as
                                    the sweetmeat syndrome[1])

[1]Mountmother, Dr. Milton J., "Manifestations of Adolescent Fantasy" paper
presented before the American Psychological Society, 1965 Convention. P.12.

...a striking similarity to what we know as The Shirley
Temple Syndrome. I am suggesting we might very well label
this phenomenon, The Sweetmeat Syndrome.

While it is true, of course, that Shirley Temple
played a variety of roles, with many fictional sets of
parents, and was herself cast in many situations that could
only be storybook in nature, nevertheless we were made to
believe those situations to be real and hence, Miss Temple
became real in them. While certain events and dramatic
episodes were improbable, they certainly were not outside
the realm of possibility. Yet, we did not mind if throughout,
the action was less than truthful or candid; we were aware
only that all ended happily and it was the ending that we
remembered most of all.

But with the Sweetmeats we were painfully aware that
this was a real 'live' family with situations that could
have only come from life itself and not from a committee
of script writers. Further, situations involving the Sweetmeats were 'supra-possible' -- we had all experienced them
to one degree or another in our own lives. During their
hour-long TV shows in the early '50s, for instance, we saw
Fay Sweetmeat make fudge, or Sam banging his finger putting
up a picture, and even then not getting it straight. We were
in Paul's room while he did his homework and in Pookie's room
as she tried out a new party dress.

And because The Sweetmeats was Everyfamily, our lives
became inexorably tied up with theirs. In time it was impossible to distinguish between their private and their public
lives. Illusion and reality blended into one. And so it was
with millions of families who emulated The Sweetmeats. What
was seen on their weekly one-hour telecast was thought to be
a condensation of a week's activities. Everything, every
problem and every joy they had, was our problem and our joy.
And when the program ended unhappily, we were unhappy until
the following week when the problem would be resolved somehow.
Fortunately, most of their programs ended happily.

The Sweetmeats were not a perfect family by any means,
but they certainly seemed more perfect than our own. In fact,
if you will recall that famous episode when Paul got a failing
grade in an English compositon, he was punished in front of
the cameras and had to spend the entire evening re-writing the
composition and was writing it still, as The Sweetmeats signed
off. How many fathers watching that program would have meted
out such punishment and embarrassment in a similar situation,
and how many children would have so obediently and lovingly
accepted his decree?

But what effect did The Sweetmeats have on children
watching in those days?...

"hello olivia..."

                                 yes emily

"i just thought you'd like to know
 that those are *cuban* paratroopers
 and submarines in california"

                                 are you sure?

"it just came over the air
 the cuban exile leader major macho
 just announced it"

                                 oh everything is so confused
                                 today!
                                      i don't even know
                               whether that's good or bad!

        good weather turns to bad
        as the first drops of rain
        reign down on big sur

                             (ric gland:
                                 about then i felt
                                 the first drop of
                                 rain
                                    but it didn't
                                 come down hard at
                                 first)

(david cohen of S.H.A.M.E.:
                        it suddenly got very
                        dark and the wind
                        came up
                             and about ten
                        minutes later i felt
                        the first drop)
                                 (colonel dipper:
 i could see a storm
 front move onto the
 mainland
        it mustuf
 been about four or
 five california time)
                        it was 4:52 california
                        time to be exact
                                 when the first drop fell

"say would you mind if i shared
 your umbrella with you"
                        says manny makemore with
                        thirty lbs. of equipment
                        still strapped to him
                                   "why not at all sweets
                                 the more the merrier"
                        says timothy queen
                        limp-wristing his parasol
                        in makemore's direction
"i'll take my chances in
 the wilderness"
                      says makemore disdainfully
                               (reverend buttermilk
                               tapes his sunday night
                             vespers sermon:
  ...are today children in the wilderness
                       they are
  lost confused without hope of the future
                    and friends
  these are our *own* children

                        not some kind of crazy
aborigines
          we must ask ourselves what we are doing to
bring our youth back into the fold and out of the
wilderness of despair
                    we must ask ourselves how we can
instill a little hope and confidence into their lives
and give them something to live for
                        well my friends
god has the answer
                  he sees their tormented lives
                                    lives
spent in the sticky web of drugs
                          in the temporal pleas-
ure of illicit sex
                in the filth and squalor of communal
living
      god sees all of this and it doesn't please him
one bit
      and yet he is powerless to act
                              powerless
                                    unless
we are willing to let him into the act so to speak
                                    unless
we turn the amber spotlight on him for a moment in
solving these problems
                  yes dear friends
                        god is waiting in
the wings
        he doesn't want a bit part
                                he wants to be the
director
        and we must give him the chance to direct our
lives because we have been floundering too long on the
stage of life without him
                    we've muffed too many lines
we don't know our entrances or our exits
                              we can't relate
to the divine author of this play
                          now just what does all
of this have to do with saint dunstan?
                        simply this...)

                                                      hello ... ?

(wearily) *KCUF - rawlins*

                                                      this is
                                                      carmella karma

(even more
 wearily)   *yes ma'am*
                                                      what is the
                                                      latest news on

      ...nothing new since
      you called last ma'am
                                                      but that was
                                                      over an hour ago
                                                      surely...

        hold on
        i've got to cue a
        commercial

                                      <u>AUDIO</u>

              (Woman) Doctor, what cigarette is

              safe to smoke?

(Doctor) There is no 'safe cigarette.'
All cigarettes are harmful to your
health according to the Surgeon
General's report.

(Woman) Does that mean I'll have to
give up smoking?

(Doctor) You'll have to weigh all the
factors. Do you want good health or
do you want a good-tasting cigarette?

(Woman) That's a pretty tough choice to
make.

(Doctor) It's a choice millions of Americans are making today. And their choice
is overwhelmingly Grasslands. Grasslands
deliver on flavor, there's no doubt on
that score. I smoke 'em myself.

(Woman) Then you prescribe Grasslands?

(Doctor) I say only this: weigh all the
factors: you only live once, you know.
Live a little...smoke Grasslands!

that is a
despicable ad!

(wearily)   *maybe so lady*
             but it sure pays
             the bills

(hey chief *says max vogel*
it's beginning to rain!)

"sweetmeat poncho
all wool
completely washable
twenty dollar"

(twenty dollars!
you were selling them
ten minutes ago for
five dollars)

"rain cause inflation"

higher and higher
it's so good
half-hour flyer
you knew we could

it's your thing
do what you want to do
it's your thing
who ya sock it to

make no difference now baby
ooo-ooo-huh-huh

"what's on television?"

olive oil is pursuing popeye

um-hum

grospekski is striking out

um

jackie gleason is sending alice
to the moon

ho-hah

lawrence welk is lip reading
idiot cards

uh-one-and-uh

lorne green is stringing fence

and there are three commercials
on the other channels (slightly mixed up in transmission)

VIDEO

OPEN ON MS OF MIDDLECLASS LIVING
ROOM WITH MOTHER KNITTING AND
CHILDREN PLAYING ON FLOOR. PAN
TO FRONT DOOR AS FATHER WALKS IN.

AUDIO

FATHER

(fatigued) Boy am I bushed.

This heat sure gets me down.

FISHERMAN DUMP HERRING INTO THE
SHIP'S HOLD. CUT TO SLOW MOTION.

ANNOUNCER (VO)

...only the finest herring are

good enough to earn YUM Kipper

DISSOLVE TO SEAL BEING TOSSED A
HERRING. SEAL IS WEARING A LARGE

Herring's seal of approval...

PENDANT. ZOOM AND CROSS DISS TO
FREEZE FRAME OF PENDANT.

ANNOUNCER (VO)

And look! Paul is actually wear-

ECU OF PAUL DOLL WITH STAR-SIGN
ON BREAST. POP ON $3.95 ON WORDS

ing a genuine Sweetmeat Star-Sign

VERY OWN.

Pin. And now you can order your

pin with your very own astrological

star-sign on it by sending $3.95...

"popeye!"

ball two strike two
on resnevpenski

"ralph
it's simply not going to work!"

FATHER

...but aren't Feel Up's habit

forming?

SEAL APPLAUDS WITH FLIPPERS.

popeye is pursued by bluto pursued by
pluto pursued by a band of rustlers
pursued by a team of wrestlers
pursued by
        "...and resnevpenski strikes out to end the inning!"
                                                    how can you
                                                    watch baseball
                                                    at a time like
                                                    this

      "but it's in the fourteenth inning"
                                      a great line-up of star-studded
                                      performers...
                you're watching television
                while our daughter is missing!
                                            she just went down to gail's
and where did gail go?
                              harry
                              i want you to call the police!
        (the kid locked himself
          in his room and wouldn't
          come out)
                                          now look mister
                                          i know my own daughter!
        i wouldn't allow it
                                                (took his allowance away)
and the kids today are...
                                    hello?
            is betty over at your house?
                                    hello?
                                                acting strangely lately
my daughter had a sweetmeat poster above her bed
but it wasn't there when i checked her room
                                        my son antonio
                                        (he's a good boy)
                                        had very good homelife
                                        i tell you mister
        "...busted every sweetmeat record he had"
went on
a rampage
                                      (cut out every clipping on them in
                                        the magazines and burnt them in the
                                        backyard)
      like she was in a trance
                              just got up and walked out of the television room
          "never before did
            that"
                              i mean
                              she adored her doll collection
                              why should she break them up like that
      i'm just beside myself with
      worry!
                                        CU OF FATHER WIPING HIS BROW

                  AUDIO

                  MOTHER

      (concerned) I think we better

      call the police. It's getting

      dark out.
                                        CUT TO TELEPHONE

192

          SFX RING

                                    CUT TO CU OF MOTHER AS SHE PUTS
                                    RECEIVER TO HER EAR

"...those wonderful little lemon sisters..."

                                    CUT TO CU OF FATHER TURNING OFF
                                    THE TELEVISION. CUT BACK TO
                                    MOTHER.

     "hello?"

                                          "hello meg
                                           this is sylvia"

     "i was just about to call you
      is linda over there?"

                                          "why no
                                           is beth over at your
                                           place?"

     "no"

                                          "i can't find beth!"

     "do you think they went to
      big sur?"

                                          "she better not have!"

     "linda was supposed to be doing
      decorations for the dance tonight"

                                          "that's exactly what my
                                           beth told me!"

     "i'm so worried sylvia"

                                          "harry refuses to call the
                                           police"

     "we tried that
      the lines are busy!"

                                          "i'm going down to the
                                           stationhouse myself"

     "ask about my linda will you
      please sylvia?"

                                    for chrissake!
                                    what is the latest news?

     T H E   L A T E S T   N E W S

1708
BIG SUR CALIFORNIA (UPI MAY 7)

HEAVY RAINS ARE MAKING THE ASSAULT ON MT. PARNASSUS EXTREMELY

DIFFICULT AS THOUSANDS OF NATIONAL GUARD TROOPS PREPARE TO

ADVANCE THE FINAL 1,000 FEET. THE 69TH BATTALION UNDER THE COM-

MAND OF GENERAL OCHRE HAS MET RESISTANCE FROM THE TENS OF THOU-

SANDS OF HIPPIES WHO HAVE INFILTRATED THE AREA. REPORTS CON-

FIRM HOWEVER THAT SUCH RESISTANCE IS PEACEFUL AS DEMONSTRATORS

ATTEMPT TO PLACE FLOWERS IN THE MUZZLES OF THE SOLDIERS' WEAPONS.

MANY SOLDIERS HAVE DEFECTED AND MANY OTHERS ARE UNACCOUNTED FOR.

                                              (swami sahalami
                                               reads over the
                                               latest teletype
                                               before return-
                                               ing to his
                                               séance in the
                                               front room)

"my ball suddenly clouds up as if
with moisture
                    i see...i see the out-
lines of many people...people in
uniforms...they are carrying guns..."

                                                    "put your hands up!"

(hey man
 cool it with that piece)

                                                    *"i'm borrowing your
                                                     bike"*

(it's not going to do you much good man
 it's spinning out under me)

                                                    "back up!"

            stuart takes marvin tempest's
            chopper and first-gears it up the
            muddy incline

                                        the rain burst upon the
                                        roadway in folds
                                        of silk and burlap

    stinging the leaves in a steady hiss

                                sending the multitudes to
                                treetrunk shelter

but it was a warm spring rain
the kind of rain once remembered in childhood

                                sweet-smelling and warm like
                                grass perfume falling from the
                                skies

the kind of innocent spring rain
spot and jane were told about from zeke
looking up into the grayness
leaning upon his leafrake
sucking on his cos cob pipe...

                                the kind of rain that fell on
                                spot
                                        and then fell on puff
                                and then
                                fell into the mold of childhood
                                fantasies

where dick and jane and sally and spot and
puff and mother and father and the grandfolks were etched in our minds
indelible
in four-colors and red binders
in the last completely happy story we ever read

                                or heard
                                    or knew of

                                            a spring
                                            rain...

        Look look, says Jane. Look at

        the big gray clouds.

                                Oh, oh, says Zeke.

                                It will rain soon.

        We should get out of the rain.

                                Come with me to the park

                                shanty. I have something

                                to show you. But it's

                                only for you. No dogs.

Go, Spot, says Jane.   Go home.

"my god my god
  stop it for godsake!"

Oh Zeke! Zeke! Stop that!

"oh no...no...no...god!"

No Zeke! No!

"oh please stop!"

Mom-my!   MOM-MY!

(lady i don't know where
  your kid is)

(please...please)

(i'm sorry ma'am
  i'm only a newsman
  i'm not running things here)

(her name is jane
          she's about this tall...)

(please lady
  i've got to do this interview)

"this is jim skinner KCUF monterey
with me is general 'chickenhawk'
ochre leader of the 69th national
guard battalion here at big sur
                            general
i understand there have been reports
of desertion in your ranks..."

"ridiculous
  some of our units have
  become disoriented in
  the rain that's all"

"roughly how many units sir"

"minor...minor..."

"have you made radio contact with them?"

"the only radio they lis-
  ten to is KCUF"

"thank you general ochre
  this is jim skinner KCUF radio monterey"

*(that looks like general ochre
says max vogel to chief broken
wind
      set me down here for a
      moment)*

"always like to help out
  the mass media anyway i
  can
      you don't have a lit-
  tle nip on you?"

"here's your twenty general"

"sorry general i don't"
          general ochre!

          um what is it

          remember me?
          i'm max vogel

          where the hell have
          you been man

          i had to shake off this
          lunatic with a rifle who was...

          you were supposed to
          report back at three

          that's what i'm trying to tell you...

          well my troops moved
          out

          you've got to stop them general!

but don't you see...

general you must stop them!

i couldn't get back in time...

general...

please...please general listen...

*i gave the order already
to advance*

*i want to get up there
before it gets dark*

*my orders were to wait until
three o'clock...*

and then take the hill

*that's what my boys are
doing
        takin' the hill*

*it's too late
i just gave the order
to take the top*

(stuart suddenly scrambles by
 kicking up a trail of stones and
 mud on general ochre and max vogel)

BBBBBBBBBBRRRRRRRRRRRRROOOOOOOOOOOOOOO
OOOOOOOOOOOOOOOOOOMMMMMMMMMMMMMMMMBBBBBBBBBBBBBBBBBRRRRRRRrrrrrrrrooooooooooo
ooooooooooooooommmmmmmmmmmmmmmmm

IDIOT!

*that's him!
that's the idiot i was telling
you about*

*look at me!
i'm splattered with mud!*

*general
he's going to kill the sweetmeats!*

$%#'@° "#$%'°@ "$#&°"!

he's going to kill them!

*well if he doesn't i
sure as hell will!*

(while there's a break in the action
 let's get this commercial over with)

("say...
 how many fucking commercials
 we got to listen to anyway")

(it's the price one has to pay in a
 lobbyistic democracy)

("i'm going to the kitchen
 for a beer")

(remember CRASS has class...)

("fuck off!")

                    TRANSMISSION
                    TERMINATION

                    POSITIVE

(did he shut off the set?)

                    POSITIVE

(is there a radio in the kitchen?)

(cue radio commercial and hold until
 transceiver is activated)

                    STANDING BY
("maybe the
 news is on")
                    SIGNAL RECEIVED

(fade in commercial...)

...much excitement puts your nerves

on edge. Relax. Put your feet up.

Take a Let Down. Let Down soothes irri-

table nerves, calms that over-all jittery

feeling you get in today's hectic society.

Contains *tetrahydrocannabinol*, the new mir-

acle ingredient that rushes its rest-induc-

ing compound directly into your bloodstream

for immediate relief. So the next time

your system cries "FIRE!" -- douse it with

(siren and
firebells)

Let Down. The one tranquilizer safe to use

when taken as directed.   (fade)

"in vietnam today
        ground action was light as mopping-up
operations continued around the beleaguered town of fuc hue
located in the strategic ying yang valley north of saigon
american casualties were reported 'moderate' with 347 men
killed and over 1,000 wounded
                enemy deaths were put at 4,500
we've just received this report from brentin strong our
correspondent on the scene..."

                (crackle) this is brentin strong with the re-
                mainder of baker battery of the 549th infantry
                battalion here in fuc hue
                                        there is a strange
                lull that comes over a battlefield after the
                shelling has stopped
                                it is strangely peaceful
                here after a night of almost continuous bom-
                bardment
                        now only an occasional burst of machinegun
                is heard every few minutes as search and destroy
                units dig out the innumerable bunkers which only
                last night held thousand of viet cong regulars
                                                today
                the hills surrounding fuc hue are deathly
                quiet
                        so far 23 enemy bodies have been found
                though estimates place the enemy death toll
                at more than 4,500
                                it is assumed that whole
                enemy units were trapped in their underground
                bunkers as B-52 bombers pounded the area with
                unceasing bombing runs last night
                                                but american
                casualties were heavy
                                also
                the 549th battalion suffered close to 200
                deaths and baker battery was especially heavy
                hit...

197

(please...
 must we go into this?)

(please...anything but this!)

(my god! no choice...anything...)

(please...please...)

(yes...no...i mean...oh please)

(yes...yes...for godsake...oh god!...)

(oh god...god...god...)

(mmm...mmm...mmmmmmmmm)

(MMMMMMMMMMMMM)

      "please general ochre you've
       got to recall your men..."

            and then all at once
            everybody seemed to hear
            'the music' together

      "what's what?"

      "i don't hear any..."

      "i just hear the rain..."

            and through the rain and
            the drop-drenched leaves
            did indeed come music
                 but with a sound unlike any heard
before
      "what is that?"

      "what?"

      "general..."

      "general..."

      "what?"

      "sounds like a sitar..."

      "general are you all right?"

(manny makemore also hears the faint strains
 of music and records for posterity the 'tape
 that didn't turn out')

*(it's getting very hard to keep
 you amused america)*

*(it's either this or another com-
 mercial or the sweetmeat nonsense)*

*(do you want to get back to the
 sweetmeat saga?)*

(the sweetmeat saga? answer me!)

(ANSWER ME! THE SWEETMEAT SAGA?)

          STANDING BY

          ACTIVATION

          VIDEO

          AUDIO

"i recall once in burma..."

"whassat?"

"...music..."

"sssshhhh..."

"sssshhhhhhhhh..."

"commie brainwaves"

"the communists!"

"hear that music mister
 not like doris day"

"commie stuff
 quarter-tone system"

"getting at us through our
 music"

"degenerating doris day!"

"...raping our wives and
 sweethearts..."

for the music was both heard
and not heard
depending on where
your head was at
it either turned you off or tuned you
in
shot you up
or brought you down
put you on
or ripped you off
blew your mind
or blued your mind
music that originated beyond the stars
somewhere in quasars yet
undiscovered
music that was formed with pure energy
somewhere in the furthest
regions of interior space
music that was played by innumerable
angels on the heads of
innumerable pins
music that emanated from every sand
grain
from every rain
drop
from
every breath of life
but music only a few heard
and fewer still would ever remember
"i don't know
what happened
to the kid..."
"one moment he was sitting there quiet as a mouse
the next moment he was running out the door"
something between the
hari krishna chant
and
row row row your boat
but can't you just hum the melody?
"i heard this...this thing in the air..."
what was it like?
i can't describe it
it was like a hymn
"like papa haydn?"
like a song
from childhood
like twinkle twinkle
little star?
"strange words
but yet i knew those words once..."
like a nursery rhyme
like a melody i knew
before i was born
brahm's lullaby perhaps?
a song every child
knows
"oh you know...whatdoyoucallit"
a song sung by my
mother while nursing
"she asked us if we heard the
music and when we said we didn't
she ran out the front door"

                                                  "what could i tell him...
                  i told him the truth...
                  i couldn't hear the music..."
      ("and yet it was so familiar...")
                               it wasn't music at all
it was just the rustling leaves and the rain
                               it was just...just nothing at all!
just something and nothing
you thought of for a moment
                    and let drift back into the mindless waves
of memory
        ah
        but then again
                you didn't hear it...

                                              did you?

"here
 take some more of my blanket
 brenda"

                                        "it's all right lou
                                         i'm not cold"

"i'm soaked"

                                        "do you want to go on?"

"don't you?"

                                        "of course silly
                                         what time is it?"

"almost six"

                                        "my parents would be getting
                                         worried about now"

"mine too"

                                        "but we must be getting close
                                         to the top
                                                    i can hear music"

"me too"

                                        "do you have another joint on
                                         you?"

          "sure"
        (louis smith pulls his blanket damp with rain
         over both of their heads and in the woolsmell
         cocooned darkness lights up a stick)

                                             a ritual that
                                             fully one-tenth of
                                             america was practic-
                                             ing at about that
                                             moment

but only to louis smith and brenda quigley
did captain francona make his muddy way just then

                                        (okay
                                         break it up in there)

  "huh" (louis comes out with a halo of high
          about him)

                                        (that smells like marijuana)

"oh no!"

                                        (let's see your i.d. kid)

"look officer..."

                                        (you got some identification
                                         on you miss?)

                        "sure"

                                        (are you louis smith?)

"yeah"

                                        (are you brenda quigley?)

                        "uh-huh"

                                        (okay you can go
                                         i don't have you on the
                                         list
                                             but keep the reefers
                                         out of sight)

"you're not going to
 bust us?"

                                        (i'd have to bust a couple
                                         of hundredthousand kids
                                         out here today on that rap)

"wow! (exclaims louis after captain francona
 leaves)
        is that outasite!"

                                   "hey you kids want to be
                                    interviewed?"

us?

          "sure i'm jim skinner from
           KCUF radio"

will our names be used?

          "not if you don't want us to"

ok

          "let me turn this set on for a
           moment...okay...good...with me
           are a couple of young people who
           are making the arduous climb to
           the top of parnassus mountain...
           what is your reason for coming
           here today?"

well i thought it would be a gas

      me too

          "where do you kids live?"

in monterey

      me too

          "and you drove down here today?"

      yeah

          "what do you think you'll find
           on the top of mt. parnassus"

i don't know
but it's a beautiful trip man

      outasite

          "do you think the sweetmeats are
           alive?"

can't you dig their sounds

          "i hear...sort of sounds..."

      oh wow!

          "if you call that music..."

you call it music man
i didn't say anything about music

      i'm having
      a déjà vu

          "then you think they're making
           these sounds..."

maybe the sounds are making them

          "i don't understand..."

      is this
      guy for
      real?

maybe the effect is cause and the
cause effect
        dig?

          "not really..."

for instance
      maybe that transmitter
is turning you on
        rather than you
turning that transmitter on
          see?

          "oh yeah...yeah but..."

maybe we're interviewing you rather
than you interviewing us

          "but..."
              before we go any
              further

    time out
    to take this

PROCEDURE EVALUATION QUESTIONNAIRE

PROCEDURE TO BE EVALUATED: _____.

A. Please answer "YES" or "NO" to the following questions:

    QUESTION #1 - Is the complete procedure (as it affects you)
                     operational? _____.

    QUESTION #2 - Are personnel available to handle all functions of
                     procedure which relate to your area? _____.

    QUESTION #3 - Have any problems developed as a result of the
                     implementation of this procedure? _____.

    QUESTION #4 - Are all required forms printed and available? _____.

    QUESTION #5 - Is the procedure "as written" being followed without
                     changes? _____.

(proceed
please)

                                              "but..."
maybe we'll never understand each
others sounds

                        i hope we
                        do

                                    "this is jim skinner KCUF big sur
and so friends
         until next sunday night at this
time this is rev. cecil buttermilk saying god
bless you all and may jesus take a real good
liking to you whoever you are
                             (organ music swell & fade out)

        <u>VIDEO</u>

    OPEN ON LS OF INSIDE OF MILITARY
    BARRACKS WITH JUNGLE GROWTH APPEAR-
    ING THROUGH THE WINDOWS INDICATING
    A FOREIGN OUTPOST. DISS TO MS OF   <u>AUDIO</u>
    MARINE AS HE SITS SOBBING ON HIS
    BUNK WITH A MOP IN HIS HANDS.   1ST MARINE

                                    Oh dear...oh dear...

                                    An inspection is due...

                                    And my barracks look like

                                    Dien Bien Phu!

    PAN TO SEVERAL RAGGED CHILDREN AT
    THE WINDOW BEGGING FOR RATIONS.

                                    CHILDREN

                                    Please G.I....please...

    MS OF MARINE AS HE CROSSES OVER TO   1ST MARINE
    WINDOW.

                                    Why don't you kids go home to

                                    your mothers...those who still

                                    have any.

                    CHILDREN

One gum...please G.I....

                    1ST MARINE (softening)

You kids know it's against code

28A section 14 subsection 6

paragraph 3 to...

                    CHILDREN

One gum...

                    1ST MARINE (ignoring them)

I've just *got* to get these barracks

clean or the general will bust a

tit!

CUT TO MARINE SERGEANT WITH SMOLDERING   SERGEANT (excitedly)
BAZOOKA AS HE BURSTS INTO THE BARRACKS.
                                                JIM! JIM! The area's been

                                                liberated!

                                                1ST MARINE (brightening)

PAN WITH SERGEANT AS HE RUSHES TO   Oh, that's wonderful!
1ST MARINE.

                                                    SERGEANT

                                                Are you out of your mind, man?

                                                We've got to get out of here!

CUT TO CU OF 1ST MARINE AS HE SALUTES.   1ST MARINE

                                                I'm staying until I can see

                                                my reflection in the floor, sir.

                                                Those were my orders.

CUT TO CHILDREN IN WINDOW.   CHILDREN (together)

                                                Hey...G.I. Joe...

                                                You need detergent?

how quick these kids pick
up everything
                                       "my little diane knows all
                                         the commercials by heart
                                                        don't you dear"

        "yes-i-do-daddy-yes-i-do"
                                       "go into your little routine dear"

"crass-in-a-glass-has-class
crass-beer
           -the-one-beer-to
have-when-you-feel-like-it"
                              "isn't that great!
                               and she's not even seven yet!"
                                                    (time for
                                                     after dinner
                                                     entertainment)
spin the bottle
                                                hit the bottle
              pin the horn on the cuckold
                                             pin the clap on
                                             the coccoid
         swap your partners two-by-two
                                         cheat a little bit
                                         if you're feeling blue
        spend a little bread and dues eat dough
                                         take the little woman
                                         to the movie show
                                                      (open a
                                                       bottle)
"...going down to the meeting hall honey..."
                                          "every saturday night
                                           every saturday night
                                           every saturday night..."
     all join hands and loop-de-loo
                                  (...all on a saturday night)
         "here we go loop-de-la..."
                                                B-7
      ooooohhhhhhh
                                                G-22
      ooooohhhhhhh
                        a hundred thousand east coast senior citizens
                        hold their breath in unison
                        for the calling of the next ping-pong ball
     while a demonstration of
     the limbo-rock by dance instructors mel and sandy
     loosen things up on the up-tight dancefloor of bar nothing ranch
                                                            while
                                                            darkness
            sweeps over the midwest like a sigh
                                    (open a bottle)
the transistorized farmer
takes a slug of silicon and scotch
                                          I-13
                        and sunday papers suddenly
                        begin to appear on stands
      (hours before the familiar
                        TWACK
                             would land them upon stoops and porches
(seen
  thru the eyes of some near-sighted
                        paperboy)
                                  in the subliminal dreams of
                                  thousands of sub-bourbon
                                  hangovers)
      a strike for a turkey
                   plump finger-bowling
                                      the boston matron
                                      turns to
                                      Klingerman's Kolumn

"...as i'm writing this the outcome in big sur is
still undecided
                    but one thing is for sure:
                                        nothing
is going to be the same after this weekend"
                                                (a favorite Klingerism)
                                    "...the
sweetmeats have become a legend in their time and
that legend has become gospel with today's kids"
                                        "when i catch that
                                        sonofabitch i'm going
                                        to kill him"
                                                mutters
                                                marvin tempest
                                                mudslogging it
                                                up parnassus
            the sonofabitch in question
            is of course stuart who at that moment was
            tearing the transmission out of tempest's beast
                                        rrrrrrrrrrrrmmmmmmmmmm
bbbrrraaaaakkkkkkkbbbrr   rrrrrmmmmmmmm ccccchhhhhhhuuugggg gggggggguuuuu
bbbbbbbbbbbrrrrrraaaaaaaakkkkkkkkk   chucghuch   brt brup
                                        (suddenly a stillness
                                        in the forest)
        raindrops on leaves
                                            grass hiss
                        a ripple of laughter
                        beneath muted ponchos
                                            the roadway rivered
                                            with spikes of rain
    how much further?
                                a little ways
            "i can hear the music already"
                                        thousands of huddled
                                        hunchbacked hippies
                                        trudging onward
        "anybody want a drag?"
                            ("did i hear someone say drag" lisps
                                timothy queen all a flutter)
so the next time someone asks you
do you have a drag
                pull out grasslands
it's the kind of cigarette freeloaders
really appreciate
                "and this is sonny swingle swinging it
your way this rainy saturday afternoon
                                but we got lots of the hots
coming up your way this next twenty-five
                                so stay tuned to the station
that radiates smiles of sunshine soundwaves...
                                    the sweetmeats and...
                                            (cue in)
                ...neon hero"
                            if on-ly tech-nol-o-gy kept pace
                            if on-ly we could turn the dial
                            what great suns of warmth we'd see
                            beyond the neon hero's smile...
        "be damned if i know what
        they were talking about"
                                    ...take that trip
                                    take that wonderful trip
                                    beyond your mind...

"a bunch of nonsense if you
 ask me"
                                                    can you hear the music?
"you call that noise music!"
                              the generation gap
                              started with potatoes in its ears
(and heads in the sand)
                                                    can you hear the sounds?
          SHUT THAT DAMN THING OFF!
                                                    can you hear the beat?
          IT'S SO LOUD I CAN'T HEAR A FUCKING
          THING!
                                                         (cool it)
     (sssssshhhhhh)
                                                         (temporize it
                                                          man)

       (ssshhh)
                                                         (sugar xxx is
                                                          giving the word)

"brothers
 this whole scene looks like a bummer to me
 like i don't see nothing goin' down 'cept
 a lot of cats breaking their chops to get
 to the top
          and i don't see no way in this
 rain and all
            how we are going to radicalize
 the situation
            so maybe we just better disperse
 and dig the..."

                                        "but whut about all these
                                         mazel tov cocktails we
                                         done brought wid us?"

"pass them out for kerosene lamps"
                                        "man
                                         we got a perfect oppor-
                                         tunity to..."
"this ain't gin-time my man
 this is something else"
                          it's quite simple explains mountmother
                          in periods of ultimate stress progressions
                          the ego and the super-ego make a pact
                          with the id in effect saying:
                                        if you don't blow
                          your cool now i'll let you blow it twice as
                          hard some other time
                                        so then the super-ego
                          says to the nervous system:
                                        relax baby
                          i got it all cleared up with the id
                                                   so then
                          the ego tells the senses to keep especially
                          alert but the...
      "THIS IS THE REVOLUTION"
                          shouts david cohen into his transistorized
                          portable megaphone
      "THROW OFF YOUR SHACKLES"
                                        but no one is stopping to
                     listen to him
      "STUDENTS LISTEN TO ME!!!"
                                        but they're passing him by

"THE MILITARY-INDUSTRIAL
COMPLEX SPENDS BILLIONS
EACH YEAR...

"hey shut the fuck up so we
can hear the music"

"yeah"
"CAPITALIST MONOPOLY..."

"hey quiet!"

shhhhh

"(i just don't understand)"
says david cohen to himself
"(they've just tuned me out
completely!)"

"do your thing later
after the concert man"

"we don't want to get
hung-up about that now"

...a real bring-down

even chief broken wind
finds the road to riches paved
with stoneheads and limited allowances

"genuine pookie and paul
tom-tom with good housekeeping
seal of approval"

no thanks chief

"how about this genuine astrological star-sign..."

("genuine fake")

"you like-um this sweetmeat
necklace?"

"like-um the necklace
dislike-um the mark-up"

"special discount to you"

come off it chief
yeah
just cool it!

it was true
that day chief broken wind
couldn't *give* away sweetmeat merchandise

in fact that day hundreds
of tons of sweetmeat dolls
were being summarily
court marshalled and exe-
cuted on the spot

<u>AUDIO</u>

(BG MUSIC: STARS AND STRIPES
      FOREVER

   ANNOUNCER (VO)

It's new...it's exciting...it's filled

with action   Pookie and Paul as Green

Berets! Now for the first time you can

be with Pookie and Paul as they patrol for

Viet Cong in foreign jungles. Share

adventure after adventure with Paul as

he goes on deadly missions through the

<u>VIDEO</u>

OPEN WITH FOLLOWING SHOT OF
BOY AND GIRL AS THEY MOVE
THROUGH UNDERBRUSH. CUT TO
REACTION SHOT OF BOY AS HE
DISCOVERS GREEN BERET OUTFIT.
CUT TO OUTFIT ON SIDE OF PATH.

PULL BACK AS BOY AND GIRL
OPEN KIT FROM BOTH SIDES.
BOY PULLS OUT PAUL DOLL. PAN
AND ZOOM WITH AS IT IS SET IN
TALL GRASS.

208

very heart of Vieg Cong territory. And
here is Pookie as Green Beret nurse, always right beside Paul when the going
gets rough.

      (CUE UP SHELLING SFX AND FADE)

Everything you need to simulate real live
battle conditions is included. Five enemy soldiers...an authentic Vietnamese village you can assemble and disassemble yourself...real ack-ack guns...two live-action
tanks...and much more!

And here's Paul in an authentic Green Beret
uniform...complete with rifle that really
fires! And Pookie's nurse's kit has a thermometer that really works!
Wow kids! You'll figure out dozens of ways
to have fun with Pookie and Paul's Official
Green Beret outfit. Make up your own war
games and record battle casualties with
this Battle Report Sheet, just like they
use wherever the fighting Green Berets are
stationed. It's included with the kit!
Get your Green Beret outfit today while
the supply lasts! Sold at fine toy stores
in *your* neighborhood. A Makemore quality
product.

      (BRING UP BG MUSIC TO END)

  "what is it pop?"

  "it looks like...a burnt...
   doll!"

CUT TO POOKIE DOLL AS IT IS TAKEN FROM KIT BY GIRL. PAN AND ZOOM TO DOLL PLACED ALONGSIDE OF PAUL.

PULL BACK TO REVEAL ENEMY SOLDIERS SURROUNDING DOLLS.

PAN TO VIETNAMESE VILLAGE. BOY REMOVES GRASS ROOF FROM HUT OF CENTRAL DWELLING.

PAN PAST VILLAGE AND MOVE IN ON ACK-ACK GUNS AND TANKS BESIDE THEM THAT BEGIN TO MOVE INTO THE VILLAGE.

CUT TO ECU OF PAUL DOLL. BOY PULLS BACK RIFLE BOLT OF GUN.

CUT TO ECU OF POOKIE DOLL. GIRL TAKES OUT MINIATURE THERMOMETER FROM KIT.

CUT TO BERET OUTFIT IN LIMBO. SLIDE IN ON TOP OF IT BATTLE REPORT PAD.

DISSOLVE TO REAL GREEN BERET STANDING OVER CORPSES. CU OF BERET AS HE REPORTS CASUALTIES ON CLIPBOARD.

DISSOLVE TO GREEN BERET OUTFIT. SUPER LOCAL SIGN-OFF.

  "rushell rushell!
   come here shun"

  "look whut i found out by
   the incinerator"

"they're lots more there"

"that's linda's doll collection!"

"'bout twenty"

"she loved her doll sets!"

the rain has turned to mist on parnassus

"my god chief i'm dying back here!
do you have to stop along the way
every minute to sell this stuff"

(sweetmeat manager should know
about sweetmeat sales poten-
tial)

"i do i do!
but the kids just aren't buying that
stuff today"

(it is great mystery to me...
get your official sweetmeat
roach holder...)

"look chief
suppose i buy all this stuff from you
could we get up the mountain faster?"

(you can have everything...
all merchandise...blanket...
saddle...horse...shoot and
caboodle -- for five hundred
dollar
          i take personal checks)

"in other words
five hundred dollars to get rid of you"

(it is known as a saskatchewan
shakedown)

"anything to get off the rear end of
this animal!"
          (max vogel pulls out his
checkbook)

(make check payable to
CANNABIS CORPORATION)

          1811
          BIG SUR CALIFORNIA (AP MAY 7)

          REPORTS REACHING AP CONFIRM FACT THAT

"swami sahalami sees all"

                    yes swami!

"my ball is very misty now"

                    yes

"i see...i see a stonehouse in the middle of
a large clearing..."

          (gasps)

"there are hundreds...thousands of people
surrounding the house..."

          TROOPS STILL LOYAL TO GENERAL OCHRE ARE
FINDING THE GOING
          DIFFICULT AS

"there are soldiers..."

          (more gasps)

"stepping over live bodies"

          MUSIC HEARD
EMANATING FROM THE
          DISTINCT SMELL OF MARIJUANA.

"they are swaying from side to side
as if in a trance..."

          oh god!

"ah! that is all i can see for the
moment! i must retire"

(hey says woody wilson
almost at the peak
look at the guy in the tree there)

"oooooooooooooooooooooooooooo
stuart!   stuart!"

(must be off his rocker)

jagoff to underwater one
come in underwater one...

one here sir

can you see my signal

yessir

how far am i from the top

about thirty yards sir

i'm going for the top now
stand by

aye aye sir

"this is jim skinner reporting from the top
 of mt. parnassus
            before me is just an unbelievable
 scene!
      i simply can't put it into words
                        there seems
to be about a hundred thousand kids up here
huddled beneath blankets in this heavy mist that
has settled on the top of this mountain
                        in the mid-
dle of this crowd
            about a hundred yards from me
                                i
can make out the outline of a small cottage which
they tell me is the stonehouse
                there are no lights
in the house because there is no electricity there
i am told
        but nevertheless there is music being am-
plified somehow coming from that general direction"

SAVAGE
GET YOUR ASS UP HERE

my god!
what a sight!

pauline please...winded...

take a look
it's fantastic!

(puff) are we on the...top?

look over there
that's the stonehouse

kids...more kids...

we've got to get
set up quickly

all of this...for that!

there isn't time
we go on the air
in less than an
hour!

...catch my breath...

it sure is!
i'll get the
interview

isn't that...general ochre...

                              "general ochre sir
                               pauline farnsworth from the
                               AGH network sir"
     "fifty dollars"
                               "what?"
     "fifty dollars for the
       interview"
                               "but..."
     "it's a new army regulation
       aimed at de-muzzling the
       military"
                               "well...all right"
     "fine and dandy...
       now what did you want to
       ask me pauline?"
                               "just what are your plans
                                general"
     "we'll give them a period of
       time to surrender and if
       they don't we'll go in
       after them"
                               "who general"
     "who's ever in there"
                               "then you really *don't* know
                                who's in there"
     "i figure if they have noth-
       ing to hide they'll come
       out
          and if they don't come
       out
          it indicates to me that
       there's a dirty commie plot
       going on"
                                        that seemed to be the
                                        black and the white of it
the red and the black of it
                                        the black and blue of it
cue: *god bless america*
                    gradually increase volume
                                        (the nigger and the jew of it)
the "america we knew" of it
                    ...one nation invisible...
                                        "subvert our highest
                                         ideals..."
          things are rotten enough without
          the sweetmeats
                                        (all of this eastern music shit)
   "...and there was that shot of pookie
     kissing that negro..."
                                              and paul saluting the
                                              flag with a clenched fist
          or how 'bout the time paul burnt his
          blue cross membership card
and pookie
her bra
          right on the stage of the miss america contest
                                                "shocking...
                                                 simply shocking!"
                    i don't know what happened to those
                    kids in the past few years
     they set the example
     for today's youth it seems

"i noticed a change in my own kids"

"suddenly it was 'if pookie can do
such and such a thing
why can't i?'"

(my kid was the same way...
he'd see paul do something
crazy and the next moment
he were doin' it himself)

absolutely no respect...

("yet i couldn't get over pookie's
fantastic set of tits...")

i mean
those shots of her in foreplay were...

i just wanted to mother paul
it was a perfectly natural thing

"i mean
we grew up with them..."

they were like children to us

(i guess i had been secretly
in love with paul for years)

"...had no parents you see
so i supposed i fantasized
a little..."

she was my little girl
don't you understand!!

"shocking...
simply shocking!"

i both loved her and hated her
for doing those things

...with libertines and
just ass for all

paul needed professional
counseling
i wrote him a letter telling him that

"...just the people
they associated with"

that great spread shot she did
in the foreplay foldout

"HENRY!"

"i couldn't take my eyes off him
he was so well-hung and all"

"PENELOPE!"

the generation gape

a decay in our
moral fiber

determined to nip it in the bud-dle

"while there is still
time"

"...carmella?..."

"hello?"

"carmella!
this is sheldon klingerman in new york
i've been trying to get you for hours!"

"well i've been tied up
on the phone all after-
noon shelly"

"look dear
i simply have to know the latest on the
sweetmeat thing
it's capital-V-vital!"

"i haven't heard anything
except what's on KCUF"

"how's fifty dollars"

                                        "you paid me seventy-five
                                         for the mario savio tip"

"seventy-five then"

                                        "well according to jim
                                         skinner from KCUF

                                                        general
                                         ochre is convinced this
                                         is a communist plot and
                                         he's ready to bring up
                                         heavy artillery if he
                                         doesn't get a response
                                         from the stonehouse"

"do you think he's serious?"
                                        "anyone who knows ochre
                                         knows he's serious"

"they've got to stop him!"
                                        "he's just re-arrested
                                         david cohen for disturb-
                                         ing the peace"

"david cohen!
 what's that punk doing with the sweetmeats!"

                                        "hold it shelly...
                                         there's something com-
                                         ing over KCUF now"

"put the telephone receiver next
 to the radio"

                            ...bringing david cohen over to
                        the microphones...

            ok ok
            let's have some room

                                                    "over here"
                        step back!

"let's get him
 over here"

                                            all right
                                            clear a path

        "mr cohen"
                            ("...your fucking hands off me")
        "mr cohen
         can you tell us..."
                            "this is a goddam witchhunt"
"why are you here"
                            "i have a perfect right to be here"
"you've used the word revolution"
                            "this is it!
                             this is the REVOLUTION!"
"are you then advocating the
 overthrow of..."
                            "we have to first de-systematize
                             the para-militaryindustrial entity"
"have you been in contact with the
 sweetmeats"
                            "the sweetmeats!
                             those brainless tools of a capital-
                             istic mono-technocratic demagoguery
                             are you out of your mind?"
all right
that's enough

                                        (mr cohen)
            let's make some room

"go ahead savage"

"fifty yards!
 i want you to get in closer"

"i don't give a damn about the kids!
 i want you to be on the front steps"

"listen savage...
 i've got everything riding on this
 10 o'clock special
                  do you realize that
 the network pre-empted a vaughn monroe
 special for this special!"

"you don't know what i had to do to get
 this prime-time slot"

"*my* job is at stake savage...and that means
 your job is at stake"

"get your ass in the thick of things
 for once in your life savage"

"yes pauline"

"very good"

"great
 i was telling savage that i want you
 to get further in"

"yeah i've heard about him
 send it through and i'll hold it
 if we need filler"
  switch system output to variable video replay
  adding target pulse electrostatically-generated signal

      ("i think people are missing the
       important part of this gathering
       pauline")

      ("it's a testimonial pauline
       a testimonial to the sweetmeats for
       all the wonderful things they've
       given us over the years")

"hy
 can you read me?"

"we're setting up about
 fifty yards from the
 stonehouse with telephotos"

"we can't chief
 it's packed solid with kids"

"you don't understand hy..."

"i know that hy..."

"i can imagine..."

"we'll try hy
 but general ochre says..."

"while we're on that subject
 here's pauline"
                "hello hy?"

"*how is the signal?*"

"*the crew is all here now*"

"*we have a thirty-second with*
manny makemore who's the
head of Sweetmeat Enterprises"

"*here goes*"

                        (eee-ooo-eee-oooo)

      ("and what's that")

      ("you mean their music and
       their...")

    ("sure their music
                   but i'm thinking
      specifically of the scores of wonder-
      ful products the sweetmeats have lent
      their name to over the years...")

                                    ("then how do you account
                                      for the fact that...")

    ("...pookie and paul dolls for instance")
                                    ("what you're saying then
                                    is that...")

MED! MEG!
MY GOD MEG!
                                        what is it russell?

get in the car!
we're driving to big sur
                                      what's happened?

louis and linda are there
i'm sure of it
                     "wow bud
                      i've never seen so many people in all
                      my life"

     "we must be near the top now
      are you all right lin?"
                      "i'm a little wet but i feel outasite"

     "me too...
      listen...
      the sweetmeats are playing
      i'm concerned"
                    (i'm ooohhh i'm concerned
                     images won't leave my mind
                     we can't be all together
                     till we right what's left behind

                     i'm ooohhh i'm concerned
                     they tell us to forget it all
                     yet i see their faces there
                     on every door and wall...)
just what the hell were those
sweetmeats talking about?

     "at least give me something that i can
      understand"
                                   ...something that
                                   makes sense
"this is brentin strong with the 432nd corp of
 engineers at the site of what was up till yesterday
the town of fuc hue
                 to combat units R&R means rest
and recreation at one of the many hospital bases
here in south vietnam
                 but to the 432nd corp of
engineers
       R&R means Refugee Rehabilitation
                         the men
working behind me are the first to arrive at the
scene after search and destroy operations are over
and the town is secure
                it's their job to 'put the
pieces back together' -- to make fuc hue habitable
once again
        and win the people back over to government
control

this stockade has the survivors of fuc hue
                                    the poor
peasants caught in the middle of this conflict
                                        many of
the men are communist sympathizers and are undergoing
interrogation about suspected viet cong activities in the
area
    but most of these people are women and children and
the very old
            with typical american ingenuity the engi-
neers have devised an 'instant city' on this crater-
pocked hillside designed to house the remaining inhabitants of fuc hue within hours after the corp arrives
    standing with me here is specialist
    2nd class george coleman
                                could you
    tell me more about 'instant city'?"

                                    "uh
                                    we can go into one of these here
                                    villages and uh put up enough
                                    housing to accomodate uh anyone
                                    who's left and uh we can do that
                                    now in just a few hours"

"and how is that accomplished?"

                                    "uh well we use existing terrain
                                    features to build on so that
                                    concrete foundations aren't laid"

"i suppose the foundations take
 a long time to set"

                                    "uh yes that's right and uh they're
                                    hard to tear down or shell later"

"in case they are later recaptured"

                                    "uh in this case re-recaptured
                                    we don't want anything we've done
                                    to fall into charlie's hands"

"how are these homes put up?"

                                    "uh these shelters are put over
                                    bomb craters as you can see
                                                        we just
                                    uh lay these geodesic domes over
                                    the implosion and uh it forms a
                                    sort of cave in the hillside"

"these are buckminster fuller's
 domes aren't they?"

                                    "uh right
                                    just miniatures of our geodesic
                                    dome at the brussels world's fair"

"and this vinyl covering
 is wind and rainproof"

                                    "uh right
                                    and fire resistant too..."

(now that's *something i can understand!*)

                                    the bright side of things
    "...the papers allatime talking 'bout
     rapin' and shootin' and violence
                            never say anything good 'bout
                            losa us hardworkin' honest people"
        never a word about all of
        the good things going on
                            "oh-beautiful-for-spacious-skies..."
...the millions of loyal patriotic
americans who have fought and died
for ideals which...

                                        (olivia dear
                                         i think there's something burning
                                         on the stove
                                                    i'll have to call you
                                         back)
          the wonderful thing it is
          to be an american
          living the american way of life
                                                        cakewalks
                                                        bake-offs
        ball games
        stuffed drains
                            parades
                            charades
                                        new cars
                                        gay bars
          freedom to worship as you see fit
                                                  freedom to publish an
                                                  unretouched tit
          freedom to smoke and freedom to drink
                                      freedom to bathe
                                      and freedom to stink
      freedom to read and freedom to write
                                (freedom to kill
                                 providing you're white)
                                                        "...waves of grain
          for purple..."
                              sewing bees
                              auxiliary teas
                                          barbecue sauce
                                          santa claus
        two-car garage
        odd-fellows lodge
                          ...for which it stands
                                        "bring those howitzers up here
                                        men"
          freedom to
                      defend our great heritage that has made america
        dental floss
        screw your boss
                          "i don't understand
                           i simply don't understand what's happening"
          things are getting
                          crazy again
        cranberries
        tangerines
        avocados
                      taste-tempting tummy-twisting good
            to the last bitesize
                                                  "ball-bustin'"
                          (are there any more aspirin?)
          deep-in-the-heart-of-texas
          the stars above...
                                      "sometimes things are clear as a bell
                                      and other times everything is hazy"
        i don't know what in hell he's
        talking about

                                        it's sometimes hard
                                        to follow

          "...off on tangents..."

                              everything was going so well
so well
                              everything was understandable and clear
        things made sense
        we knew in which direction we were heading
                                                west
                                                were we going young men
        west and then up
                    as far west as the sea
                                      and up
                                      up
                                      up into outer space
        hawaii
        midway island
        the philippines
        japan
        korea
                    west and then up and out
        vietnam
        laos
        cambodia
        thailand
        burma
                        west
                        as far as columbus sailed from
                                            when he went west
        west and up and out
        and over the edge
                            "underwater one
                            underwater one
                            i've reached the top"
be-be-beep-be-beep-be-be
                        crown thy good with
                                    "hey man
                                    the scene is all into it"
        follow directions and you can't miss it
                                    can't mess up
i'm lost
i'm simply lost
                what in god's name does it all mean?
                                            thorns
        (it's not a christ-crucifixion allegory
        i can tell you that!)
                            574620167   46586920987   5637=83656
    "circuit open"
                        (i thought they'd include an index or a
                        glossary or a concordance -- anything!)
        "line check"
                                            "testing testing
                                            one-two-three-four..."
        "stand by for ten-minute mark"
                                    ...so inconsiderate...
            they just go ahead as if we
            didn't exist at all!
"mark!"
                                    never bothering to explain
            never so much as one word of
            explanation
                        much less an apology!
                                            "video sync"

bud bud
it's so beautiful...so beautiful!

> *wow!*
> *it was worth the*
> *climb all right!*

ZOOM BACK TO REVEAL FOGGY
PANORAMA

my god!
all these people!

> *all beautifully*
> *stoned*

(bud and linda spread their
 poncho and lie next to each other)

oh wow bud...

> *wow...*

PICK UP MUSIC

"we gonna have to make a move
 before this fog rolls in"

"but general ochre sir..."

"are the men in position lieutenant?"

"sir...the men..."

"well what is it man!"

"most everyone is gone"

"gone...GONE! what kind of an answer
 is that!"

"...eh...deserted...sir?"

(six minutes
 to air time)

but here's a word from Princess Gefilte Fish

<u>VIDEO</u>

OPEN ON ELS OF GRAND BALLROOM
WHERE A REGALLY DRESSED MATRON
IS SOBBING ON HER LOUIS XIV
LOVESEAT

(...over there...over there)

converting rotary motion to lineal
ball movement using a rack gear and
pinion assembly

"...cayce and castor oil"

(slight trouble on the random jammer)

57673110   46563645
10897261

stuart thinks to himself:
i'm getting hungry

woody wilson
is too zonked to move

meg and russell mom and dad
take to the hills

oh dear....oh dear...

i don't know what to do...

the coast of california
is coming up on the horizon
reports colonel dipper

my caterer's on strike!

it's my daughter's debut!

what does it all mean
what's he driving at?

"what's happening now jim?"

("nothing much happening 'cept the music
and it's getting very foggy out")

                                                    "can you..."

("hold it for a moment
somebody is using a bullhorn")
LISTEN IN THERE
THIS IS GENERAL OCHRE OF THE 69TH NATIONAL GUARD DIVISION
STATIONED AT FORT ORD AND IN CHARGE OF THESE OPERATIONS
NOW I WANT TO WARN YOU FIRST THAT THE ENTIRE AREA IS SUR-
ROUNDED WITH MY MEN AND THEY HAVE THE CAPABILITIES OF WIP-
ING YOU OFF THE MAP OF CALIFORNIA

                                        (hey who the fuck is that?)

        (hey cool it man)
                            "...some uptight freak i dunno..."
I'M GIVING YOU EXACTLY FIVE MINUTES TO COME OUT OF THERE

                                                hey man
                                                cool the jewels huh?

        wow like uptight man like the cat...

                                        ding-ding-ding-ding-ding

    "SAVAGE SAVAGE"

                                        yes hy (wearily)

    "i just heard what ochre said"

                                        i know i heard it too

    "you've got to stop him!
      he's going to give the ultimatum
      just as we go on the air!"

                                        i'll try hy...

    "my god!
      he can't start things now!"

                                        he's way over on the other side hy...

    ("where the hell are those pills")

                                        "wow" says marvin tempest "zap me!"

1756
BIG SUR CALIFORNIA (UPI MAY 7)

                        (isn't this great brenda)

                                            (oh louis louis...)

                        (i can't believe we're
                        really here!)

                    VIDEO
                    ‾‾‾‾‾

CUT TO AN OLD-FASHIONED FISH   AUDIO
PEDDLER STANDING IN THE THRESH-   ‾‾‾‾‾
OLD. CU OF PRODUCT AS IT IS
HELD UP.   PEDDLER

                                            Hey lady let me tell you...

                (five minutes)   For a real quick dish...

                                            Go out and get yourself...

                                            Princess Gefilte Fish

    "i'm going to kick that goddam
      set in!"

                                                    "harry
                                                    control yourself...
                                                    take a LET DOWN"

    "lemme at that set...!"

                                                    "HARRY!"

                            TRANSMISSION
                            TERMINATION

(lock-in video census)

                                        video census as follows...

                16,548,952 for NBC
(check)

                18,056,431 for CBS
(check)

                8,967,102 for ABC
(check)

                34,645,909 for AGH
(check)

                                        "arbitron scanner on"

      percentage breakdown to follow
                                        correction-error
                                        followup ready

                                                        (relay
                                                        please)

    "hello?"

                                        "mrs douglas of 435 harbor
                                        drive?"

    "yes"

                                        "this is the Big Neil rating
                                        calling"

    "oh yes..."

                                        "what station are you pres-
                                        ently tuned to?"

    "channel 8"

                                        "that is the AGH network?"

    "i think so
    i really don't know"

                                        "um-hum it is dear
                                        and how many people beside
                                        yourself are watching
                                        tonight"

    "uh...four"

                                        "we see five in our monitor
                                        mrs douglas"

    "oh...you must see grandad in
    the back
        well i didn't count him
    because he's stone blind"

                                        "he can hear though
                                        can't he?"

    "oh yes...yes!"

                                        "we'll put him down for
                                        one-half then
                                                        thank you
                                        mrs douglas"

    "thank you for calling"

                    (make that 34,645,909½ please)

(correction noted)

                                                        "time check"

        "9:56:10 mark!"

                                                        "roger"

YOU HAVE FOUR MINUTES BEFORE WE START SHOOTING
I WANT EVERYONE TO CLEAR THE AREA IMMEDIATELY

                                        (hey tell that guy to
                                        shut his fucking face up)

        just as his horse drops dead
        from under him
        max vogel reaches the summit
        and literally
                falls into the
        arms of manny makemore

"manny?"

"max! ba-by
what are you
doing here?"

"long-time-no-see
how's the wife?"

"fine and yours?"

"great
and the kids..."

"in school
so what's new?"

"have you ever seen such a
mob before in all your life"

"excuse me please
excuse me
getting through please..."

but it was hopeless

seymore savage
was a bottle bobbing in a sea of humanity

zzzzz-zzzzzzt

ooo-eee-ooo

("is this jim skinner")

("who the hell are you?")

("this is swami sahalami
calling")

("how did you get on this
band!")

("never mind that
what's happening now")

("the crowds are starting
to move back")

("what is ochre doing")

("hey you can't jam this
station
it's illegal!")

analog storage through the use of high grade
capacitors is a proven technique

"everything movin' so fash
thesh days"

"eh...eh ..? how's that?"

a signed decimal number denoting the
exponent of the floating point constant

"oh yes...yes i see..."

FOUR MINUTES!

465638

(SAVAGE!)

"...i'm here hy"

(where?)

"...in the crowd...it's
impossible to get through!"

(farnsworth?)

"yes hy"

(we're going on
with a direct)

"but hy..."

(there's no time
for a lead-in)

"really squeezed in here..."

(i want three
minutes of savage
before a breakaway)

          3:00:00 mark!
                                              "louis!"

  "linda!"
                                          "i thought you were at home!"

  "i thought you were sis!"
                                          "thanks for covering me!"

  "thanks for covering *me!*"
                                          "oh wow
                                            mom's gonna bust a tit!"

  "they're probably on u.s. #1
    right now"
                                          "right in the middle of life's
                                            traffic jam"

  "oh dig dig dig little sis
    how i...how i love you!"
                                          "oh wow louis
                                            it's so good to be so together!"

ENTER BRENDA AND BUDDY
FROM EITHER SIDE AND THE FOUR
OF THEM EMBRACE EACH OTHER
                                          "i love everything...everyone..."

          sunshine and angel dust
          descend into darkness
                                                  can you begin to
                                                  taste the music?

ENTER MITCH FRANKLE AND CAROL RICHARDS
FROM EITHER SIDE AND THE SIX OF THEM
EMBRACE EACH OTHER
                                              together...
                                              together...

        "carol richards?
          where did i hear that name before?"
                                                  i mean for chrissake
                                                  how in hell am i
                                                  supposed to remember

  and john and brenda quigley...
                                                  didn't make
                                                  the connection

now we're expected to remember every detail!
                                                  just sorta scanned over
                                                  that part

    didn't realize they
    could be related!
                              i both remember and forgot
                                                              both
        remembered and forgotten
                                                              both
                              the parts would become whole
                                                              both
      a waste of time!
                                      all of this...
                                      for this?

      a time of waste!
                                                              together
louis and linda
brenda and buddy
mitch and carol
                              and hundreds of thousands
                                                              together

assembled there
                                      while you asked
                                              america

            "what in god's name is going on?"
                                          getting there...
                                          getting there...
and the past and the present
blending into the future

                                          while you stood there
                                                          agape
                                                            a
                                                           gap
                                          generation-wise
and asked
and asked
        "what in..."
                          the world is happening
                                          "came all this way
                                            for that!"
                    a let down
                    come down
                    bring down
                                          (up and over and out...)
       paid good money!
                          never heard any music
                                          came all that way...
    "no sir
     didn't hear no music"
                              paid good money
                              and got gypped
  those kids
  robbed us blind!
                    i don't see...
                                  "after going through it
                                   i knew no more about what happened
                                   than before"
       (though some heard the melody
         some heard the words
         and some heard both together)
                                              all together...

the gathering of the holy tribes
                                              coming together...

one head and one heart and one body and one soul
                                              getting together
                                              as one

          bringing it so far down
          that the ground trembled
                              rocked with electrified angels
          air earth fire water
                              all opposing forces
                                      all together
        (the ying and the yang of it)
                                      gandhi and jesus
                                      walking alm in alm
(...and they shall beat their golfclubs
 into pruning hooks...)
                              a whole-in-one
(...their putts runneth over cups)
                                          mitch and carol
                                          take communion
that even god smiled
                                          BLASPHEMY!
yes
even god smiled with approval

                                          HERESY!

        Genesis 1:31 And God saw every thing that he had
              made, and, behold, *it was* very good.
                                    getting there...
"come along with us"
                                   (my god!)
"domino fields dropped with acid"
                    (it's not an adam-eve-cain-abel
                     creation allegory
                           i can tell you that!)
something
more molecular
        interstellar
              both into it and out of it
                              NO! NO!
"linda?"
                       "i've never..."
"it's time"
                       "...oh i...i..."
                                my god!
"louis"
                                oh please
                                stop please
               "i've never...
               mitch?"
"go ahead"
               "oh god...
               please let it be a good trip..."
                           (oh no no no)
"go on"
                              STOP!
                              GODSAKKE!
        do you hear the music
        do you hear the music!!!!!
                            NO! NO! NO!
"go...go..."
               "god...god..."
                    "good...good..."
                       (lord...)
  that can't be it!
  they wouldn't dare!
                     absolutely repulsive
                         "an obscenity"
(i still
 don't understand)
                     they dropped acid man!
(acid?)
            you mean
            we came all this way for an acid trip?
(acid trip?)
                            partly man
               and partly to find out
               about the sweetmeats
(the sweetmeats?)
               together as one
                     when the parts
                     became the whole
               giving them life
                   us life
  dontcha get it?
                     we were the dead ones

                    repeat please...
                                                    WE WERE THE DEAD ONES!
what are they trying to say?)
                                    repeat please...
                                                        operator
                                                        i can't get through...

                        THREE MINUTES!
                                                        number please
    stand by for transmission
                                        68473658
                                        59392843
                                                    (...reason to believe...)
applause
                    "but what does it all mean
                        after all?"
                                            ("my god meg...oh my god...louis and
                                                our little linda up there...and
                                                we're stuck in a traffic jam!")
                ...shades of fellini...
                                    "tangential tangerine
                                        is this spring's fashion color..."
        lines of communications are still
    open
        lines of communications are still
    open
                                                                i repeat...
                "mr. president
                    we're trying to get general ochre on the phone sir"
still trying
                                            please deposit another...
                                two minute
                            i'm passing over the
                            coast of california
                                                        any ELDMK's?
    "the fog is getting pretty thick general"
                                            "well keep me covered captain
                                                i'm going in there myself to
                                                bring them out"
    "but general..."
                                            "git outa my way boy"
                zzzzzzt zzzzzzt
                                    circuits are all busy...
                                                        58673726453
                                                        84658104134
this is brentin strong with another report from
                                            (can't you get that greener
                                            tina?)
        B U L L E T
                            what's wrong?
ONE MINUTE
                                        I N
                                            T H E   H O U R
            (a special courier brings brenda quigley's
            mom the news
            that her dear son john is coming home...
            boxed in pine)
                                                    "my god!!!!"
                                        i wasn't prepared
                                        for that
                                                (must they include
                                                every detail?)

"...the nation's attention is turning this"

TURN ON
TO AGH-TV

(who?)

<u>AUDIO</u>   <u>VIDEO</u>

DOCTOR

OPEN TO A SURGEON COMING OUT
OF AN OPERATING ROOM.

Whew...I'm glad that mess is over..."

"oh no...no!"

"what is it hy?"

"they've sched-
uled a 60-
second commer-
cial in a 30-
second slot!"

"just break in on it!"

"i can't...
it's computer
programmed!"

("...standing by hy...")

"savage!
SAVAGE!"

CUT TO INSIDE OF WASH-UP
ROOM AS DOCTOR BARGES THROUGH.

...win a fortune in oil

BILLION HOTEL MOBILE WELFARE

...hello?

number please

sunny swingle cutting away for five of the
latest jive from jim skinner down at

eee---ooo---wee---ooo---

(so you can imagine
my embarrassment)

my lights began
to dim

my horizontal hold
began flipping out

"this is pauline farnsworth
general ochre is making his way
over thousands of bodies
towards the stonehouse"

"can you hear the music"

"i think..."

"here
 take this"

"one moment please..."

"hey lady with the
 hookup"

do you want to be interviewed?

"we're not interested
 flora scope"

my name is pauline farnsworth
WAGH in new york

"come along with us
 pauline"

come along?

"take this"

this...this piece of sugar?

"sweets for the meats..."

i...what is this...

"lysergic"

acid...lsd?

"come with us"

(thirty seconds seymore)

what is happening
can you tell me that?!

No rubber glove smell!

"when i say that something
i want to hold your hand..."

"SAVAGE!"

lines of communications approaching
danger
overload

half minute mark!

i repeat

danger
overload

1900
BIG SUR CALIFORNIA (UPI XXXX)

DANGER
OVERLOAD

(they must have their
amps blowing full gas)

listen...listen to the music...

there isn't some other way?

"it's the only way"

(but there was
no electricity)

"oh wow!"

(twenty seconds)

"doncha see the music?"

listen...
you can
touch it now

NURSE

Haven't you heard about the new
Digitdouchet Handy Towelette?

THIS IS GENERAL OCHRE AGAIN
I'LL COUNT TO TEN
THEN I'M COMING IN

(now that's something i can understand!)

getting there
getting there

(ten seconds)

"SEYMORE!
IT'S A 60-SECOND SPOT!
SEYMORRRRRRRR..."

(stand by for audio level)

"check"

1-2-3-4-1-2-3-4

"ok on two"

(camera three on close-up)

check

(move in on stonehouse door)

two check

(five seconds)

"full on two"

audio level
maximum

(don't hear anything...)

(repeat...)

                                                    maximum level

(ready for direct)

                                        "roger"

(cut to black)

                                                        ready
                                                        on hold

            DANGER
                    OVERLOAD

                                "SEYMORE
                                CAN'T YOU HEAR ME DAMMIT!"

(ready)

                                        "shoot"

(you're on)

                                                O N   T H E   A I R

            PEAK
                    OVERLOAD

                                        "this is seymore savage from the crest
                                        of mt. parnassus high atop
                                        big sur california..."

"YOUR LAST CHANCE!"
                                doesn't that idiot know
                                he's not on the air yet?

"I'M COMING IN!"
                                        "general ochre is standing before
                                        the door of the stonehouse..."

    (who's ever in there
     please come out!)
                                        "he is alone
                                        having been deserted by all 600
                                        of his troops"

    (don't hurt me when
     i come in please fellows)
                                        "and now he is moving forward
                                        up the front steps"

    (i have a machine gun
     with me fellehs)
                                                so handy for pocket or
                                                purse

zzzzzzztt
        zzzzzzzztt
                                                "GET FARNSWORTH TO
                                                DO THE OPENING"

...come in pauline...
pauline...
                                        "...he's at the front door"

    I'M COMING IN!
                                        "and he's going in!"
                                                            (YYYYYYYY
YYYYYYYYEEEEEEEEEEEEEEEEEEEEEE)
                                zzzzzzttt
                                    zzzzzzzzzztttttt
                                                VIDEO POWER

        "...G-I-T-D-O-U-C-H-E-T"
                                                BLACKOUT
    "no video signal"
                                        "he's just come out
                                        he's...he's...

        ten seconds to breakaway

"shaking his head..."

PAULINE GODDAMIT WHERE ARE YOU!

"seems there's no one there..."

no one

no one

not a soul there

"no video signal"

not a soul

"the stonehouse is empty
it's absolutely *empty!*"

nothing

but...but that's impossible!

empty and dark

blacker than the heartfelt void

absolutely empty

five seconds

"relay power overload
is...it's gone!"

flowing back to the
heartbeat of creation

wait! wait!
you're going too fast!
wait for chrissake!

begin slow fade

while you
america

pinned to that ghostly fading image

CAN'T GET NO PICTURE!

(your face peering into that reflective grave)

saw nothing
but death

"...nothing...nothing..."

on the air!

what's wrong?

what's wrong with the set?

can't get a picture

CAN'T GET NO PICTURE!!!!!

blew

every cathode tube
from mendocino to millinocket

some kind of interference

KINDLY STAND BY
WE HAVE LOST THE VIDEO PORTION

zzzzzzzttttttttt

i told you to
fix...

"I'M GOING TO BLOW THIS PLACE
TO KINGDOMCOME!"

(time to unplug)

5848576747
5130671 9 8

"everything
went blank"

the goddam sound is
fading too!

this can't be the ending!

(time to ascend)

america

(time to come with us)

can't you get that better
hedda?

            "KINDLY STAND BY
      WE HAVE TEMPORARILY LOST
        OUR VIDEO PORTION"
                                 (time to come)
  can't you...?
                               (time)
america
          audio signal out
                                    eh whashesay?
  "can't hear you"
                           out
         KINDLY STAND BY
      WE HAVE TEMPORARILY LOST
        OUR AUDIO PORTION
                         OUT
    (time to unplug and ascend)
                                     what?"
 my god!
            can't hear you
                             nothing...
                             nothing...
  nothing
         (dissolve to nothing)
                             0000000000
                             0000000000
               my god...my god...
        KINDLY STAND BY
      WE HAVE TEMPORARILY LOST

EPILOGUE

"Okay, take it from where the music stops."

> *. . . and now the music has stopped and she still stares straight up these steps . . . and as the hymn plays . . . the honor guard begins to move forward . . . the American Flag and two clergymen . . . now . . . flag-draped casket . . . of the President of the United States begins to go down the steps . . . the pallbearers are extremely careful at this point to . . . keep that casket level as possible . . . the steps are quite steep . . . and as I look around I see all the people . . . many as this reporter . . . looking with tear-filled eyes at this particular moment . . . because as our former executive chief leaves the capitol building it's . . . a reminder in everyone's hearts that . . .*

"Hy!"
"Ssssshhhhh!"

> *this is his final trip from the capitol . . .*

"What do you mean the Sweetmeat piece is cancelled!"

> *and now . . .*

"Okay, hold it. Hold it, fellows."
"What do you mean by cutting . . ."
"Now just calm down for a minute, Pauline."
"Savage tells me you're cutting the Sweetmeat footage."
"Well, I am. Sorry."
"For Chrissake why? That's the most fantastic stuff we've got!"

Frisbee pushes a button on the console and the projection room overheads come on. Before him stands a teeth-clenched Pauline Farnsworth—a videotape can in one hand. The rest of the staff wisely make for the nearest exit. "Why don't you fellows come back in a half-hour," Hy suggests, but they're already gone.

"Hy, listen . . ."
"What do you mean barging in like that?"
"You're cutting the Sweetmeats?"
"We can't use it, Pauline. Things are very tight as it is."
"But Hy, this is a real coup. Did you take a look at it?"
"No."
"Then how can you . . ."
"Look," says Frisbee, his voice beginning to quiver, "I'm running this Special. It's *my* baby. See what it says on this clipboard—SIXTIES SENDOFF—FRISBEE. That's me, and this is *my* show!"
"We've worked together a long time, Hy."
"I know that."
"Hy, it's 1970 next week. We've worked together for almost five years!"
"Congratulations. And Merry Christmas."
"Hy, listen to me. I'm not expecting favors, but it took me two whole weeks to locate this tape. Two whole weeks!"
"You shouldn't have wasted the time."
"Hy, listen to me. This is the missing tape. It's the Rosetta Stone of the Sixties!"
Frisbee releases a groan.
"Take a look at it, at least."
"I can't use any Sweetmeat footage, Pauline. I don't care what it is."
"Some journalist you turned out to be!"
"For Chrissake, Pauline, get off my back with this crap. That's all I've been hearing from you for years. Big Sur this and Big Sur that! You just stick with the weather reporting; I'll take care of the news department."
"Stick with weather reporting! You know damn well I want to get out of weather reporting!"
"Calm down."

"I'm not expecting favors, Hy. I don't care what your excuses have been for passing over me, but . . ."

"I can't pull you off just like that. You know you have a fantastic rating in New York and besides . . ."

"You haven't put me on a straight news assignment in years."

"Nothing's come up in your area."

"Nothing! You knew I wanted to cover Woodstock. I got down on my hands and knees."

"There were reasons why . . ."

"Ever since Big Sur. You haven't put me on anything since Big Sur as if that whole thing was *my* fault."

"Let's not go into that again."

"Was it my fault the transmission went dead, Hy?"

"Pauline . . ."

"We were still recording until the very end."

"I know all that."

"Hy, the transmission went dead but it wasn't our fault. We were still recording on tape. We have it all on tape!"

"I don't want to . . ."

"It took me two weeks to locate it, Hy. There are parts of it that are absolutely . . ."

"I can't use it. We're too jammed up."

"Just a couple of minutes."

"Sit down, Pauline," Hy sighs, "Now look. The Sweetmeat thing is a dead issue. It was the biggest bummer, the biggest nothing of the Sixties. A hoax. Nobody . . . nobody wants to be reminded of it. Nobody saw them. Nobody heard them. Nobody remembers them. Their manager—Vogel—he retracted his story about talking to them through the door of the shack. He never made it to the top in the first place. That crap about them asking him to set up a concert was a complete and utter lie."

"And General Ochre taking off the top of the mountain with a ton of explosives. Was that a lie too?"

"The man was deranged. He's still basket-weaving at Bellevue and no one knows why he flipped out up there, least of all you. According to Savage, they found you half-naked in a stupor in the back of the press tent. The crap I had to go through to kill that story . . ."

"That's not important. It's what happened up there that's important."

"Oh sure. And you have that on your tape?"

"Nearly two hours. From the time the transmission went dead until just before Ochre blew up the Stonehouse."

"Sounds like wholesome family entertainment."

"But there is a part . . . just a couple of minutes before the end that you've got to see."

"I can tell you right now that . . ."

"Please, Hy. It's all ready to be set up."

"We just can't use any of it. I've told you that already."

"What are you afraid of, Hy?"

"Afraid of! You know me better than that."

"You're even afraid to screen it here."

"C'mon . . ."

"I wonder what people will say when I tell them that Hy Frisbee was too scared to look at a tape I brought in."

"I don't have time to look it all over."

"Just two minutes, three at the most. Please, Hy."

"Christ, all right already." Frisbee sighs and reluctantly pushes the lights off as Pauline dashes back to the projectionist's booth. Moments later a strange, eerie grayness flickers onto the screen.

```
                                                    here we
        are
          here
                                    we are
                                                                over

                    over here
                                              we are over
                                                        over here
        we are over
```

                              up and over
                and through
                                  t
                                  h
                                  r
                                  u
                                                    (over
                                                    here)
s l i p p i n g
                                on crystal icefields
                                upward
                                    upward and out
                                    through mind doors
floating over crystal palaces
                        (here we are)
                                    interstices of
                                    interstellar space
s l i p p i n g
                    through leaf clots
                                        higher than birds
                                            bats
                                            bombers
                                                    higher
than spires
and campfire sparks
                        zoetropes of spinning starslots
s   l   p   p   p
                        i
                            n
                                        g
                back
    back
        to energy sources
        beyond the void-illumination of the stars
                                            so...
                                            so beautiful...
oh...
                here we are
                over here
                                        up and out and over and through
        cell-burst and blastulas
up and...
        pulsing beneath icepanes
                                        o
            u
t
                        so beautiful...
                                        together in a
                                        communal consciousness
        voyagers free floating past temporal palaces
time locks
mind doors
body holds
                                                s
        l
                                        i
                    p
                                            p
        i
            n
                                                    g

rabat
kathmandu
hilversum
chiclayo
                              beyond the last horizon
                              the terror of the unknown
                                                          listen...
do you hear it now?
                                        "listen..."
                    past the heartbeat
                    the pulsebeat
                    the lifeflow of flooding bloodstreams
(the rush of leaf waters)
                                                          listen...
                    past the earlap
                       cochlea
                       eustachian tube
                       auditory nerve
                                   layers of brain tissue
                                   to the deepest region of the
                                   cortex
                 (and then through several
                  information storage areas
                  the size of football fields)
           back
back
                                        to those rosebud
                                        memories of childhood
      "listen!"
                       h
                                a
                                      p
                                              p
    y
                            ...something...
          --.- .-. -.
                                                   ...---...
.---
                    hello?
                    hello?
                                   beyond radio waves
                                   the van allen belt
                                   the atom handball court
beyond...
             t
                o
                                         y
                                            o
                                               u
         h
            a
              p
                                   into orange sunshine fields
    flowing
    in radiance down to a speckled sea
                         "i can see the music now!"
    notes cresting off the breakers
                             b
                                i
                                   r
                                     t
                                           h

239

(the faint bell-tones of a celesta)
                                          t
                                              o
                                                        y
                                                            o
                                                              u

(waves of gold and silver hammered glockenspeils
 wash upon a foamy shore)
                                                  b
                                                    i
                                                      r
                                                        t
                                                          h
                                                            d
                                                              a
                                                                y

                    flutes and oboes and clarinets
                    flutter in the inlet reeds
can you touch
the music?
                                        the violas and the violins
              the cellos and double basses
                                              sitars and harps
                                              pianos and organs
        every string that was ever strung-out
                                          every guitar and banjo
cigar-box balalaika
wash-tub bass
                                  d
                                    a
                                      y
                                          d
                                            e
                                              a
                                                r
                                                    p
                                                      o
                                                        o
                                                          k
                                                            i
                                                              e
              and the horns
                                blasting on flashing clouds
        riding the soundflow
        in muted fury
                                              french horns and trumpets
                                              forming the heads of horses
          (hoofbeats added by the percussions)
                                              dissolving to don quixote
                                              and other literary figures
        so...so beautiful
                              as minds break free
                              float collectively
                              in staves
                              that become bars
                                        across the american flag
(the stars dance out to become notes)
                                              marital music is heard
            wind and thunder
            rockets and roman candles
                              dear
                                        can you see the music?

"marching down every mainstreet u.s.a.
 just like bob preston in *the music man*"

                                         that's right
except with a
billion and 76 trombones

(gulp!)

              with a *trillion* and 110
cornets right behind

(ggggaaaaa!)
       tubas cymbals bassoons tambourines
                 moogs
                 and fugues

happy birthday to you
              through the perilous night
happy birthday dear paul
             o'er the ramparts we watched
happy birthday to you...
                        lutes psalteries
                        dulcimers zithers

you
through
 paul
o'er
                  tabors and fifes
     kazoos and combs
                             beercan bongos
                           stump drums

birthday dear sweetmeats happy
             breaking the sound barrier
             into hemidemisemiquavers

splitting the darkness
into silver shards of sound
                 "come with us"

rolling back the stones
that caved the light of heaven
                 "come with us"

into the perfect eternal sunrise
                 "come with us"

the perfect ending
           c
               o
                   m
                      e
                                 ("*lights!*")

                         ("lights!")

     ("wait hy . . .")
"Lights, dammit!"
"Hy, wait a minute. There's more."
"Not for me there isn't. This is garbage."
"Garbage!" Pauline shrieks. "Garbage?"
"I can't understand a word. Nobody will. What is all of this . . . some kind of lightning storm?"
"It's a light show, Hy. It's what Colonel Dipper saw when he . . ."
"When he said later at a press conference that what he saw was water vapor particles form on the spacecraft's window that created halos, a perfectly natural phenomenon. Case closed."
"And how about Forest Jagoff who swears that no one jumped off the cliffs behind the Stonehouse."
"So?"
"So what happened to them? What happened to the Sweetmeats? Their bodies were never found. Did they disappear, just like that?"
"How the hell should I know. They're probably in Cuba having a drink with Judge Crater right now."

"Oh Hy, be serious. It's one of the great mysteries of the century."

"You mean, one of the greatest press agents goofs of all time. A bunch of amateurs. A great build-up. All the media, the press services, prime-time, hundreds of thousands of kids . . . then poof! Nothing. Somebody really got their wires crossed. A fantastic cop-out."

"It wasn't a cop-out, Hy."

"Let's understand one thing, Pauline: I'm willing to make allowances for a point of view, but I'm not going to change the facts. The Sweetmeats were never found—not in the Stonehouse, not on the cliffs, not in the wreckage—nowhere. The Stonehouse was empty, isn't that right? A thorough search was made, right? In fact, the whole thing was a case of mass hysteria according to . . . what's his name . . . Mountmother. No one saw the Sweetmeats and no one heard them playing."

"I heard them, Hy."

"What did you hear?"

"Why . . . why *you* must have heard it! Don't deny you didn't hear it. It's right on the tape!"

"Music?"

"Right! MUSIC!"

"I wouldn't call that music."

"What does it sound like to you?"

"It's . . . I don't know . . ."

"It's 'Happy Birthday,' Hy. 'Happy Birthday' amplified and electrified."

"Electrified? With what, Pauline. There was no electricity up there."

"Batteries."

"Why didn't Savage hear any music? Answer me that. Why didn't any of the engineers hear music?"

"They did. They just won't admit it."

"Afraid of appearing foolish?"

"I guess that's it."

"Well, frankly, Pauline—you do look a little foolish. In fact, if you want my honest opinion, I think you look downright unprofessional about it."

"Unprofessional! Is that your euphemism for nuts?"

"Pauline, ever since you got back from covering that story . . ."

"Like, flipped out. Is that what you're telling me! I know. You've never given me another news assignment, Hy. You've been trying to ignore me. You probably want to get rid of me. But I'm such a fucking good weather girl . . . such a FUCKING GOOD WEATHER GIRL . . . tell me that again, Hy. Tell me what a GOOD WEATHER GIRL I AM!"

"Pauline . . . look, you're a fine weather girl, but . . ."

"But I'm a lousy reporter, right?"

"Pauline . . . we've all covered certain stories that we have a personal interest in, or that some-how become personal because we've become emotionally involved in the issues and the personalities of the thing. But in this business you can't let personal sentiment dictate the importance of the event. You can't let your own interpretation color the facts. That's editorializing, in the same way that certain stories are presented with a decidedly biased point of view. I want to be fair about this, Pauline. The Sweetmeat story just isn't worth any time devoted to it on this wrap-up program. Some other program, maybe."

"Five years ago you went out of your head with it. You sent Savage and me 3,000 miles to get an exclusive. You scheduled prime-time for live coverage. Why, you even . . ."

"Because at the time it was important. But seen in context, seen against the backdrop of the entire decade it doesn't rate a footnote. Ask any ten people you meet on the street to list the most important events of the sixties and I'll bet not one mentions the Sweetmeats."

"Because it *was* so important. Like taking something for granted, forgetting to mention it."

"C'mon . . ."

"But there is a story there, Hy. An important story. It should be told."

"Not on *Sixties Sendoff*. I'm presenting news stories here, not hairbrained theories, or ego-tripping, or psychic phenomenon findings. I've got just 60 minutes to capsulize the Sixties. One damn hour and they expect me to cram ten years into it. I've got three assassinations . . . two election campaigns and three inaugs . . . five big riots . . . four space spectaculars . . . the Cuban missile crisis, the Berlin confrontation, the astronaut funeral, campus unrest, slums, pollution, poverty and peaceniks. And that's not to mention the war. And you think the Sweetmeat story should be in there?"

"Do you have to put in Julie Nixon's wedding and the Mets?"

"Balance, Pauline. I've got to keep things balanced. Right now we're running 40 minutes of blood and gore and 10 minutes of light stuff. That has to be balanced off—more weddings, births, sports events, beauty contests, animal stories, whatever. The Sweetmeats don't qualify. They typified a tiny minority of screwed-up kids out on a free-for-all."

"But it *happened*, Hy. You can't deny that."

"Like hell I can't!"

"And the Sweetmeats? Do you tell your kids they didn't exist either?"

"Stevie is too young to understand. I tell Benjy . . . I told him they died in the car crash. They were killed along with Fay and Sam. That's the end of it."

"Like dirt under the rug, cover it up. Don't bet on it. They'll find out about them sooner or later."

"Well, they won't find out about them on *Sixties Sendoff*. "

"Don't trouble yourself about that. May 8th is already an underground event with the kids."

"What the hell are you talking about?"

"I mean the kids didn't forget—not then and not now. It gets bigger each year. They celebrate the Sweetmeats' birthday like a national holiday."

"Something between Christmas, Easter and Memorial Day, huh?"

"You can laugh all you want, Hy, but it's still a fact. The Sweetmeats were born on V-E day in 1945. They were the very first of the post-war babies and they came of age and died exactly 21 years later at Big Sur. That was their birthday party. That's what the whole thing was all about."

"So they were 21 that weekend, what of it?"

"They became legal-age adults, Hy, and when you become an adult, you lose your innocence . . ."

"Innocence? Those two kids corrupted a generation."

"And who, corrupted *them*, Hy?"

"That's exactly what I mean, Pauline. You're trying to blow this thing all out of proportion. Stop romanticizing this Sweetmeat stuff. Let it drop, for Chrissake. That's not where it's at today. People want to be shown how everything is *together*. Isn't that the expression these days, 'getting it all together'?"

"That's what I want to do, Hy."

"Well, get off this Sweetmeat thing. I tell you, kids today don't know shit from shinola. I'm not going to come down to their level. If they want to take off their clothes and drop dope and screw in the streets, that's their business. I'm not going to give them the satisfaction of seeing themselves over nationwide T.V. getting their filthy message across. Some of those kids are . . . they're goddam little anarchists, that's what they are! And the drugs, that's another thing. You ask them a question and they look right past you like you didn't exist. And all that crazy kid does all day is listen to that rock music. With earphones yet. I'll be damned if I'm going to give them five seconds!"

"Hy . . . ?"

"You know what's wrong with this country? We've given it over to the kids. It's the kids this, the kids that. Like I'm running hoops for the kids. I'm sick and tired of hearing about them."

"You can't stop the tide, Hy. Half the country is under 25. The country is in their hands now. Ever since Big Sur things have been tipped to their side. That was the turning point."

"Crap! I had some respect for my elders when I was their age. I didn't go putting on a pair of earphones when my father tried to talk with me."

"It's you who has the earphones on."

"Huh?"

"You're shutting out the voice of 100 million Americans. They're not going to go away all by themselves, Hy. You just can't crawl into your shell and live a phantasy of the good old days."

"Me, phantasizing? That's what I mean about respect, Pauline. Your attitude. I've been noticing about your attitude lately."

"Oh, I see. And what about my rating?"

"You've put me in an awkward position with the staff about this Sweetmeat thing."

"Shit"

"I can't have this kind of carping behind my back."

"Are you going to fire me?"

"I'm considering it."

"Save your consideration. I quit! And you can take your fucking clipboard and shove it." Pauline, in a movement, flings Frisbee's clipboard across the seats and bursts out of the screening room.

"Do you want to see that Kennedy footage again, Hy?" asks the projectionist after a thoughtful interval.

"Yeah, yeah."

"From the beginning?"

"Take it from where the music stops."

"Okay. Hit the lights, will you, Hy?"

> *. . . and now the music has stopped and she still stares straight up these steps . . . and as the hymn plays . . . the*

Savage catches up to Pauline running down the corridor: "Pauline!"

"Not now, Sy."

"Why, you're crying!"

"It's nothing. Just a blow-up."

"About Hy yanking the Sweetmeat footage, huh?"

"As if you didn't know!"

"Look, it's his show. Besides, that whole weekend was just a blur to me anyhow."

"You're a real friend, Seymore. Thanks a million."

"Say, listen, before I forget . . . there's been a guy from Columbia University calling up every ten minutes or so, says his name is Doc and wants to talk to someone regarding the Sweetmeats, so I gave him your name."

"You don't want to get involved in other words."

"It's not that, Pauline. It's just that . . . well . . . you have this special interest in them and . . ."

"What does he want, creep."

"Something about him discovering the significance of the Sixties."

"Forget it. Nobody's going to believe him either."

New York City

November 1966
   through part three

December 1969
   epilogue

(WE'RE GONNA) TAKE BACK AMERICA

Words and Music by
POOKIE AND PAUL SWEETMEAT

Once a shin-ing cit-y... Built up-on a hill...

Now the people wonder ... is it shin-ing still? (We're gonna)

TAKE BACK A - MER - IC - A ... Take back the dream ...

TAKE BACK A-MER-IC-A ... Make our al-a-bas-ter cit-ies gleam!

Once the torch of freedom	Once our nation's leaders	Once a hopeful people
Lit a future bright	Walked with nations tall	Grew this nation strong
Now a rocket's fire	Now the men who govern	Now we ask each other
Boasts our nation's might	Turn faces to the wall	Where did we go wrong?
We're gonna	We're gonna	We're gonna
TAKE BACK AMERICA	TAKE BACK AMERICA	TAKE BACK AMERICA
Re-light her flame	Restore our pride	Reclaim our land
TAKE BACK AMERICA	TAKE BACK AMERICA	TAKE BACK AMERICA
Let her beacon shine on our good name!	So there's no place left for them to hide!	Plant it firmly in the people's hand!

ACKNOWLEDGMENTS

The publisher extends his profound thanks to the following for their
generous financial support which helped to defray some of this edition's
production costs:

Ted Adams   Theo Alpert   John Alvey   Ashley   Ivan Babanovski

Thomas Young Barmore Jr   Nick Barry   Sam Bertram   Brian R. Boisvert

Ian Braddy   David Brownless   Blake Butler   Chris Call   Captain Awesome

Scott Chiddister   Chelsea Clifton   Joel Coblentz   Randy and Haley Cox

Malcolm & Parker Curtis   Victoria Elizabeth De Maria   Curtis B. Edmundson

Isaac Ehrlich   Joshua J. Erb   Pops Feibel   John Feins

George and Jean Fischer   Dennis Forsgren   Tom Foster   Jesse James Fox

Stephen Fuller   isaac hoff   Justin Gallant   Pierino Gattei   Katja Gifford

Stephan Glander   GMarkC   Mark Godenho   Sam Goldstein   B F Gordon

Dr. Natalie Grand   G.F. Gravenson   Stan Halstead   Ham   Aric Herzog

Hall Hood   The Jewett Foundation for the Arts   Erik T Johnson

Fred W Johnson   Gautham Kalva   Stefan Kruger   Kyle   Mark Lamb   J. A. Lee

Gardner Linn   Nick Long   Brian de León Macchiarelli   Jonathan Leyva Mack

Jim McElroy   Donald McGowan   Dr. Melvin "Steve" Mesophagus   William Messing

David Miller   Jason Miller   Spencer F Montgomery   Steven Moore

Geoffrey Moses   Gregory Moses   James Munro   Scott Murphy   Matt O'Connell

Michael O'Shaughnessy   Andrew Pearson   Ry Pickard   Pedro Ponce

Stephen Press   Waylon M. Prince   Ned Raggett   Judith Redding

Patrick M Regner   Ethan Rodrigues   Luel Rosa   Alexandyr Makani Rycroft

Rebecca S   George Salis (Interview with Gravenson at www.TheCollidescope.com)

Christopher H. Sartisohn   Don Schulz   Spike Schwab   Jason Smith

Yvonne Solomon   Sid Sondergard   K.L. Stokes   Tango Tango   Evan Thomas

Tousedsa   Elisa Townshend   Christopher Wheeling   Isaiah Whisner

Charles Wilkins   Jeff Wilson   Brad Wojak   Marcel Wolf   T.R. Wolfe

The Zemenides Family   Anonymous

Lightning Source UK Ltd.
Milton Keynes UK
UKHW030722050422
401124UK00004B/318

9 780578 383255